# THE
# JUKE

## BOOK II OF CHANGES

# TED PERSINGER

ISBN 10: 098625214X
ISBN 13: 978-0-9862521-4-3

Formatting by L.J. Anderson - Mayhem Cover Creations

Editing by Lisa Aurello

Cover art and design: Monark Design Services

Published by Farfalla Press

Farfalla
Press

# DEDICATION

*This novel is dedicated to my two grandsons:*

*Kurt Mitchell Persinger*

*and*

*Lucian James Persinger*

*I don't see you nearly enough, but I love you both so much*

# CONTENTS

"For one sweet grape who will the vine destroy?
Or what fond beggar, but to touch the crown,
Would with the scepter straight be strucken down?"
*William Shakespeare, The Rape of Lucrece*

# PART I: PRIDE COMES

# I

The bars rattled and scraped, clanking steady after a sudden, jerking start. He sat bolt upright, eyes locked on the entrance. His hand found the shank he had wedged in the grating under his cot. When nobody entered his cell his hand relaxed, though his eyes stayed narrowed. Ready. He remained physically tense, but then again he was always physically tense. Lately, he had been focused on trying to do good time, but staying alive was always the first order of business.

"Joseph!" He heard the shout down the block.

He turned, feet to the cement floor, then stood up slowly. Time, after all, moved unhurriedly here. Agonizing boredom punctuated with terrifying violence. He looked in the reflective plastic mirror and smoothed his thinning gray hair. He saw his own dangerous eyes glaring back at him with gray steel. His heart was a stone. His wit was a keen blade, sharper than his shank. He was ready to respond to any situation, with deadly violence if required. Hundreds of push-ups and sit-ups in his small cell made his body hard. He pumped weights on the yard when his privileges weren't suspended. His mind and heart were hard as well, crafted from years of brutality. Honed. Shaped. Though older, not a person on his cell block was stupid enough to challenge him. He had earned respect the hard way…the *only* way you earn respect in prison.

"Joseph! Hurry the fuck up!" The voice was commanding now.

That didn't concern him. He knew the game.

He took slow strides as he moved out, turning left and down the long corridor. This was the pace of his life. This was his world. This was his house. Now. He was a creature of the moment. He had adapted to it as surely as he had adapted to other worlds and other houses in his life. Many lives. Many deaths. He was Kali: life, death, rebirth…both creating and destroying.

"Got a visitor. Get downstairs," the blue-suited CO shouted to him from the overlook.

"Yeah."

Down the grated stairs. Slow steps. He heard the shouts as he moved past cells. A few called out to him. A few just called out. He nodded to a few friends. He glowered at a few enemies. He had to keep the veneer. The frightful visage. The iron mask. Weakness here was blood in the water, and vicious sharks swam all about him. Face of a killer. Eyes cold, dead. The disguise had to be on at all times. Keep the wooden presence but be coiled and ready to strike when needed. He had to interpret every sound and every movement through a lens of violence. Let your guard down, and it was stitches in the infirmary, filthy blade ripping holes in your skin. Or the last ride out, buried in the yard—the backdoor parole. Nobody would claim his corpse, he knew.

She would have, but she was gone.

He moved to the visitation corridor and knocked twice. The guard inside turned. He pressed his ID to the glass. The bull called out, and a buzz unlocked the door.

Inside, he turned and faced the wall. Though he had few visits, he knew the routine. The CO called out steps he knew without being told.

"Shoes off…strip…hands on the wall…bend over…cough…" He complied—no smoke. Resist an officer out here, away from the observation cameras, and the resultant attitude adjustment could be permanent.

Strips had humiliated him once, so long ago. The violation of his most personal space. Now, it was barely a flicker of indignation as he coughed to open his anus for inspection. He put his clothes back on casually. The guard tapped the cuffs of the shackles against his own wrist impatiently. A *tsk* escaped him, watching the prisoner taking his time of the process.

The longer a prisoner was inside, the fewer his visits. At first, family and friends would come often, though sometimes just to say they did. Clear their conscience. Tell their friends that they were visiting their husband, brother, uncle, son. But each year the frequency decreased, as their own lives took hold of their hours. As their incarcerated relative became more institutionalized: new prison tats, darker attitude, more distant, angrier. *Masque de la mort. Visage horribles.* He could no longer remember his last visit, but he remembered it being uncomfortable for both parties. He wasn't the man who walked into this prison, not by a long stretch.

"Okay, hands out," came the next order but they were already extended. Handcuffs, chain around the waist, cuffs on ankles. The last tug and jerk he gave simply for his inconvenience. But Joseph never let out a sound. Just a taut jerk with his wrists.

"Open door two-oh-three!" the guard shouted out. An unseen hand pressed the button, and another loud buzz sounded. The guard yanked the door open, and he pushed his ward through.

The hack walked quickly, and the short steps the manacles required had to come fast. It was a trot. He was as a geisha, bound feet following his master. Each clinking jerk rasped the metal against his chafed bone and tendons. He knew he wouldn't dare move slowly now; down this corridor, it was just him and the CO, and he was in manacles. A quick strike from the baton to the unprotected solar plexus and he'd be on his knees sucking air.

The corridor to the visitation room was long and had two turns. He knew the way. His small world was fully mapped out in his mind. He knew every spot in the tile. He knew every entry door and side room. He could visualize every inch he had walked here. His mind was bent to the task of analyzing his environs. Every rat, after all, seeks to escape its maze. Every mole knows the roots above its head. He took it all in and looked for changes from his last visit. He would cross talk with his friends later and share anything new he had seen. Someone was always trying to find a way to escape, though it never really happened. He guessed it was sport. Yes, sport. Something had to keep them mentally occupied, and dreams of freedom topped the hit parade.

As he reached the final steps, the door opened in front of him. He was pushed by the bull behind him, one last hard jerk of his leg cuffs. He would remember that. If he ever caught him alone, he might just even the score. Inmates earn cred inside by attacking guards. One was as good as another, but it was special to exact a tiny amount of revenge on a CO that fucked with you. He would tell his row, *He had it coming...I owed him one.* That would earn him a toast of pruno and more wary respect.

In the anteroom, two COs stood regarding him. As the door clacked shut behind him, he held out his fisted hands, wrists up. A rough grip and a hard thumb to the joint of his pinky finger and then a turn. A submission grip. He felt the hard twist, but surrendered to it. He had no choice anyway. The buzz and snap of the cuffs. First one, then the other loosened, then off. As one officer bent down to unlock his leg irons, the other held his baton with a menacing glare, showing him the response to any action. He only smiled back at him, the cool smile of a dangerous man. Batons didn't scare him... anymore.

Once the shackles were off and the waist chain unwrapped, he turned to face the wall. He was patted down one final time. He looked through the glass in the door to his right to see if he could recognize his visitor. No face caught his attention, and there were too many facing in different directions.

"Visitation ends in two hours, Joseph." He flicked his head in acknowledgment.

He stepped through the door and felt the whoosh as it closed tight behind him.

Snack and drink machines lined the wall to his left. Lightweight tables with even lighter orange chairs were spread around them. At several of the tables sat prisoners in their matching denim shirts and trousers. Around each sat family and friends. He scanned them. Nobody he knew. No trouble here. No beefs to be had. Bulls in each corner of the room.

One man sat at a table alone. He was slender. A light-skinned black man. Hair trimmed short and neat, razored along the edges. He wore gray slacks, expensive leather shoes, and a navy sport coat, obviously tailored. Bright gold buttons. White shirt, no tie. He saw the young man stand up and smile at him. Reflexively he smiled back, though no kindness was contained within. He could play the part, but couldn't really make himself feel any longer. Instead he was sizing him up. Measuring. It was a habit now. It would never leave him, he knew.

His mind, though, considered the face, and he compared it to his mental library. He scanned pictures of the faces he knew but couldn't find a match.

The young man stepped forward, hand out in front of him.

"Hi, Frank. It has been a long time…" he said, and their hands met. The voice. The gait. The smile.

Remembrance came roaring like a prairie fire.

## II

He lost everything that night. In seconds. He lost all he had to give. Isn't that always how it is? The shit-show started with little fanfare. A small tremor before an earthquake. A few drops of rain before a hurricane. Frank expected challenges in his life. He prayed for them, in fact, as *trials turn to gold*, or so his pastor told him. He knew challenges come to everybody, and learning to handle them was part of maturing, both in life and in the path of a good Christian's walk with God.

But it was the overwhelming force of that change that surprised him. Change hit him like a fully loaded semi, unrelenting and unstoppable. No screaming brakes. No last-second swerve. Pedal to the floorboard. Needle pegged red. Change crushed him under its massive spinning wheels and left him broken. A smashed, twisted ruin. Squeezed out. Lifeless. It happened so suddenly and forcefully that all his structure and preparations for his life turned to vapor. The cackling Fates changed everything in the twist of a knot, a snip of the shears. Frank was left in the smoldering remains, wondering what happened.

And why.

But is there ever a why? Instead, our numbers just come up, don't they? We're due. The big spinning wheel goes around, and then tick, tick, tick…stops on you. Me. Us. There's no reason, no rhyme. It's just our turn. Sometimes the change is small, like a car accident or slipping on ice. Sometimes, though, the change is momentous. Heavy-handed. A knockout blow. Frank found out how drastic change can be. That night. So long ago.

A wildfire, after all, is just dramatic change. It burns and ruins all in its path. Life ends quickly and savagely. Yet in that decimation the fire breeds new life, and often that new life is stronger than the old. More resilient. The sprouts of new life are formed from the hot fire of destruction. Seeds cook hot and then burst, destroying their outer shells to push forth into their new forms. Calamity is rebirth. Black cinders transform into green nativity.

Genesis.

*All* the life we know came from ruin. Every molecule in our bodies came from an exploding star. Did that star know it was giving its life to create new, more complex life? No, it was oblivious to its role, and only knew its own destruction. Like a seed, it also cooked hot and then erupted from within, spreading new elements and creating new forms. Will our star create new yet-unforeseen life in the future? Nobody reading this will ever know.

But we know about Frank. Frank was a fair-weather kind of man. He was prepared for a middle-class life, fully accessorized with the skills he would need. A tempest would expose the holes and cracks in his upbringing.

Frank tipped back his head and finished his second beer. He let out an *ahhh* and then a stifled burp, enjoying the throat burn. He put the glass down on the bar.

"Do you want another one?" Tony asked.

"I'd better not. Driving."

"There's still lots of time left in the game," Tony said. He motioned the waitress over.

It was rare for him to even have any alcohol at all, but tonight was a special night. He hadn't seen Tony for over a year. Tony's job had kept him traveling, and Frank missed him immensely. Monday nights were usually church evenings, but he had to see his best friend.

"Another round, gents?" the waitress asked. Frank read the "I-

Ball" logo on her blouse. She smiled at him as his eyes focused on her chest. He blushed when he realized where his eyes were, and she looked away so that he could finish his ogle.

Tony looked at Frank. Frank nodded. "Okay, one more round," Tony replied. The waitress left to fill their order. The I-Ball Sports Bar & Grille had terrible parking but good beer. Tony had always loved coming here for games, but Frank would have preferred to be home. He was glad he acquiesced to Tony's requests, though, as it was a great atmosphere for a big game.

"It's so great to see you again," Frank said. "I've missed you since you moved to LA."

"Yeah. I miss spending time with you, man. And my job keeps dragging me all over. Road-dogging. I'm on the road more than I'm in LA."

"I don't know how you can do it...I couldn't handle a job that made me travel that much. I'd miss my family too much."

"How are Michelle and the kids?" Tony smiled as the waitress approached. "Everybody doing well?"

"Great!" They both turned and received their beers. Frank took a pull from the frosty glass, then put it down in front of him. "Shelly is homeschooling our youngest. Matt just turned fourteen...can you believe that?" He stared into the bubbles floating up inside the glass.

"Fourteen already?"

"Yeah. He's a young man. He helps out at church and is even teaching a youth Bible study on Sundays."

"Oh, that's great." Frank knew Tony didn't share his faith, though they used to attend the same church before Tony divorced and moved south. "How about Mark and Luke?"

"Mark and Luke are both in middle school, and Ruth just started first-grade lessons. I'm so blessed." His wallet was out, and he handed Tony their most recent family picture. Little Ruth was in a white dress that matched his wife's. Both had the same light blue eyes. The boys were all in white shirts and red neckties. His wife's hand rested on the shoulder of his dark suit. Her once-playful curls were now straightened, and a few streaks of gray showed through. Her once-slender form now showed some matronly curves.

Tony smiled at the photo. "Wow, they're growing so fast." He handed it back. "Beautiful family," he added, then looked away.

"Thanks, Tony," and he held up his beer. They clinked glasses.

"Next time you're in town, please be sure to stay at our place. There's no need for you to stay in a hotel when you have us nearby. I'm sure Shelly would love to see you again."

"Yeah…that would be great, Frank," Tony said, taking a drink. "Thank you for coming out tonight. I was worried you wouldn't get out of your church meeting."

"Don't you feel special?" Frank said with a grin. "I do love Monday Fellowship meetings and leading them is such a rewarding experience."

"Well, it's greatly appreciated. I don't know when I'll be in Sacramento again." He was tapping two fingers on the rim of his glass.

"I hope often, but I guess I need to take the family down to LA once in a while as well."

"Yes, you do, man!" Tony let out a laugh, then took a long drink. "Since the divorce, I could use the company. Hard to catch me though…I'm usually on travel."

"I'm just so busy with work and the church and the kids. You know how it is. Tech is busy these days, and now that I'm a deacon at church I find my evenings and weekends disappearing quickly."

"Do you ever think about taking a break from all that? You're working so hard."

"No…not now anyway. It's too rewarding. I feel the Lord using me, and it feels so wonderful to be a small part of God's great plan."

Tony smiled.

As they turned their attention to the big-screen television above them, they saw quarterback Steve Young throw a touchdown pass to tight end Brent Jones. A loud shout went up around the bar. Glasses clinked all around them.

"Young is hot tonight!" Tony shouted above the din. "I think this could be our year!" He tugged on his red shirt emblazoned with Young's No. 8. "I think this is the year we win it all."

Frank wasn't as much of a fan as Tony, but he was wearing his Joe Montana No.16 jersey in road white. "Well, Young is great, but he'll never beat Joe." He said this confidently, but knew he didn't know enough about football to really judge anyway.

Tony said loudly, almost shouting over the din, "Joe is gone, Frank! Let it go! Steve is our guy now!"

The both chuckled into their beers. Frank looked up at the television and saw the score was 30 to 14—a comfortable lead for San Francisco.

He heard a tumult behind him and turned to look. At the backside of the bar sat three Raiders fans, dressed in black, perched on tall stools around a high, round table. He heard them grousing. "Running up the score." "It's the fourth quarter." "What are they trying to prove?" *Sore losers,* he thought, and turned his attention back to the replays.

Transformation was moments away.

It was a cool fall evening, that September 5th, 1994. So cool that Frank wore a light jacket over his Montana jersey. Normally, Sacramento Septembers are furnace-hot, but not tonight. He welcomed the change and hoped the coolness would last.

At a commercial break, the bartender put on some music. Gin Blossoms.

*All last summer in case you don't recall*
*I was yours and you were mine forget it all*

"So do you think Jerry Rice is going to break the record tonight?" Tony asked, looking into his nearly empty beer. "One more ties it."

"Nah, it's the fourth quarter. I can't imagine he'll score two tonight. Maybe one, and tie it. But two? He already scored in the first quarter…"

"Yeah, you're probably right. They like to spread the ball around. Would be nice to see them do it at Candlestick Park." Tony checked his watch.

"Do you need to get going, Tony?" Frank asked, turning toward him.

"Not yet. Hope to see Rice score one more tonight."

"Okay, man, just let me know." Frank was nursing his beer, but he noticed it had gotten below half. Tony had the look of a man who was ready to go, so Frank thought he should finish his beer and be ready.

Abruptly, the music in the bar softened, though it still played in the background.

*Rumors follow everywhere you go*
*Like when you left and I was last to know*

As they both turned their attention to the large screen again, they saw Jerry Rice, No. 80, take the football on a reverse and speed to the end zone, a quick fake right, then hard left, knifing through the defense like they were standing still. Once again the place erupted.

"That ties the record!" Tony shouted. He was on his feet pumping his fist in the air. He threw his arm around Frank and they were shouting. No words, just sounds. Tony held up his glass to toast with Frank again.

All around the room, people shouted, "Jerry...Jerry..." Football friendships were forming, as people high-fived and hugged men they didn't know. Frank and Tony couldn't hear the announcers, but saw the play from nearly every angle possible. Reverse handoff from Watters. Jerry streaking around the corner. Long, lithe strides. A terrific shoulder fake. He squeezed between defenders and battled through a tackle to fall into the end zone. Touchdown 126.

Tony shouted again, "Why didn't we go see this game in Candlestick?" The roar in the room was nearly deafening, and Frank had to lean over to him to shout his reply.

"I know, right? What a great night to be there." Of course, Frank knew that even getting a couple hours out of his busy life had been a challenge. Getting the afternoon off to fight Bay Area traffic just for a football game wouldn't have happened. Not just getting off from work, but how about Shelly and the kids?

Jim Brown's touchdown record had stood for decades and seemed insurmountable. Yet here was a receiver in his prime, and he had just tied that record. Frank was so glad he had asked for the night off from Deacon Trenton. While he enjoyed, truly *loved*, the fellowship from his church brethren, he was glad to see a bit of history with his best friend. Who knew when he would see Tony again? He really didn't know.

Tony checked his watch again, then said, "Hey Frank, I'm going to take a leak, then I'd better get back to the hotel. Early flight."

"Yeah, okay, man. I understand."

Tony slid off his stool and moved behind him on his way to the bathroom. The waitress returned with questioning eyes. Frank said, "No more for us old guys...just the check." She smiled and went back to clear their tab.

He was staring into the bottom foam of his beer when he heard a loud groan from the bar. He looked up to see that the Niners had fumbled and that the Raiders now had the ball. Of course there was no worry; with the score 37-14 late in the fourth quarter there would be no stunning comeback. Though early in the season, a win gave them momentum in a season filled with expectations.

When the waitress returned with the check, Frank stood up to fish his wallet out of his back pocket.

The smashing of glass behind him caused him to jerk his head around.

As he focused on the source, he saw Tony standing near the bathroom, being faced by the three Raiders fans. Their black and silver shirts seemed menacing, and each seemed larger than Tony, who was shorter than Frank and slender. These men stood towering over him, and even from this distance he could see the worry on Tony's face.

Frank moved quickly and involuntarily, and as he approached he heard one of them shouting loudly in a tense voice.

"Take your fucking chump-ass Forty-Whiners bullshit and go fuck yourself." The man's curly red hair went down his shoulders enough to cover the name on the back of his jersey, with No. 12 on both shoulders. Red was tall and thick, and his hands and wrists said construction. Frank was next to Tony in a second, and stood directly in front of Red.

"I'm trying to," Tony replied. "Why are you hassling me?"

"You bumped us, asshole," the heavyset Latino man said, jabbing his finger at Tony's chest. Tony looked down at the finger, then to Frank.

They heard shouts from the bar. "Take it outside!" "Settle down, guys!"

Frank tried to make peace. "Whoa, whoa, guys...easy..." with his hands outstretched in front of him. Red's gaze burned into him, and Frank saw his body flexed and fists balled.

"I didn't bump you," Tony protested, not stepping back from the finger in his chest. Though small and slight, he wasn't backing down. He looked more confident when Frank arrived. "Why don't you leave me the fuck alone, man?"

"Take your friend and get the fuck out of here, fuckhead." This time, his finger thumped Tony's chest. Tony pushed the finger away with a swatting open hand.

And then it started. There was no turning back.

As Tony's hand swiped the finger, the man's hand folded into a fist and struck Tony on the side of his face, sending him stumbling into the table behind him. Frank felt the first punch from Red swing by his head. Though it missed him, his forearm struck his shoulder and sent him back on his heels.

"What are you doing?" Frank shouted as he backed up, looking for space. Another punch whizzed by his face. He looked over to see the third man now throwing punches at Tony, who was on his knees with one hand on the floor. Both men were going at him, punching downward. Strikes rained down on his ears and shoulders.

Again, Frank shouted, "Why are you doing this?"

There was no response from Red, only grunts and the whoosh of air as more punches missed him. He could smell the beer on Red as the man swung his arms erratically but violently. Nothing was landing, but Frank was out of space. His heels found the wall behind him.

He wondered how this could happen to men their age. Then he felt the air from another punch that again missed him, if barely. Red had closed the distance and his punches would soon find him.

Judgment fled him, and he became primal response. His fists balled, and he swung with all his might. He grazed the man's ear, and his right fist was in his red curls. He grabbed those curls and pulled his head toward his left fist. He pumped three successive left crosses into Red's face, opening a cut above his right eye. Red staggered, but Frank still held his hair. Red was no longer throwing punches.

Now, with his adrenaline flowing hard, he threw a hard hook, which landed flush on Red's nose. Blood sprayed out. With his balance off, vision blurring, and blood flowing, Red used his size and threw himself on Frank. Their bodies smashed together, and Red's weight sent them to the floor. Frank landed heavily on his back. Red let out *puhn* as they hit, and his blood sprayed into Frank's eyes and mouth. Blood was spilling freely, and both men were quickly slick with it.

Frank twisted his body and pushed Red away from him. Though he had a huge size advantage, Red's balance was off still, so Frank quickly reversed, moving to a top position. He pushed his left hand down on Red's chest to steady himself, but even through his adrenaline he could now feel his left hand throbbing angrily. Frank threw down piston-like punches on Red's face, and blood coated his forearms. Red jerked suddenly, arching his back, sending Frank onto the floor. They rolled and twisted, each struggling to better their position. Red was panting loudly through his mouth and spraying blood with each exhale. Frank could feel the man was strong, but alcohol and hard punches must have made him unsteady. Still he struggled. The stink of stale beer, bad breath, and body odor was overpowering to Frank. How had he ended up on the floor with a man he didn't even know? How had he found himself touching and pushing and punching and wrestling a man who reeked of construction sites and unwashed clothes?

The struggle continued, and Frank's shoulder hit a nearby table, dumping beer on both of them. A heavy mug rolled off and struck the back of Frank's head, then fell to the floor with a crash and tinkle. Instantly he saw gray and silver stars, and felt a deep throbbing from his neck up.

And then there were hands on his shoulders, and he was pulled roughly to his back. A large bald man in a white I-Ball polo shirt put his huge flat hand on Frank's chest, pinning him to the ground. Red was struggling with a bouncer just a few feet from him. Frank saw that Tony had already been separated from his attackers. He was surprised to see Tony wasn't bleeding, though he was being pushed up against a wall. He noted the third man in Raider-black was blonde haired and gangly, and a bouncer had him in an arm lock.

He attempted to sit up, but the bouncer held him down. "Not yet, buddy...wait for the cops."

"I just want to sit up."

"Not happening." He smiled down at him, but his force was unrelenting. As he lay there covered in beer and blood, he regarded the man above him. He looked at the logo on his white polo shirt. A large eyeball, complete with red capillaries, with the letter *I* on it. *Who thought of that logo?* he wondered. *Such an ugly logo for a sports bar.* It's funny what a person notices in moments like these.

He also felt the adrenaline begin to purge from his bloodstream, and the dull aching throb in his hand and head became sharp staccato. He let out a groan as pain grew within him. His elbows and knees began to burn. His shoulder felt bruised. All the sensations from his tumbling fight found him, as if they had traveled far to get there.

Nobody in the I-Ball that night saw Jerry Rice score touchdown 127. Nobody saw the beautiful spiral snatched from the air between two defenders. They were all too busy looking at the men on the ground, each with his own personal bouncer. Beer on the floor. Stools upended. Broken glass. Bloody fists. Sirens in the distance. People clucked their tongues, and were glad they hadn't been involved. They all looked with sour judgment at Frank and the others. Adjudicating eyes. Contemn. Many would tell the story of this fight later, adding embellishments to make it more interesting than it had been in reality. Frank could feel the heavy, reproachful looks, even as he looked down at his split knuckles and bloody hands, and tried to wipe Red's blood from them.

Then the police arrived in numbers. Black shirts and creaking leather gun belts. Fingers pointed them to the men on the floor and against the wall. Cops swaggered over to where the bouncers held their charges. No discussion. No investigation. Instead, Frank was pulled roughly up to his feet, where he felt something he had never felt before: the cold, metallic grind of handcuffs on his wrists, tightened to just short of bone-cracking. His left hand sent shooting hot currents up his arm.

In complete disbelief, he tried to turn to look at what was happening to him. He received a hard shove from the cop. He then demanded, "Why are you arresting me?"

"Disturbing the peace, buddy…assault…battery…public intoxication…you want me to go on?" Derision in his tone.

"I didn't do anything. I was only defending my friend. Arrest those fucking Raiders fans." That word leaving his mouth shocked even him. It wouldn't be the last time tonight. "*They* fucking attacked *us*, man!" and now his voice was shouting.

"Watch your mouth, sir…don't make it worse for yourself." He was given another shove.

But now his blood was up. His heart was pumping. "Listen, we didn't do anything except try to have a couple beers and watch the game. These assholes attacked my friend, and I just tried to help him out."

"That's not the call we got. They reported it as a bar fight. But don't worry…we arrest you all, and let the judge sort it out in the morning."

"Judge? Morning?" Frank was now being led out into the cool evening. The black-clad officer had his gloved left hand on the chain between wrist cuffs, guiding him to the car. Metallic shoe-taps clicked on the concrete. "No way am I spending the night in jail," Frank protested. He stopped and tried to turn to address the officer. For his efforts, he received a hard forearm on the back of his head, which intensified the ache.

"Sorry, pal," and then he added a shove to the cuffs, sending more jagged pain up his forearm. "I don't make the rules. You're in a fight in a bar, you go to the lockup."

Frank began to dig his own grave. "Listen, officer, you don't know who you're messing with. I'm Frank Joseph, vice president of Niver Technologies. I'm not some jerk off the street. You don't just arrest me. My hand hurts. Take these cuffs off and let me call my wife, or my first call is to your police chief. I need medical care, not fucking handcuffs."

Officer Whalen took great pleasure in shoving Frank hard up against the side of his car, then kicking his feet apart. With his feet out, he fell over the trunk of the cruiser. Frank had to squint against the blinding, flashing lights atop the roof. Even with his eyes closed, he could see those lights. He hadn't known they clicked as they turned.

"Well, *Mr. Vice President*…let me make sure you don't have any weapons on you." He ran his hands roughly over Frank. Neck and shoulders. Sides. Thighs. Ankles. A rough grab on his crotch. His wallet and car keys were placed on the trunk of the car. "Now let me read you your rights, Mr. Vice President," and he was already opening the car door. Frank was shoved in roughly, head forward. The metal grating between the front and back seats left him little room, and his knees scraped across the sharp frame. The cuffs pinched and bit his wrists. "You are being arrested for the crimes of disturbing the peace, assault, and battery. You have the right to remain silent. You may refuse to answer any or all questions. You have the right to an attorney…"

As Frank sat in the back of the black-and-white, he saw the red and blue lights flash against the badge and the buckle of Whalen's gun belt. He heard the hissing, static-strangled voices of the police radio on the other side of the cage. He knew the conversations would be about him, but couldn't understand much of what was said. Ignoring the officer's practiced Miranda-drone, Frank looked to his left, and he could see Red over the hood of another black-and-white, while a black-clad officer rifled his pockets. Frank saw he had broken Red's nose, and every word he said flecked blood, even now on the hood of the black-and-white. Blood also dripped from his swollen right eyebrow, and it was pooling. Red looked over at Frank, even though he was still bent forward. Their eyes met for the briefest of moments. Both men knew their futures were intertwined. Both men knew they were going to pay for this evening in the future. Both men would never be the same again, and both men knew it.

And then he saw a smirk on Red's face just before he was placed in the back of the patrol car.

# III

"I said, I want my phone call! How can you deny me that?" Frank's voice was raspy, his throat sore, and he was exasperated. Though never in jail before, he knew he had certain rights, chief among them a phone call. He wanted to call his wife. He wanted her to call a lawyer and get him released. He wanted out of his meshed-glass-and-metal cage. It smelled of vomit and urine, and he could hear his breath echoing. He was sweating freely, and the orange jumpsuit smelled of mold and chafed his skin.

Most and worst of all, he was left alone with his thoughts. The panic of those thoughts made him want his phone call more than anything else in the world. He wanted to hear his wife's voice. He wanted to hear that somebody knew of his plight. He wanted to know somebody was working on his situation. He knew his life had taken an ill turn and sitting there waiting was more than he could bear. He anticipated what was to come and wanted to get working on it immediately. This was a problem, a big problem, but he made a career out of solving problems. He knew the worst thing he could do was sit and not take action. He had to bend this problem to his will; he had to reshape reality. The sooner the better.

"Just sit down and shut up," the deputy said. He checked his watch. *Where is Pete?*

"Look, man, I'm bleeding, I'm tired…I need a two-minute

phone call. My wife is probably worried to death..." He yelled as loudly as possible, as the thick glass muffled sound. It caused an echo in the room. He knew it was nearly midnight. He hadn't even been fully booked. He had been breathalyzed and tossed in this stifling, poorly ventilated room. No toilet. A flat white metal bench along one wall.

"Well, you're not bleeding much. Shouldn't get in fights, buddy." Another irritated glance at his watch.

"I didn't get this from the fight, asshole. I got this from the cop car." He turned his face to show the checked print of the grating over his left eyebrow.

The deputy let out a dry laugh. "Oh, you got waffle-faced? Tough luck, man." He let out a sigh of relief when he saw Pete Jensen key in through the security door. He checked his watch again. *Fifteen minutes late!* He wanted to yell, but knew that would just delay his departure. Instead, he feigned concern. "Pete, you okay?"

"Yeah, sorry..." he began as he moved to him. "Traffic..."

"Monday at midnight?"

"Yeah, sorry, man. Won't happen again."

"No worries." Half-hearted. "So watch this guy. He's some VIP, or so he claims. I think he got booked in, but he says he never got a call. He only blew point-oh-eight-five, but he could draw a drunk and disorderly as he was involved in a fight. I'm kinda babysitting him a bit. Don't think he'd do well in GP." He turned as he heard the flat hand slapping the heavy glass. "Just wait, man!" he shouted back.

"He causing problems?"

"Not really...just expects to be in control, I think."

"I hate that type," Pete said, teeth gritted.

"Well, he'll definitely bond out in the morning. He came in with a few others. We cut the rest of them loose...a couple of them knew the chief, and he called to have them released. We only have this guy left. He'll see the judge at eight."

"Cool."

"Okay, well, that's all then...I'm shoving off. Have a safe night."

"Yeah, thanks, man."

Deputy Jensen turned and regarded Frank, who had taken a seat on the bench, eyes to his feet. He moved to the nearby desk to sign in and start the evening paperwork.

But Pete wasn't fully there. He was back home. He was roiling in his problems that night.

*"I told you, I need these clothes for work! I can't sell women's clothing if I'm dressed like a bag lady,"* his wife had shouted at him. He had heard their kids scurry to their bedrooms, which they always did when she started shouting.

*"Goddamnit, Crystal, we're in debt…you can't keep buying clothes like this. We're going to lose the house, for fuck's sake!" They always went back to the same argument. Every single time.*

*"If you want me to work, I need to dress the part. I'm already the poor girl at work. Maybe if you got a real job I wouldn't have to work and spend money on clothes!"*

He could still see her. Little fists curled up. Brown eyes afire. She knew right where to hit him. She knew right where to go.

*"I can't believe you make such a crappy salary…you've been a sheriff for ten years…yet you get paid the same as a teacher…"*

Right to his manhood she had gone. They did that to each other. Both were unhappy, and both knew it. Both would move on at some point, and the divorce would be ugly. They both knew the kids would never recover from the damage. The daily damage. Both children saw both of their parents berate each other, so they would both grow to adults without gender models.

"Hey man, come here!" he heard Frank shout through the window glass.

"Not now, buddy," he mumbled to himself. "Not tonight." His stare was miles in the distance.

"Hey…yeah, you…come here…"

Frank couldn't live in that claustrophobic room a minute longer. He couldn't take the heat. He couldn't live with the idea that the police officer had purposely slammed on his brakes to make his face mash into the metal screen. He couldn't stand the indignities he had already suffered. He had been searched. He'd been forced to wear a ragged orange jumpsuit. He'd had his belongings confiscated. These things didn't happen to people like him.

He had reached his breaking point. He failed to consider that others had breaking points as well. He was completely locked in his own head, experiencing his own problems.

But it was beyond him to bear those without protest. Frank wasn't a man who could take slights or suffer fools. He had rights. He was somebody important. At work, people stepped out of his way. He certainly wasn't about to be abused and mistreated. He knew he had the right to a call. He knew the deputies were *required* to uphold his rights. He knew he was a pillar of the community and deserved better treatment. Worse, the hot, room was stuffy and stank horribly, and he knew a phone call would mobilize forces to get him out. He expected that phone call, and he wanted it. He wouldn't wait for the deputy to solve his personal problems; he was drowning in his own at the moment.

"Seriously," he shouted from within, "I want my fuckin' phone call. I have that right. Read the Constitution...I have rights." He didn't bother to mask his supercilious attitude.

Deputy Jensen moved back to the glass. They looked at each other through the crisscrossing wire reinforcements. "Sir, I'm not going to put up with this all night. You were given your phone call when you were booked. I'm just here to make sure you don't hurt yourself..."

" I *never* got my phone call! What part of that don't you understand?" He yelled loud enough to make his own ears ring.

He couldn't see the turmoil in the deputy. He couldn't see how close to the edge of breaking the man was. He didn't realize how deep was the rabbit hole he was tumbling down. At this very moment. The deputy's stare was far away, his face without affect. Inside, though, was a storm.

"Look, I don't have time to argue with you, sir. I don't do phone calls...not in my job description. Just step away from the glass, sit down, and shut up. It'll be morning in a few hours, and you can talk to the judge."

"You're making a huge mistake, deputy," Frank said, and had he thought about it, he would have realized his tone was condescending...dismissive. "I'm a senior vice president for Niver Technologies. Our taxes pay your salary. I have a legal team at my company that will crush your balls when they find out you are denying me my rights. I want my phone call. Give me my *fucking* phone call." His accusatory finger pointed right to the deputy's face.

And that was enough. That was all it took. Just that amount. Nothing more required. Jensen snapped inside, like a taut guitar string turned one too many times. It wasn't the first time, but this time was bad. He snapped in a way that his accumulated frustration ensured was his most violent, most extreme response possible. After all, these releases are really about escape. When someone blows up, they're really seeking a violent way out of their situation. Jensen really wanted a divorce. He really wanted to file for bankruptcy. He really wanted a new job, one that challenged him in a different way. But he lacked the courage of his convictions. He lacked the ability to take the leap of faith needed for these changes.

So he turned to violence to escape his problems.

The flush in his face burned hot. He was vertiginous. Hands trembling as the adrenal fuel flooded volcanically into his bloodstream. That momentary rush reassured him that what was next was the right step. It just had to be this way.

He turned the key on the door almost automatically. Eyes focused afar. Frank stepped back with a relieved look on his face. The door swung open, and he was in the room. Frank's look of surprise as the door slammed continued as the black baton slid from its leather loop with a *whisk* sound.

There was a moment of silence. Calm. But only because Frank couldn't read the deputy's body language. The blank façade was gone. In its place were tense shoulders, bowed forward. White knuckles on the baton. Teeth grinding. They made eye contact, and only then did Frank see it coming. He saw the boiling hate in the other's eyes. Hate not for him, but hate all the same.

Pete Jensen swung his baton with precision. He had received training on it, after all. He knew where to aim. Each stroke had a purpose. As the left arm rose to protect his face, the baton smashed down to break the small, slender bones of the lower arm. Next swing to the head to stun and compromise vision. Then, a hard shot to his knee, which dropped him to the ground.

Frank looked up through his tears and saw the raw fury on the deputy's face. Eyes of fire. The hard, bony thumps on his legs and arms echoed in the room. He could hear both of their breathing, each gasping with the hard strokes. "Why are you doing this?" Frank cried out, but in answer the deputy stepped over his legs and made a downward stroke with his baton. Frank threw up his already broken left arm, and he could feel the small bones in his hand snap from another blow. He shrieked in agony, which brought the deputy's work boot down on his face, flashing stars into his vision.

He knew without it being said that he should not utter a word or even a sound. He was to lie there and receive damage until the deputy was satisfied. Tears streamed as more blows rained down on him. Shoulder. Thigh. Ribs. He stroked the baton to be sure he caused damage to every structure of Frank's body. Hip. Lower leg. Ankle. He continued striking with all he had. Sick thuds, heavy breathing. More thuds. Gasps. Groans of pain.

The deputy began to breathe heavily, and his blows weakened. His face lost its rage.

Then all at once the door flew open, and two other uniforms were in the room. One grabbed Jensen and pulled him back. The other stood over Frank, baton at the ready.

"What happened, Pete? You okay?" The man was holding the baton like a miniature baseball bat, squeezing his fists to secure a tighter grip. Frank wondered if more blows were coming, and he braced himself.

Deputy Jensen was panting heavily, gasping for air. He lowered his baton and made no reply. He was still looking down on his victim. Frank began to groan involuntarily. The ache of each baton strike began to burn and throb. He could taste blood pouring into his mouth from his smashed and swollen lips.

Frank's groans brought out the last bit of bile from Jensen, who stepped forward and stomped on Frank's knee. The officer next to him grabbed him and pulled him back again.

"What did he do? Pete, what happened?"

Frank noted that the officer behind him, a heavyset black man, had three stripes on his tan uniform. "What happened? Did he attack you?" To keep from vomiting, Frank turned his head and was spitting some of the blood out onto the cement floor.

Deputy Jensen made no reply. His eyes were still miles away, but all malice had now left them. They were vacant and distant again. He slid the baton back into its leather loop. His face was slack. His affectation was limp, like a man just awoken from a deep sleep. He looked at his supervisor, then turned and shuffled to the door. He opened it and walked out, moving in a slow, deliberate fashion.

The two officers stood over and looked down at Frank, who was holding his left forearm with his right hand, gently wiggling his fingers. He could feel the broken bones grating from his elbow to his fingertips. The deputies had sharp eyes as they looked from him to each other and then back to him.

"Help me," he spat, and more blood flecked from his lips.

"Sit him up," the sergeant commanded. The other officer, young and slender, kneeled down and lifted Frank by his left shoulder. As he sat up, blood coursed from his nose, and he spat out another glob of blood. He used his tongue to wiggle two teeth that felt loose in his mouth.

"What'd you do, man?" the sergeant asked, with hands on his hips.

"I asked…" he spat again, "I asked for my phone call."

"Bullshit. What did you do?"

"I told you…" His voice was a croak now. He could feel heat as his left eye began to close.

Both men helped him up to the long white bench. Frank lay down on it, breathing heavily, turning to spit often. The sergeant stepped out of the room and radioed for the night medic.

Sergeant Aldis Franklin then moved to the tape room.

Something was wrong. Pete's face was wrong. The amount of blood was wrong. Deep down, he already knew what he would find, and one replay of the grainy tape showed him what he feared to be true. He still watched it several times, wincing as the blows rained down. The images sickened him.

He found Jensen in the break room, eating a bag of chips and sipping water. He was wan, eyes downcast, chewing slowly.

"Pete, why aren't you at your post?"

"I needed a break, Sarge. I'll get back in just a few minutes. Gotta get some energy."

Sergeant Franklin pulled up a chair and sat across from him.

"Pete, I just watched the tape of what happened. You attacked him with no provocation. This is bad."

"He was being verbally abusive, Sarge," Pete said with a reflexive response. He immediately went to, "I felt threatened. He attacked me." He had learned that response on the streets a long time ago. Never accept responsibility…it was always self-defense.

"Don't bullshit me, Pete. I watched the tape. It has audio. He was asking for a phone call. What's going on?" His eyes locked on Pete's, and they were all business. Pete understood.

"What do you want me to say?" He took a sip of water.

"The truth."

"No, you want me to give you a reason, Aldis. I don't have one." His voice was resigned.

"You don't have a reason?"

"I just snapped, I guess…just snapped…" and his voice trailed off. He focused in the distance. He knew his career hung in the balance of this conversation. He knew he was now under investigation. He knew the routine, the process. He had been there before.

"Pete, you've snapped too many times. You've been warned before. You can't go around beating people. This guy is somebody… he's not some homeless guy we picked up. He'll have lawyers and media. We don't need this."

"I'm sorry."

"Pete, I'm filing this in your report. You're on leave while I investigate."

"Sarge, I don't…"

"I have no choice, Pete. If this turns bad, I have to have shown that I took action. I've already got a call into HR. You'd better hope the tape of this beating doesn't come out. You'll be brought up on charges. You could lose your job over this."

Pete looked down at his chips. He wasn't hungry anymore.

"Pete, I've known you a long time. You and I were trainees together. I'll do what I can to help. Let me start here…this is the number for the union lawyer. Call him. Protect yourself." He slid a slip of paper over to him. "The second number is for a psychiatrist. You get ten free visits as part of our medical plan…no questions asked." Pete looked up at him. "You have issues you're not addressing in your life. You need to talk to someone."

Jensen didn't protest. Sergeant Franklin left without another word. He went back to the tape room, retrieved the tape from the VCR, and took it to his office. He put it in a locked drawer, where it sat for some time.

At the end of his shift, Pete called the union lawyer.

He never did call the psychiatrist.

# IV

"Christopher Francis Joseph, please step forward."

The shackles yanked as Frank stood up. The shackles only allowed him short steps. Each of those small steps pulled on the waist-chain, which in turn jerked the handcuff on his left wrist down on his swollen, broken hand and arm. Though they were bandaged heavily and the cuff opened the widest possible, the pressure forced a grunt out of him. He stepped up to the podium gingerly, feeling his joints ache with the exertion. He scanned the room for Tony, but didn't see him.

"Mr. Joseph, this is an arraignment. Have you been read your rights and do you understand the charges that have been filed against you?" The judge looked above the bifocals perched on her nose.

Frank's left eye was nearly closed, but he made eye contact with his right. He spoke through swollen lips. "Your honor, I was beaten in jail last night. I demand that charges be…"

"Mr. Joseph, you are in no position to *demand* anything from this court," she shot back. "You are being arraigned for the charges you were arrested for last night." Her voice was sharp, like the crack of a whip. "Disorderly conduct, assault, and battery. Other charges may be forthcoming." She was filling out a long form with multiple carbons as she read the charges. He was now part of the machine, after all, and the machine had to be fed paperwork.

"Your honor, I was beaten by a deputy last night simply for

demanding..."

"Bailiff, help Mr. Joseph."

The thick-necked, crew-cut uniform stepped to the side of Frank and grabbed the waist chain with his right hand, sending it up his back. The sudden sharp motion jerked hard on his cuffs, and he let out a yelp of pain. The uniform stood beside him and held the chain in this position. Tears fell from Frank's eyes.

"Now, to be clear, Mr. Joseph, you are being arraigned on charges related to California penal codes 240, 242, and 647. These charges together carry possible fines of up to ten thousand dollars, and/or a sentence of up to two years in jail. Other charges could be included for what happened in the jail last night, but for those there will be another arraignment. Now, I see you have been read your rights, and I see you have waived an attorney..."

"I never waived..." but the jerk of the chain made him yelp again.

"...you have waived an attorney being present this morning. Therefore, I'm going to ask you to enter a plea. How do you plead to the charge?"

This time Frank did not respond. He looked at the bailiff next to him. The bailiff made a side-tilt of his head, toward the judge. "I'm not guilty." He braced himself for another jerk of the chain, but none came.

"There, that wasn't so hard, was it?" He winced at her arrogant sarcasm and her leering smile. She scratched her pen across a long white form with yellow copy underneath. She tore the yellow copy off and handed it to the clerk next to her. "Bond is set for five thousand dollars. The case will be referred to the district attorney. Mr. Joseph, when you bond out, be advised that you are responsible for appearing at subsequent hearings. I do highly advise you to consider hiring an attorney. A man of your means can certainly afford representation."

There was no clack of the gavel. The bailiff simply turned Frank by his chain and pointed him to another deputy who stood near a side exit. He moved toward him, and the deputy took his arm and moved him through the door. Beyond the door was a short hallway and then a glassed window. An officer appeared, and his shackles were removed. He was handed his clothes and personal items, which he signed for. He was pointed to another window, where he used a credit card in his wallet to charge his bond.

"Has my friend Tony Santos come through this morning?" he asked.

"Move along, sir," the man behind the glass commanded and then returned to the magazine in front of him.

He was glad to shed the orange jumpsuit, covered in his rough, dried blood. He didn't immediately put on his clothes. He stood there in his white briefs, examining himself in a long, pitted mirror in the changing room. The frightful visage reflected in it shocked him. He stepped to it and touched his heavily swollen left eye with his right hand. He pushed on it gingerly, trying to see the white beneath the swelling. He managed to see dark red only, and pressing more was too painful. He gently curled up his smashed, swollen lip to see the split tissue on the inside. His front teeth still felt loose. He attempted to remove the elastic and gauze bandages on his left arm, but they were clipped tightly, and any pressure was too much to bear. He would need a cast, he knew.

He stepped back from the mirror and examined the rest of his body. Besides his soft paunch and white skin, he had black and green bruises on his legs, arms, sides, and hips. They were long and slender, matching the baton that made them. He could feel each stroke as he viewed them in the mirror. He looked like someone who had crashed a motorcycle or fallen off a building. He carefully pulled on his clothing and winced often as those clothes slid over bruises, cuts, and swollen tissue. Pulling with his left hand was impossible, so he had to adjust with his right often. The Joe Montana home white jersey looked ridiculous on him now, and Red's brownish dried blood stood out in thick blotches. He couldn't slip on his jacket as his left hand wouldn't fit through the sleeve, so he carried it out.

Once dressed, he looked very much the same, minus the swollen eye and lip, and the heavily bandaged left arm. However, the image in the mirror was very much a new man. He was different now, and he knew it. He was not the same man who met Tony at the bar a half-day before. External and internal bruises and deep, rutted scarring. He was scarred in a way he wouldn't fully comprehend for some time. He only knew that the face looking back at him was changed. He was as a man arising from the dead, unable to forget the Hell he was returned from. Once seen, Hell cannot be unseen.

Outside the changing room he signed a few more forms, which directed his appearance at hearings. He was handed several copies of other forms and then was shown to the exit. He folded the forms with one hand, shoved them in his pocket, and stepped outside.

The glare of the morning sun stung his good eye. He had no car waiting for him, and he was downtown. He watched the commuters go by for a few moments. He had no idea how he would get home and wondered if his wife knew where he was. He didn't see a payphone.

By the time Trenton Yamaguchi picked him up, it was almost noon.

"Frank, oh my God."

"Hi, Trenton. Yeah, I'm in bad shape. Just drive." He struggled with the seatbelt, but the leather seat felt smooth under him.

The BMW moved out of the gas station and out into traffic.

"Thanks for coming to get me. I didn't know whom else to call. When I was finally able to speak with Shelly, she said they impounded my car, and I couldn't walk to the impound lot. Probably couldn't drive in this shape anyway."

"Of course, Frank. No problem." He felt his friend's eyes examining him.

As they moved through the one-way streets toward the highway, Frank was glad to be leaving the downtown. He tried to unwrap his hand again, but it was still too painful. His fingers on this hand were black to the middle knuckles. He heard himself hiss with each frustrating effort. The throbbing was intensifying and it was hot from the swelling.

"Frank, I have something I have to talk with you about. I hope you don't mind. I know you have a lot to deal with already."

"What?" Frank turned in the passenger seat and regarded him. Trenton turned to look at him and smiled when their eyes met. He turned back to the road.

"After you called me, I called Pastor Probst and told him about your arrest. He asked me to talk with you about it."

"What's there to talk about?"

"Well, he's worried what the congregation will think if they find out about what happened."

"Like I told you on the phone, it was self-defense in the bar, and then the cop just attacked me for no reason. I'm going to win this case and then sue the hell out of the sheriff's department." He gave up fumbling with his bandages and just left them.

"I'm not judging, Frank. We all get put in bad situations sometimes. I'm just telling you what our pastor said. We've worked so hard to make First United Church something special. We don't want to have people questioning one of our most senior deacons..."

"I'm innocent, Trenton. Did you guys talk about that?"

"Frank, please...don't lash out at me. I'm just telling you what the pastor said."

"Go on, then." Frank felt nauseated.

"Well, he asked me to ask you if you wouldn't mind staying clear of the church for a few weeks. We have that big fundraising push over these next two weeks and then *The Bee* is doing the story for the Sunday section. Maybe after that you could come back." He turned his face to him and smiled as if it was already agreed.

"Maybe?"

"Well, that's not what I meant. I just meant that if you wait until those things get behind us, it would be a better time..."

"Trenton, no offense, but that's absolute crap. I'm innocent, as I said. I have been with First United since we worked out of that warehouse on Watt Avenue. I helped build the church membership..."

"Nobody is..."

"Wait a damned minute, Trenton, you are...you very much are! Remember me? I helped design that giant black and gold building. I helped choose the illuminated cross. I tithe ten percent of my gross income *upfront* and you have always counted on me to provide extra. I'm in for over one hundred grand over the last five years alone, plus what I've done to get others to contribute..."

"You've been at the vanguard since the beginning, Frank. That's not what we mean..."

"The hell it isn't, Trenton. You're embarrassed by this incident. You're worried it'll hurt donations. You're worried I'm a liability. You haven't thought twice about all the work I've done or all the money I've contributed. You're worried about getting more money moving forward..."

"You *know* this is a tough stretch for us, Frank. You know that..."

"I do...I've been helping you plan for the last year. I've given everything to this church. My family has been in this church longer than you have..."

"And everybody appreciates what you have done. Please calm down, Frank..."

Voice raised. "Calm down? I've been a church leader from the start. I've donated a small fortune. I've brought hundreds of people to First United. Then I get falsely accused of a crime and you're telling me to stay away? I might hurt your image?"

"No, Frank...don't put words into my mouth..."

"What is it then?"

"As I said, this is a tough patch for us...we just don't need any negative publicity. It could hurt our fundraising and then we might not be able to pay for the landscaping project. You know how critical that is."

"Yeah, the landscaping project *is* important. But without me you wouldn't even have that giant black and gold building. You wouldn't have people driving by and seeing that amazing structure...seeing God's church on the highway. Landscaping? You'd all be back in the warehouse if it wasn't for me."

"And everybody knows that, Frank. We know you've been so critical to our rapid growth. And the new building. We just don't want to see your good work go to waste. I'm sure all this will blow over, but in the meantime we just want you to lay low." He wasn't turning to look at Frank anymore, and Frank knew it was intentional. He could feel the scalding anger boiling inside him.

"That's it then. I need to hide out. Stay away from church."

"Just for the next few weeks."

"You know, Trent, when I sat in that disgusting cell last night, just before the deputy beat me bloody and broke my arm, all I could think about was getting back to the House of God. Singing hymns. Praying. Feeling the Spirit move through me. That's all I thought about…even before my family."

"Frank, it's just a couple of weeks…"

"No, it's not." Frank saw that they were a block away from his home.

"C'mon, Frank…"

"It's not a couple weeks."

"Seriously…just until after *The Bee* spread."

"No, it's much more than that." His voice was soft now, his gaze out the window.

"I don't understand you…"

"Trenton, if Pastor Probst, you, and First United turn your back on me now, I'm done. Do you hear me?"

"Frank, c'mon, man…don't be childish…"

"No, *you* c'mon. If you're not going to support one of your most senior deacons in his time of need, then I have just realized this church is not about serving God's will. Would Jesus turn his back on a man in his hour of need?"

"Of course not, and neither are we. Hate the sin, love the sinner…" Trenton said, as he pulled up to the front of Frank's large brick home. A dog barked nearby.

"Well, I have a message for you and Pastor Probst." Frank pushed his right hand forward, and his middle finger nearly touched Senior Deacon Yamaguchi's nose. He blinked hard at it, but didn't react, as much as Frank wanted him to. Frank regarded the eyes staring at his finger. Empty. Dispassionate. Dead. How he himself was feeling inside at that moment. *The eyes reflect the soul,* he thought. He also knew he was walking down a path from which he would not return. A singular, narrow path. *Narrow is the gate.* Though he had no idea how accurate that was, he was beginning to understand. The door was cracked open, and he could see what was ahead. Dark clouds. Detritus. Death. The scattered rubble of once-proud homes. Bones turning to ash.

"Frank…"

"No, fuck you, man. I guess you find out who your true friends are when you're at your lowest." He opened the door, stepped out, and closed it with a bit more force than he had intended. He didn't look back as he walked up to his house. He heard the BMW drive away.

As he neared the door, he stopped. He regarded the house.

# V

Terry Lawrence motioned Frank to the chair in front of his large polished wood desk. He was turned sideways, finishing his phone call, one foot up on an opened bottom drawer. Fumbling at first with his cast, Frank pulled the door closed behind him, moved to a chair, and sat.

"Yes, senator, we'll be sure to contribute again. We've always got your back…"

Frank looked around Terry's office, casting his eyes to the plaques and mementos he had seen hundreds of times. They had worked together for years, but he knew this would be the last time they would be together in this room. He saw the folded *Sacramento Bee* on his desk. He had been mildly surprised they had used his mug shot in the paper. *So much for privacy.* Though it had been three weeks and his physical wounds were mostly healed, minus the cast on his arm, he had known the day would come when he would have to answer for the event.

"Okay, senator. No problem. See you at the Capitol Ball next week. Give Carolyn my best."

He hung up the phone and turned to Frank. Terry was his friend, but he had no illusions about what this meeting was about. He knew what he would have done in his place.

He was a bit surprised, though, when Terry got up and came around the other side of the desk. He pulled the other chair sideways and sat facing him. He was still flashing his million-dollar smile, emphasized by his tanning salon glow and cosmetic dentistry. Terry pulled on his cufflinks to adjust his monogramed shirt under his suit jacket. His guise was always on here in the office.

"Hey Frank, thanks for coming in. How are you?" *Eye contact, face tilted to show concern.*

"Well, mostly healed…just the arm…" and he held up the cast. His left sleeve was open around it.

"Shelly and the kids doing well?" *Working through the concern checklist.*

"Yeah, all things considered." He hated this dance and just wanted to get it over with.

"Yeah, I see what you mean." Terry looked down at his shoes for a second.

"Look, Terry, I know why you called me in. I understand. I saw the article. I get the position you're in."

He saw relief all over Terry's face. "Yeah, thanks, Frank. This isn't easy. You and I have been friends a long time."

"Sure, we both climbed up out of middle management together. You and I took this place out of the mainframe age."

"We did, Frank. We certainly did." *Warm, reassuring smile.*

"Don't worry, Terry…I understand what you have to do. I know you met with the board last night. I completely understand. I guess I just need to know the particulars."

"Particulars?"

"Well, I'm hoping you'll send me off with a reference. And, of course, there's my severance package. I need to transition, and need some time, especially while I fight these charges."

"Yeah, see…that's the issue…" Now he was staring at his expensive shoes.

"What's the issue? My severance package?"

"Yeah. The board directed me to withhold any severance. I'm sorry…"

"Why? It's in my contract."

"Yes, I know…this is tough, Frank…" His eyes flicked up, met Frank's, and then were right back down to his shoes.

"Tough? Yeah, no shit. So how could they deny me a severance?

You and I negotiated these contracts together..."

"You see, it's the officer clause in your contract. They said that since you are an officer of the company, your misconduct—their word, not mine—precluded the award of a severance."

"How is that even legal?"

"Well, they're serious about this, because they don't want anybody to think you cashed out on the way out...they're worried it would reflect on them...the *optics* in the community."

"But I have to find another job, Terry. We built in a one-year severance so we could transition. This is bullshit and you know it!" The math was beginning to become more challenging for him.

"I totally understand your anger, Frank. I don't like it either. But this is a board decision, and they've already conferred with the legal team. They think they'll win, and it's a lot of money."

"Goddamned right, it's a lot of money, Terry....goddamned right..."

Terry looked up. He had never seen Frank flushed, angry, and swearing.

"So what am I supposed to use to pay my mortgage, Terry? How the hell do I feed my family?"

"I'm sorry, Frank...there's nothing I can do about it. Surely you've saved..."

"I have, but I give a lot to my church, and much of it is in investment accounts...401ks and bond funds. I can't just pull that out. Plus, I have legal fees, pending the hearing. I need that money. This is unbelievable..."

"I'm sorry, Frank. There is nothing I can do. I fought for you...I want you to know that. They were adamant and unanimous. No severance, and they want you out today." He reached over and put his hand on Frank's knee. They made eye contact. "I want you to know that I personally am so sorry. You've always been a true friend, and you're a fantastic leader. It'll be so hard to replace you."

"I guess you have it pretty tough, huh?" His snide tone wasn't lost on Terry.

"Frank, let's not do this. I understand you're hurt..."

"No, Terry, you don't understand. I figured I had a year to get things together. Now I'm walking out with nothing. Everything I have worked for is gone."

"I understand…"

"The fuck if you do!" Frank bolted up, erect as a post, back of his knees pushing his chair back. He stood over his friend, looking down. What he saw surprised him. A flash of panic. As if he expected Frank to throw a punch at him. That told him everything he needed to know. And for a moment he liked the power. He liked that his friend feared him and perhaps felt him dangerous now. Respect of some kind, anyway…better than no respect at all. At that moment, it was enough. It would have to do.

Without a word, he turned on his heel and walked to the door. He didn't acknowledge Terry's admin, instead walking with pace two doors down to his own office. On his desk was an empty box. Someone put that there while he was meeting with Terry.

"Motherfuckers…" he hissed under his breath.

He packed his pictures, diplomas, and a few files. He took the elevator down, left his keys and ID badges at the front desk, and then loaded the box in his trunk. He never set foot in that building again. He started the car and moved out of the parking lot. He was lost in a forest of thoughts, trying to find a path, but with no success. Instead, he now felt there *was no path*, and he felt desperate. He had never been lost before. He had always had a plan. Ever since he was a young man, he had always wanted to do exactly what he had been doing… up until that moment in his life. He had pictured himself successful. He had pictured himself well-dressed and professional. His self-image had been exactly what he had built, now cracked and threatening to fall to pieces.

He was tangled in his thoughts and drove reactively. He didn't even realize where he was driving. He was on the freeway. Then he was off. He found himself pulling into the parking lot of the Providence Memorial Assisted Living Center. He parked in visitor parking and walked into the sprawling building, past the newly planted trees.

"Hi, Mr. Joseph, we weren't expecting you. Are you here to visit?"

"Yes, I guess." He hadn't been sure until that moment.

"Your mother is just finishing breakfast. She slept in this

morning. I'll have her cleaned up and ready for you in just a minute."

He was waiting outside for her as she was wheeled out to the small patio behind the center. His face was in his hands. He wiped the tears quickly and stood up as she was rolled out to him.

"And here's your son, Mrs. Joseph." The nurse put on a happy voice, as if his mother were a child seeing her birthday cake.

She didn't look up. She looked ahead, eyes vacuous. As blank as the stare Trent had given him. Wispy cotton-candy hair thinner than the last time he had seen her. A million miles away, also seeking a path she would never find, lost in a forest that was consuming her.

"How has she been?" he asked the nurse.

"She has been...fine..." and her hesitation told him everything. He knew she could be combative; Alzheimer's patients often grew frustrated and angry as their minds worked hard to try to put together missing pieces. Work across plaqued-over brain tissue. Over the last year, she had lost so much and was now nearly a clean slate. A newborn, with only biological needs making her a person.

"Okay, thank you," he said, letting her off the hook.

He dragged a cast-iron chair next to her wheelchair and sat.

"Hi, Mom, how are you?" he asked her. She didn't turn to his voice and maintained her distant stare. "How are you feeling?" He hated that he always spoke too loudly to her, as if her issues started with hearing. No response, only looking forward.

"I need you now, Mom. I wish you could understand me."

For a moment he sat, eyes tangential to hers, both gazing into the distance. Both trying to sort out the fragments of their lives. Both missing pieces they could never fill. Both wishing for better days. They were both living the same surreality of that moment.

"I'm in trouble, Mom. I just lost my job...." and now tears were rolling down his cheeks. "I lost my job, and now I don't know how I can take care of my family. Take care of you." Voice trembling now. "I don't have enough saved to cover everything. We have a big note on our house. I gave everything I could to help the church." The tears were hot now. "I don't know how long I can keep you here, Mom. I don't know how long I can afford anything."

He put his face back into his hands. The hard cast smelled, but he still pressed it against his face. Tears ran down his palm and down his wrist. His tears wet the plaster. He spoke through it.

"I have all the rest of my money tied up in court. The union is representing the deputy sheriff that beat me, and now he's suing me...claiming I attacked him. I don't know what to do, Mom. I think I'm going to run out of money before I run out of things to be sued for."

And then he openly wept. Hard. He wept as the small child did to the woman who sat beside him. He wept the way he had when he had fallen off his red Schwinn and tore the skin off his hands and knees. She had held him then, softly cooing and shushing. He cried the way he had when his father, her husband, had died; and then they had cried together. He cried the way he had when his high school girlfriend dumped him when she went off to college, and while he had wept she had gently assured him he would find another love someday.

He cried hot tears. Loud cries of pain. All that he had held in him came out. He shuddered from deep within his soul. This was a loss he wasn't sure he would or even could ever recover from.

He hadn't noticed that the cold, soft hand was touching his. It stirred in the back of his mind. His sobbing stopped, and he pulled his hands from his face. His mother's cold, liver-spotted hand touched his. He took her hand, and he held it. She turned her distant gray eyes to him. He didn't even think she could see him or perhaps even comprehend him. But her hand felt comforting on his.

How that hand had consoled him, nurtured him through the years of his life. How those hands had washed him, changed him, wiped his tears, cleaned scrapes and cuts, ironed his clothes. Those hands had been the connection between him and his mother. Her touch had joined mother to son. Her touch was life and love to him. Her touch had raised him, from boy to man.

Now their hands held each other's.

And he saw it. Ever so slightly. He thought he saw a flicker of recognition in her fading vision, though perhaps he just wished it to be there.

# VI

Her gray-blue eyes were earnest and imploring. Frank knew she felt vulnerable, more than she ever had in her life. It was new to her. It was new to them. Everything she had known about her life felt balanced on a knife's edge. Her voice was as sharp as that blade, and it cut him to the quick.

"How are we going to take care of the kids?"

"Don't worry, everything will be okay." He was doing his best to project confidence, but he wasn't optimistic. He could feel it, off in the distance. He knew the storm was coming. His brave face hid many cracks. Pretense crumbling.

"How can you know that, Frank? How can you say that?" She looked away from him, cheeks angry red.

"God will see us through this, Shelly. We'll make it through this tough time. We have to pull together and support each other."

"I think this is getting worse, not better." She crossed her arms, appearing authoritarian as she leveled her gaze at him. He saw judgment.

"It's a tough challenge…it definitely is…" He couldn't hold her gaze, and his eyes fell.

"You made a choice that night…you went to the bar instead of taking care of your family. You weren't being responsible. Now we all have to suffer for *your* mistake…"

"We've been over this. I'm sorry. I wish I could go back, but I can't."

"I have to think about me and the kids." She was looking past him now. "I have to do what's right for us. You don't know how vulnerable I feel right now."

"Don't I? I'm the one with the court date."

"I'm worried about my children, Frank. *Our* children. You're worried about yourself. If you go to jail, how will we afford this house? How will we eat?"

"Haven't I always taken care of you? Haven't I?" She was still looking afar. "I've always handled things. Trust me to handle this."

Shelly looked back at him, then down to his hands. She stood up from the bed, straightened her blouse, and then turned. Her back was to him. He could see the few light streaks of gray in her shoulder-length hair. "Frank, you need to solve this. You need to get this fixed soon. This is embarrassing for me. My family. The kids. We have lives too. I'm not going to let you screw up all of ours. I'm not going to toss away my life because of your lapse of judgment." *Properly stated,* she thought. She left the bedroom and walked to the front room.

Frank would have been better served to have understood what she was telling him in that moment. Instead, he continued to look at his hands, assuming she was venting. His mind swirled. His thoughts collided and mashed together. He couldn't get his thinking lined up and organized; he couldn't find a sequence or pattern to solve. Too much. It was all too much. He was overwhelmed. Drowning in the wave that crashed down on his life. His thoughts cast shadows around the room, too quick for his eyes to follow.

*How had it come to this?* he wondered. How could his perfect life collapse from under him? All he had done was stand up for his friend. They were both outnumbered, and nobody was hurt badly. Then in the county lockup, he had only asked for a phone call. How had such simple things derailed him? And Tony wasn't returning his calls.

*What on earth is going on?*

He had immediately sought counsel. He hired the best money could buy. His lawyer set to work immediately. Both incorrectly assumed the case would be reviewed and dismissed. They hadn't dismissed it, though. Far from it.

"Frank, there's something amiss here," Kevin Matthews, esquire, had said, fiddling with his Stanford tie. "The DA seems to be pressing this case. I don't know why...and the judge is blocking many of my requests for information, especially about the deputy and some witnesses. Something is very odd about this case."

"What does that mean?"

"It seems they're going to press this case for what happened at the lockup...they're going to come at you hard on this one, and then when they bring the next charges, they'll already have proven you to be a violent person. They are refusing to talk about plea bargains and want this first case to go to trial...and they want that soon. They need to move through this one, so they can get to the charges for what happened with Deputy Jensen."

"What?"

"Yeah, they're planning to go all the way; the sheriff's union is demanding you be held accountable, and since both cases are tied together, they are demanding jail time for each. Your second case should be presented to the grand jury soon. Is there anything you want to tell me? About that incident, I mean. Deputy Jensen is claiming serious injuries sustained that night. He has been out of work since then. He said he experienced physical and emotional trauma and that he may not be able to work again. What happened?"

"I told you already. I was asking for my phone call. The officer simply opened the door and beat me with his baton. He had only just arrived...maybe ten minutes. I didn't do anything except demand my call." Frank was lightheaded. His fingertips were tingling. An icy sweat coated his forehead. Tightness in his throat and chest.

"I subpoenaed the surveillance video from the lockup, but nobody can seem to find that tape. They're saying it must've been accidentally erased."

"Erased?"

"Yeah. Coincidence, right? Plus, the union is pressing in support of their officer...they've met with the mayor twice. They're demanding the DA support Jensen with an all-out prosecution. No pleas will suffice. They keep talking about officer safety. They say you need to be made an example of, or others will do the same." After a pause. "And now they're holding the civil case until the criminal trial...they think it'll increase the award of damages."

"What could happen to me?"

"Assaulting a police officer is a felony...this could be some serious jail time if they don't accept a plea deal...plus what you're facing from the bar. Civil trial could result in a serious cash award, including levies against future earnings."

Frank could feel it slipping away from him. He knew this was breaking in the wrong direction. Like a Reno slot machine, every crank of the handle showed lemons. He had left his lawyer's office in emotional rags. Since their meeting he had been home, trying to make sense of the calamitous turn his life had taken.

He heard his children playing outside in their backyard. A thin wall of stucco, two-by-fours, and insulation were all that stood between him and them, but they felt miles away. He normally loved to hear the sound of their laughter, but tonight he had other thoughts. Dark ones. Tonight he was a defeated man. He was lost in the harsh hurricane in his heart and mind. All was tumult and despair.

He slipped off his bed and down onto his knees, barely able to stay upright. He smoothed the white duvet and then turned his eyes up to the ceiling. He spoke his prayer aloud, voice pleading, straining with every ounce of his body to push his prayer up toward the heavens.

"Dear Father, I know I have prayed that you give me trials in my life. I know I prayed for you to forge my spirit in the crucible of spiritual challenges. I realize now that I wasn't ready. I am not strong. I'm weak. So very weak. Lord, please take this challenge away from me. I'm not strong enough to take any more. I want to stay in my walk with you. I don't want to lose everything I have. I don't want to see my family hurt. I have worked so hard..."

He jerked when the phone rang. He tried to continue praying, but the ringing made him lose focus. Shelly answered, then called out from the kitchen.

"Frank, it's Matthews!" She had expectation in her voice.

He stood up heavily with a great weight between his shoulders. He felt decades older than he was and was drained from all the emotions he'd had coursing through him these last weeks.

He picked up the phone. "Hi, Kevin," he said. He waited for

Shelly to click off the line, but she didn't. The ambient noise made his lawyer sound far away.

"Hi, Frank. I have some news for you."

"Yeah, go ahead," he said, but he knew from his tone that this was going to be bad.

"Like we talked about, it's not looking good. The DA is still playing hardball...no plea bargains. They feel they have a strong case. Your friend Tony has agreed to testify against you and claim you started the fight that night..."

"He what?" Frank couldn't contain his shout. "Tony?"

"They're already planning their initial prosecution against you for the bar fight and are wrapping up a second for the county jail incident. The first met the grand jury this morning, and they returned an indictment. And as I said before, the union is demanding action to support the deputy, and they hope to have that case ready in two months. I'm sorry...wish I had better news."

"Oh my God," Frank said, sitting down on the bed. His elbows were on his knees. Trembling left hand rubbed his eyes and forehead. He could barely hold the phone to his ear.

"I pressed for a plea down. Usually for these types of cases and someone without a record you can work down to probation and fines, but they're not bargaining. I do have an offer from the DA. It's not great, but I want you to consider it...going to trial is dangerous. I just want you to think about it. The DA is willing to accept a one-year sentence, and good time could cut that in half. Five years probation. Hundred-thousand-dollar fine, for court costs and damages."

He could hear Shelly's excited breaths and movements in the kitchen.

"Kevin, how can this be?" Frank felt the phone trembling against his ear.

"I'm sorry, Frank. You know I pushed for no jail time, but there are forces at work here."

"Forces? Yeah, forces of corruption!" He felt his face flush with rage. "They beat me..."

"Frank, I know..." he tried to interject.

"...and then not only do they get away with it, but I'm the one looking at jail time? How on Earth is this possible?"

"I'm sorry, Frank. You're a citizen and they're the authorities. They hold the strings, and from their viewpoint you hurt one of them, and they want you to pay. I'm meeting with the DA again on Monday. I'll try to work down the jail time more. But your friend's willingness to testify against you...that's an ace they have in any negotiation."

"I can't go to jail, Kevin. I can't. I have a family."

"I'll see what I can do. Our only other option is to go to trial, but anything can happen there. You could end up with a lot more. It's risky."

"How much more?"

"They have those three charges they've already listed: disorderly conduct, assault, battery. Plus they could list damages to the bar... could be a lot. You could end up with two to three years, perhaps, though I imagine it would be less. We also have to consider whether they'll file more civil charges, and guilt in a criminal court furthers that civil case."

"Do they understand I have no prior record? Do they know I am a deacon in the church and all that? Was..."

"Of course I told them, Frank. Of course I did," almost indignantly. "That's why they're offering this deal. At first, they weren't bargaining at all."

He sat there rubbing his eyes. He was trembling uncontrollably.

Michelle Joseph filled the momentary silence. "Kevin, what happens to me if these fines are levied against Frank and he goes to jail?"

"What do you mean?"

"Do I have to pay?"

"As husband and wife, the fines would go against your family assets. Any joint funds would be levied."

"The house?"

"Yes, the house. Savings. Investments."

"You can't let that happen, Kevin," she insisted. "I have to think about the children if Frank goes to jail. Who is going to take care of us?"

"I understand, Michelle. I'll do everything I can."

"Thanks, Kevin," Frank said, resignedly. He hung up and set the phone on the bed next to him. He heard his wife continue in the kitchen. He lifted himself slowly to his feet, and then stepped into the bathroom. He opened the toilet and vomited. One single watery heave. It came out of his nose and his mouth and burned fiercely. He spit to clear his mouth, then flushed the toilet. As he cupped his hand to get water from the sink, he looked into the mirror. His eyes seemed so vacant, so distant. He felt like he was seeing himself across a divide, seeing another him…an older one. His cheeks sagged. Gone were his open smile and happy eyes.

He walked back to the bed and sat on the edge for just a moment. He slid back to his knees. He body was nearly limp, and his hands clasped weakly.

"Father, please help me. I can't do this. I need you to help me. Please show me what I should do. I'm not ready for what I'm going to face. Please…" His face was shedding tears into the white duvet.

"Dad?" Soft voice at the door.

"Mark…what's up, buddy?" He kept his face down.

"Is everything okay?" His son took a tentative step forward.

Frank looked up at him. Mark saw his father's face and stepped back. "Yeah, everything is fine." He tried to smile, but it just made him appear gruesome.

"Dad, I can help you. I can work. I can cut grass…"

"No, everything is fine, son. Run along, Mark. It'll be okay."

"But Dad…"

"*Not now, Mark!*"

Mark turned and left the room.

Frank squeezed his hands together and prayed with all his emotional strength. He prayed for an end to his struggle. For an end to his suffering. For an end to his trauma. He prayed that the onrushing change would stop in its tracks even though it was picking up speed.

# PART II: THE FALL

# VII

The two men sat closely together, speaking in low tones. The flags. The wooden barrier railings. The high seat and the judge's black chair. The jury box. It had the look of every courtroom he had seen on television. *Is there a rulebook somewhere for courtroom construction?* Frank wondered. *Some master plan for the room where guilt and innocence are decided?*

Frank had never imagined his entire life would be judged in just two hours. He sat there hunched over, holding his stomach, which felt like it was twisting inside him. Eyes down, nervously rocking. *Any time now…any time.*

Two hours. That was all it had taken.

Opening arguments. Witness testimony. Motions to dismiss. All so very swiftly managed. Rote even, as if everybody had done this a hundred times, and they were just going through the motions. Performing in the same roles they had acted for years. This was a play, and all the actors performed it every day, with one guest performer after another. Today it was Frank, and tomorrow it would be someone else. A theater of life changes and heartbreak. *Théâtre de la ruine.*

His life now hung in the balance. All that he had worked for. All that he had accomplished. Everything he would be in the future, now just a matter of decisions and forms. It didn't matter what he thought. At this point, it didn't matter what he did. Determinations would be made about his life, and they would be made by others. Others who only knew him by what they read and the testimony given. Here, in those two hours.

He could walk out of this room a free man, or he could leave it in handcuffs, based solely on what a jury found after two hours of testimony. They knew him enough to judge him, and that's all that mattered, it seemed. They didn't know who he was; they knew what other people portrayed him to be. Good? Bad? Innocent? Guilty? Each had made their case.

It hadn't been like he had expected. He was expecting Perry Mason moments. Shouts of "I object!" and witnesses exposed on the stand, acknowledging their deceit. "Okay, I lied...Mr. Joseph is innocent!" and sharp intakes of breath as the judge dismissed the case.

None of that had happened. No game-changing revelations. No exculpatory evidence. No witness breakdowns.

Instead, it was a mostly rehearsed performance. The court followed a script. The judge read long, meaning-filled passages, giving points of law and directions to the parties involved. Witnesses, the jury, and Frank all heard more about legal proceedings than they could ever care to know or could even remember. Opening statements were flatly given. No shouting or theatrics...each side simply stating what they wanted the jury to believe. Witnesses related what was given in sworn statements, carefully rehearsed so as not to contradict themselves.

And he learned everybody's name. People he had been with for just minutes turned into real people with full lives. Just like his. The bouncer who had held him down was named James "Jimmy" Huber, and he was the evening security supervisor at the I-Ball. The pretty waitress who served them beers was Lisa Everson, a student at Sacramento State University, studying education. Red was Randall Karrick. He lived in Alameda, but that night was in Sacramento visiting his friends Hector Garcia and Tommy Laughridge.

The I-Ball witnesses had all refused to pick sides, and instead simply identified the people they saw. "I didn't see who started it" and "I came in after the fight was almost over."

"They are probably fearful of being sued," Matthews had told him. "It's smart business on their part to stay out of it." So, then, it had become Frank's word against everybody else, and he knew that wouldn't end well for him.

All of them wore their best clothes. Red's hair was cropped short, devoid of its curls. He looked different in a suit—almost looked like someone Frank might hire in another situation. Something about a dark suit, white shirt, and good tie…they could make anybody look respectable. Frank knew this himself, so he wore his navy Hugo Boss two-button and Versace tie. His Italian shoes cost more than Red's entire outfit.

Randall Karrick's testimony was lucid, and that surprised Frank. His deep, growling voice gave him a presence on the stand.

"What happened when Mr. Santos exited the restroom?" the DA had asked.

"My friend Hector was bumped from behind. I don't know who did it. We all stood up, just to figure out what had happened. We spoke to Mr. Santos for a minute. Out of nowhere, I saw Mr. Joseph. He was standing in front of me."

"Did Mr. Joseph strike you when he arrived?"

"No."

"When did he strike you?"

"At one point, I remember him swinging at me. I don't know what made him start, but I remember being hit in the face."

Matthews had tried to crack him on cross.

"Mr. Karrick, you swung first at Mr. Joseph, didn't you?"

"No, sir, I did not."

"Why would a smaller man attack a much larger man?"

"I don't know, but my guess is he knows how to fight, based on my face afterwards."

That had earned a chuckle from those in attendance. His otherwise unremarkable testimony was brief.

Frank had been wounded to the soul when his best friend took the stand. He had expected Red and his friends to testify against him. But Tony? Why would he? What was his motivation? Tony never once looked at him. He sat erect, eyes only making contact with the attorneys and the jury. His best friend was the best witness for the prosecution. His best friend became Brutus, driving a sword into his friend's innards. *For what? What would Tony possibly get out of this?*

The district attorney had gotten right to the point very early in his questioning. "How did the physical altercation begin, Mr. Santos?"

Frank could only stare dumbfounded as his best friend, whom he had known for decades, said, "Things were settling down. I had been talking to them, and things seemed to calm a bit. Then Mr. Joseph arrived and threw a punch at Mr. Karrick. Then the fight began." He could feel the weight of the jury's eyes on him. The rest of his testimony painted a portrait consistent with that of Red and his friends.

After his testimony, Tony left the stand and stared blankly forward as he walked out of the courtroom. It wasn't the last time Frank would see his best friend, but it was the last time he would consider him in that way.

When Frank himself took the stand, he did all he could to remember every detail of the night. Matthews felt it was important to show recall. He recounted the colors of shirts, hair, brands of beer. He blushed when he recounted his eye contact with Ms. Everson's cleavage. He reported the initial swing of fists and how he had just missed being hit by several punches.

On cross-examination, he had held up well, keeping calm despite the accusations. He had stayed even-tempered and had not risen to the response-bait the prosecutor threw his way. He stuck to his own script and held firm to his view of events. He was clear, concise, and made confident eye contact. Years of leadership gave him a professional presence.

He could feel his stomach turn, though, when the prosecutor produced poster-board images of their mug shots, State's Exhibits 4 and 5. Frank's face was unchanged, and even his profile shot didn't reveal the large knot on the back of his head, and the small grill-print above his eye seemed more like a scrape. Though later his face would change after the beating in the jail, the booking image was of someone who had not been in much of an altercation.

Randall Karrick's mug shot, though, showed much worse. His eyes were swollen and black from a broken nose, which had obviously been fixed since the fight. His lip was split, and his hair was clumped with dried blood. Frank couldn't believe that his fists had done such damage.

"Tell me, Mr. Joseph. How did Mr. Karrick receive the injuries we see on this mug shot?"

His voice stayed cool, and he replied, "Yes, we were in a fight. I've never denied that."

"But what I don't understand is how two men could have such different results from a fight if they were both fighting. Mr. Karrick's injuries that night include a broken nose, multiple abrasions on the face, and a separated shoulder. He required multiple stitches." Once again, the jury locked on him. "You, on the other hand, arrived at the county jail with only skinned knuckles, which seem to have been split when you repeatedly hit Mr. Karrick."

The room was now silent, and he could hear people move in their seats. Frank knew he needed to say something.

"Success in a fight doesn't indicate the cause of the fight, does it?"

"What do you mean, Mr. Joseph?" The DA immediately regretted asking that question. He knew better, after all: never give the accused a platform.

"I mean, just because I won the fight doesn't prove Mr. Karrick didn't start the fight, does it? There were three of them and two of us. We were outnumbered. I was defending myself..."

"Just a minute, Mr. Joseph..."

"...and Mr. Karrick obviously had too much to drink that night. When the punches started flying, I hit back, and I hit back with all I had. Which of you..." and he turned directly to the jury, "wouldn't fight for your life if you were cornered like we were?"

"Cornered, Mr. Joseph?" The DA felt the momentum change and had to regain control.

"Yes, cornered."

"Funny, Mr. Joseph, but all the testimony we've heard previously indicates you initiated the fight that night. Did you call for a bouncer? Did you call for the police? No, you simply attacked another man and injured him badly. I have no further questions, your honor."

As he sat in the courtroom waiting for the jury, he could feel that it didn't go his way. He felt that the evidence all went against him, including his best friend's testimony. He had tried to read the eyes of the jury, but they were inconclusive; most of the jurors just looked away from him. He knew enough to know that wasn't a good sign.

"Court will resume in five minutes," the tall bailiff announced, startling Frank. He hadn't seen him enter the room.

"That means the jury has made its decision, Frank," Kevin Matthews said.

Instantly, his heart began to pound furiously. *This is it then,* he thought. *I'm finally here.*

"I'm scared, Kevin," Frank said. "I'm not ready for what could happen." His voice wavered and his hands were shaking. His mouth was like cotton, and he couldn't swallow.

His lawyer looked at him with consolation in his eyes. "Remember that whatever they decide doesn't change who you are. You're a good man…don't let it fuck you up if the verdict goes against you." Frank again felt his stomach flop inside him, and he hunched over again, holding it tightly. He knew he wasn't built for prison.

People began to move. Papers were shuffled. The DA returned to his chair at the next table.

"All rise!" came the call. Doors opened, the jury filed in, and the judge took his seat on high. "Be seated," *Hizzoner* called out. As they sat, Frank felt Kevin's hand grab his. He couldn't look up.

"Madame Foreman, has the jury reached a decision in *State of California vs. Christopher F. Joseph?*"

"We have, your honor." Frank now hated the rehearsed sound, like a synchronized gambol around his grave.

"How do you find the defendant in the charge of disorderly conduct?"

"Not guilty, your honor." Clerks marked forms.

"How do you find the defendant in the charge of assault?"

"Not guilty, your honor." More forms were marked and shuffled.

Frank's heart leapt. *Could I walk away from this?* He felt the briefest moment of elation. His head jerked left in the direction of the jury.

"How do you find the defendant in the charge of simple

battery?"

"Guilty, your honor."

Frank's head dropped again. His elbows went to his knees. The room was spinning. He took deep breaths to keep from fainting. He felt Matthew's hand on his back.

There it was. His entire life. Career. Gone. Burned before him. All that he had known was about to be swept away. Guilty of a crime. A record. On every job application for the rest of his life, he would have to list this crime. A violent crime. He knew how he would have viewed the same. He would never hold a senior leadership position again. No company in its right mind would hire a manager with a violent history. He'd be lucky to get a job turning a wrench, and he didn't know any trades. And before all that…prison. Frank knew he wasn't ready for that.

The words that followed were a blur. The jurors were asked if the responses were unanimous. They agreed. They were thanked for their service and then excused from the courtroom. He heard the judge speaking, but he couldn't understand the words.

"Frank, you need to stand…Frank…" Matthews said to him.

Frank pulled himself to his feet, but was unsteady. Matthews put his arm around him for support.

"Mr. Joseph, the events of that night were egregious. Fighting another man in a bar may seem fine in the movies, but our society cannot support such violence. We rely on people to follow rules. We expect peace in our cities."

Frank felt faint.

The judge shifted papers in front of him. "However, when I look at your life, you have been a model citizen. You haven't received so much as a parking ticket in your adult life. You pay your taxes. You have a family. You've been very successful. You don't strike me as a man who would attack someone wantonly."

He nodded, but didn't have the strength to look up.

At the table next to them, the DA sat up, as if to make a comment. The judge stared down at him above his reading glasses, and the DA slid back into his seat.

"Therefore, Mr. Joseph, I'm going to assign the maximum fine of two thousand dollars. I'm going to assign one year of probation, in lieu of jail time. Do you understand?"

Frank looked up. He wasn't really comprehending more than basic ideas. He nodded, though, as he knew that was expected.

"Therefore, you will be required to meet with a probation officer, and any offenses will void that probation and earn you jail time. In simple English, if you so much as jaywalk, you'll be doing time. Are we clear, Mr. Joseph?"

Frank again nodded.

"Court is now in recess," the judge announced, and his black robes whisked as he swept out of the courtroom. All around him, people moved. More papers. Doors opening. People talking. Frank sat down hard on his chair.

Kevin Matthews shook the hand of the DA, and they spoke briefly. Frank just looked at his hands, which were trembling. He heard his lawyer and the DA laughing. *Old friends, I see. Everybody in this profession is tied together…only the defendants and jury are interchangeable. This is their business. Do they even give a shit about whom they work with?*

"Frank, you okay?"

"I don't understand, Kevin. What happened?"

"You got off *very* easy, Frank!" he said with a big grin, slapping him on the back. "You were only found guilty on one of the three charges, and the judge went light. He based his decision on your clean record. No prior arrests for anything. A citizen in good standing. Those were our points for the plea bargain we attempted, which the DA turned down. Anyway, I guess the judge got it, even if nobody else did. He gave you probation. Considering the testimony, the fact that we went to court, and the verdict, you were lucky to avoid jail time, though you probably wouldn't have gotten much for the single offense…maybe a few months. Still, you're going home today, so be glad!" He clapped him on the shoulder again, but Frank was unmoved.

"But I'm guilty."

"Yeah, you have a record now, Frank." Kevin was putting his papers in his briefcase. His voice was conciliatory. "Sorry, we did the best we could. I think those photos…"

Frank cut him off. "So what happens now?"

"Well, you'll need to complete some paperwork. Then you have a week to see a probation officer. They'll require you to take periodic drug tests, most likely, and see that you're working and staying out of trouble."

"But I lost my job." Frank's face was blank. His stare was a thousand miles away.

*I'm a convicted criminal*, he thought. He remembered how he felt about convicted criminals he saw on the news. Whose applications he reviewed. He was now in that same group...an ever-growing fraternity. He was guilty of a crime, a crime he didn't commit, though he was the only one who felt that way.

"Don't worry, they'll help you get another one. It's not like that."

"But then what?"

"Then you find a job, work, wait until your probation is over, and then you're in the clear. On this case anyway."

"What about the other?"

"I can't say. I just asked the DA if they were moving forward with the case. He said, *'It's being reviewed.'* After this long, I'm thinking there are issues...perhaps some evidence we don't know about. Not sure, really...we'll have to wait and see."

"How long could it drag on?"

"There's no timeline. They can wait months if they want. The longer they wait, though, the better it is for you."

"Why?"

"Well, time fades the issue...the testimonies. Memories become less clear. No guarantees, but I'd say if we don't hear anything in a couple more months then we know there is something terribly wrong with their case. We'll just have to wait and see. Be patient, Frank." He again smiled at him, but didn't see any return.

"Should I be worried?"

"Yes, very worried. Assaulting a police officer is a serious charge, and juries tend to favor the testimony of uniformed officers. If it's your word against his, they'll take the side of the officer almost every time. You could be facing some serious jail time. Years."

"So how will we find out?"

"They'll contact me first. I have a friend in the DA's office, and she'll let me know if they start to empanel a grand jury to hear the evidence."

Frank was still trembling.

"Frank, relax. You just won the first battle, all things considered."

"I don't feel like I've won. I was just found guilty."

"You got no jail time, and they were pushing hard for that. I had offered a plea deal that was exactly what you ended up getting, so that's a victory. Don't discount the impact of that…you're very lucky, considering how hard the DA went after you."

"Yeah."

"Listen, don't think about anything else tonight. Go home. Have a drink. Hug your kids. You avoided jail, which isn't a small thing. Once you're over this, you can start thinking about your career and all that. These things can spin you out of control if you're not careful. Don't let it do that to you."

"Okay. It's just…I don't know."

He sat down next to Frank and put his hand on his shoulder. Frank looked up to him. "Frank, you're in a tough stretch. You're in a winter. Spring is on the horizon. Just bear it. Handle the tough weather, and then you'll find things green and sunny again."

"Thanks, man."

"Is your wife here? Maybe she can take you out to celebrate."

"No, she said she didn't want to be here, just in case I was sent to jail."

"Oh. Okay. Understand." But he didn't. "Well, do you need a lift?"

"Yeah, thanks, Kevin. I honestly thought I was going to jail today, so I took a taxi this morning."

As Matthews collected his papers and signed forms, Frank pondered his life. He decided to take the positive view. He had, as his lawyer said, avoided jail. Dodged a bullet. While he might be facing further lawsuits and trials, those were out of his control. He could only take things as they came to him, and fight through each obstacle. Frank decided to push forward. To struggle on. To fight. He would work his way through his problems and find himself on the other side someday, somehow. He was intelligent, resourceful, and hard working. He would come through, he determined, and be a better man for it. He had his family...four children who loved him and a wife of sixteen years. He would find another job and get things back in order.

# VIII

Frank opened the collar of his white dress shirt and pulled loose his red necktie. The heat in his eyes made him turn his head. Outside, December rain poured from heavy black clouds. He lost himself in them for a moment. The weather matched his melancholy. Competing storms. Black against black.

"Mr. Joseph, are you okay?" the magistrate asked. She was older, and her voice cracked as she spoke.

"Fine. Yeah, I'm fine," he said, and turned back to the large table.

"If you need some time, sir, we can take a short recess…" she offered. He saw sympathy in her eyes. No sympathy from Shelly.

She sat directly across from him. Next to her sat Tony, his best friend of twenty years. The best man at their wedding. They were holding hands. Tony was stone silent, but his eyes never left Frank.

"If you're okay to continue, we need to work out the division of property and custody of your children."

Shelly's lawyer, a slender black man, resumed, speaking toward the microphone in front of him. "My client is seeking full custody of all four of their children: Matthew Joseph, Mark Joseph, Luke Joseph, and Ruth Joseph."

Frank wiped away a hot tear as the names were read.

"As such, she will require substantial child support, in an effort to maintain the home and their respective activities. We request the court direct Mr. Joseph to find employment, due to his current inability to provide any substantive support to my client and the children."

Frank sat up and leaned toward the microphone, looking directly at his wife's lover. "I provided full, complete support until I lost my job. I lost my job because I was defending my *best friend* in a fight, for which I was convicted of battery." He sat back, never breaking eye contact with Tony. Tony looked back firmly, but then blinked twice and looked away.

"Your honor," her lawyer replied with huff, "please direct Mr. Joseph to refrain from further outbursts such as these. They are not substantial to this hearing, nor are they constructive."

"Mr. Joseph," the magistrate asked in a soft voice, holding open her flat hand to the attorney, "are you sure you wouldn't like to seek counsel and convene this hearing at a later time?"

This time his eyes locked on his wife's. He again spoke directly into the microphone, as if the magistrate wasn't in the same room. "No, your honor. I'm fine. Thank you."

The magistrate didn't comment, but cast her eyes down on the forms in front of her. She ran her small, knotted fingers over her thinning hair, which was pulled back tightly. All legal proceedings relied on paperwork, and she had plenty to complete today. She took up her pen and nodded to the attorney.

"If I may, your honor, I'd like to continue with the points we were discussing. As you can see, we are requesting full physical custody based on Mr. Joseph's history of violence, which potentially endangers the children. We ask that his visits with the children be supervised at his own expense. We ask that all savings and investments go toward the maintenance of the family unit..."

"Family unit." Frank spoke into the microphone, then sat back, eyes on his wife and her lover. All eyes turned to him, and then away.

"...the family unit. As Mr. Joseph is currently unemployed, all investments must be used to pay the significant expenses my client is incurring in the support of their children."

"*Their* children." Frank had again spoken into the microphone, then sat back in his chair.

"Mr. Joseph, please hold comments, sir. I understand this is difficult…" the magistrate spoke soothingly, trying to keep calm and order. "Please understand that this is a legal hearing, and there is a process to follow."

"Yes, your honor. A process. I'm very familiar with legal processes lately. I'm sorry. I will withhold comments." He settled back in his chair and set his eyes on his wife. He put a crooked smirk on. He glared, eyes directly on the eyes of his wife, as her lawyer continued detailing the support she needed. She looked away, eyes panning the room. To Tony, with a wan smile. Then to her lawyer. To the magistrate. She could feel the weight of his stare, and it was heavy on her. Those eyes singed her. They burrowed under her skin and crawled on her nerve endings. They itched at her soul. She tried to focus on her lawyer's description of her needs, but those eyes were on her.

She turned her eyes back to Tony, looking down to his lap. She had lost some weight, and her dirty-blonde and gray hair was now colored auburn. She had too much makeup on. *Ah, cling to the last vestiges of your youth,* Frank thought. *You need to hold on to the last of what you're losing quickly.* The pretty wife who had grown matronly as she approached middle age now dressed like a woman half her age and wore more makeup than a circus clown. *You'd better hope Tony doesn't lose interest in you,* he thought. *Then where will you be?*

She could still feel his eyes moving over her.

Her lawyer continued, "So the investment accounts we're discussing are complex, but I'd like to detail them here…" but she could no longer hear him. She could only feel Frank's eyes on her. Biting her. Grinding her bones. Judging. She tried to keep looking at Tony, but he was looking away, averting his own gaze from his former friend. She looked back to her husband, and the eyes were there waiting for her, sharp like a slap. Needles in her mind.

*"STOP FUCKING STARING AT ME, FRANK! GODDAMNIT!"* she shrieked, slapping her hands on the table. Her lawyer stopped and looked at her, mouth open to say something that would not come out. A brief moment of absolute silence followed. Frank's crooked smirk broadened to a smile. A tiny victory after a string of defeats.

"Mrs. Joseph, I will not tolerate language like that…" the

magistrate began, but she was cut off.

"I'd like to request a short recess, your honor. I think my client is a bit tired from all the events of these last few months…"

"Your honor, I'd like a short recess too," Frank interjected. He had accomplished what he had wanted. "If given a short recess, I think my wife and I can work out the arrangements of our divorce. Would you please give us ten minutes?"

The eyes all flickered around the room, briefly finding others, then moving on. Frank sat back and smiled. Michelle Joseph nodded to her lawyer. That was the cue, and everybody filed out. Three people sat still.

When the room was emptied, Frank smiled at his old friend. "Well, I understand your testimony at the trial now."

"You don't know shit, Frank!" Tony's voice was sharp, hissing.

"You wanted my life, and now you have it. You could have just asked…"

Still flushed, Michelle Joseph spoke up, putting her hand on Tony's. "Frank, you said we could work this out…I'm not going to sit here while you insult Tony. He has been a rock to me during these last few troubled months." She leaned closer to him.

Frank didn't need to see any more.

"I'll bet he has. Okay, Shelly. I'll get out of the way. That's what this is all about, right? I'll step out. Full custody? Yours." He leaned back in the chair and regarded them. He put his fingertips together, his index fingers to his lips.

"I would probably have gotten that anyway," she sneered at him.

"Maybe…but I'm going to let you have them without a fight. You'll at least save legal fees. I'm not sure if Tony is really ready to parent four kids and take care of things, but you're welcome to them. Good luck."

Tony smiled over to Michelle. Frank thought he saw just a bit of a flutter in his eyes.

"And you want all the money? You want all the property? House? Everything?"

"I need those to take care of the kids…you know that's only fair, Frank. Since you're unemployed now…"

"Yeah, I guess it's fair you take everything, and I get nothing.

Yeah? Sound like a square deal?"

"I have to think about me and the kids first, Frank. I have to protect *us*."

"By *us* you mean yourself, right, Shelly?"

"Frank, goddamnit…"

He again regarded them. They seemed so small and so far away. Kids caught cheating on a test. Tony's suit was cheap; Frank wore suits daily and could spot something off the rack. Shelly's skirt was too tight for a woman her age, and her heels were too high.

"I loved you so much, Shelly. I never thought I'd have seen the day when you and my best friend were together. I never would have thought…"

"Our love died a long time ago, Frank," she said, exhaling with exasperation. Her pallid eyes leveled at him, and he saw distance. They were the eyes of a dispassionate observer. "I stopped loving you years ago." She turned to Tony, who looked back. "Tony and I have been seeing each other for longer than you think, Frank."

"Really?" And now he could feel himself going pale. "How long?"

"You worked too hard, Frank. Too much time at church. You were never there for me…"

"How long?" he demanded, teeth together.

She smirked. "Almost two years."

"Almost two years…" he repeated. *That night at the I-Ball? Tony worked in Los Angeles…how did they carry on their affair? Or did he work there? Tony's divorce?*

The accumulation of lies from both of them began to tally. So many lies are required for infidelity. How many hundreds had both of them told him? One doesn't carry on an affair without obfuscation. Little lies. Big lies. Misdirection. Truth is murdered, one cut at a time.

"Yeah," Tony said. "Sorry, man, but that's just life sometimes." Tony tried to appear smug.

"Yeah, I see that." Frank let it sink in for a minute. His smile was gone. He felt nauseated. Vertiginous.

"Frank, you are a good man," Michelle began her consolation, the last concession to the loser of the game. "You always took care of your family. Your church. You worked hard and never complained. But you were never home. I loved you once. So much. But I need more out of life than a provider. I need a man I'm passionate about. Our marriage was like a dead star…it took a while for us to see its passing, but it died ages ago."

And it all came to him. The half-smiles. The headaches. The distance. Visiting friends while he was at work. Asleep when he came to bed. *Not in front of the kids.* Too frequent periods. Skipping church to have lunch with her mother. Shopping with her sister. Her cousin in Fresno. Late-night chats with her friends. *Can you watch the kids while I go over to Ellen's? She's going through a rough patch.*

The futility of it settled over him. Why fight it? She was gone, and cleaved to another man. Their love was indeed dead. It deserved a burial.

"Okay, okay…" he began, still fighting the need to vomit. "I get it. You can have it all, Shelly. All. You can have the savings, 401k. House. Cars. Whatever you want. Call your lawyer in…I'll sign. I don't have money for support, but you can have everything else."

Tony and Michelle looked at each other, then back to Frank.

"We can arrange visitation, if you want…"

"No, you take them. It's going to take me a while to get myself together."

"Thanks, Frank," she started, "it's the right thing…"

"Fuck you, Shelly, you lying, cheating cunt," he growled with grinding teeth and fury in his eyes. "Get your lawyer in here before I change my mind."

And they did.

And he didn't.

# IX

"I'm sorry, sir, but your card isn't working."

"Try it again, please." He felt the hot stares on the back of his head. The line behind him was long.

"I've tried it three times, sir. It rejects each time."

He could hear the exasperation behind him. A long line of people carrying far too many presents. He could feel the impatient shifting.

"I'm telling you, this card should work. Please try it again."

"Okay, sir," she said, but he could see her eye roll. She pressed the buttons, swiped the card, and waited. "Same issue again," and she pushed the card back to him. He looked at the register and read $123.22. He pulled out his wallet. Only a few small bills. "Is that all, sir?" and now he could hear the mumbling behind him.

"Look," he said, "I know I have available credit on this card. I need these presents for my kids…" and then the chorus behind him became raucous.

"C'mon, asshole…" someone shouted.

Frank was relieved when a manager stepped to the counter. The young woman slid his items to the side as the manager moved to Frank.

"What seems to be the problem, sir?" the manager asked, already agitated.

"Hi, thanks for coming over." He smiled at the manager but

didn't receive one in reply.

"How can I help you, sir?"

"I was trying to purchase these toys for my kids…Christmas in two days. There was a problem of some kind…my card wouldn't read properly or something. But I know it works…"

"I'm sorry, sir, she already attempted it…"

"You're not listening, sir," Frank interrupted. "I have more than enough to cover this purchase. I need these gifts. I just need someone to call the bank and see…"

"I'm sorry, sir. She tried multiple times…"

Frank heard the people judging him as they were rung up next to him. *Oh Christ, there's always one, isn't there? Some people just can't manage their money. Tell it to the Marines, pal.*

"You're not listening to me!" Frank said loudly. The buzz next to him stopped. "Please, I'm just trying to get someone to do their job…"

The manager waved to someone in the distance. "Sir, I'm going to have to ask you to leave our store."

He flushed again. "I'm the customer here. I just need you to do your fucking job…"

And then there was a mall security guard next to him. He was thick, and he breathed through his mouth. Frank could smell his old sweat.

"Sir, let's take this outside," the guard said.

Frank looked at him. He already had a hand on the can of mace on his belt. He looked between the guard and the manager.

Without a word, Frank turned to the door. As he began to walk, the security guard grabbed his upper arm, as if to push him toward the door. "I'm going, motherfucker!" he shouted and yanked his arm free. The buzz of judgment continued, and the guard's boots thudded along with Frank as he reached the door out to the parking lot.

"Have a nice day, sir," the sneering guard said.

Frank turned just outside the door. He extended his finger. "Go fuck yourself, mall cop! You're doing this job because you can't get anything else. You're a loser!" He could feel his rage boiling inside him. The guard rested his hand on his baton and nodded his head at Frank.

He turned and stormed off. He was in the parking lot, but he had parked on the other side of the mall. *Fucking retail assholes. Who the fuck are they to judge me? I make more in an hour than they make all week. Used to...*

When he came to the mall's side entrance, he could hear the incessant ringing of the Salvation Army Santa Claus. Even from a distance, the ring was intense. The sound was aggravating. As he grew closer, it grew earsplitting. He could feel his shoulders bunch up. He was flexing his hands. He jaw was working, grinding on his indignations.

"Merry Christmas!" shouted Salvation Army Santa, in a fake Santa voice, and he rang the bell even louder as Frank approached. Frank was boiling in a stew of rage, and his face was aflame. "Ho, ho, hoooo!" bellowed Santa.

That was it. The last indignity he would accept that day.

He grabbed at Santa with both hands, slapping at the bell. It clattered to the ground. "Asshole!" shouted the Santa as he stepped back. Frank pushed him again and grabbed a leg of the kettle tripod. He threw it sideways, and the bucket fell with a crash, tripod legs akimbo. Coins and small bills fell and tinkled on the concrete. "You motherfucker!" shouted Santa with his fists up, ready to swing.

"Eat my asshole!" Frank shouted back, moving away. "Everybody in this fucking city can blow me!" He stuck his finger up behind him.

"Yeah, fuck you too, motherfucker!" shouted Santa.

Frank stomped off to his car, satisfied that he had at least ruined one other person's day. When he reached his car, he slid into the driver's seat. It all seemed clear to him now. There was no turning back, and it was pointless to try.

# X

He pressed the release with his thumb, and the cylinder flipped out. All the chambers were loaded with Winchester .357 hollow points, though he would only need one shell tonight. He flicked his wrist, and the cylinder locked into place. His hand was slick from gun oil.

"This is it then," he mumbled to himself. He opened and went through the contents of the plastic box one last time. Notes to his children, an envelope for each. Notes to his few remaining friends. Pictures. Hastily drawn last will and testament, signed last week.

And a copy of the life insurance policy. Last payment made that morning. One million dollars, put into a trust for his children. It was all he had left to give them. It would pay for their college and give them a shot at a world he could no longer provide for them. He hoped they would forgive him and have good lives. He was glad he'd had the policy long enough to avoid the suicide clause.

*There's no turning back now.*

He looked into the envelope of pictures. He had included his favorites. Coaching Luke's Little League team, and their team photo. Holding Ruth after she was born. Wrestling on the floor with the boys. And one special picture, enlarged for this final package: It was taken a few years before, all their family around his mother at a visit to the home. He pulled out this picture and looked at it. The boys were young, and Ruth was just a year old. His mother looked much the same as the last time he had seen her. Eyes distant, hair wispy. He wanted his children to remember their grandmother. He knew Shelly had made sure they didn't attend her funeral, now just three weeks past. Perhaps for the best—he had bawled like a small child as she was lowered into the earth. Still, he wanted them to know about his family, and perhaps this picture would make them curious someday.

And lastly he had something special for Shelly. He had prepared a cassette tape with a single song on it. *Found Out About You* by the Gin Blossoms. It had played at the I-Ball that night, now six months past. He pulled the tape out of the manila envelope. He had written the song lyrics out by hand:

*All last summer in case you don't recall*
*I was yours and you were mine forget it all*
*Is there a line that I could write,*
*Sad enough to make you cry?*
*All the lines you wrote to me were lies*
*The months roll past the love that you struck dead*
*Did you love me only in my head?*
*Things you said and did to me*
*Seemed to come so easily*
*The love I thought I'd won you give for free*
*Whispers at the bus stop*
*I heard about nights out in the schoolyard*
*I found out about you*
*Rumors follow everywhere you go*
*Like when you left and I was last to know*
*You're famous now and there's no doubt*
*In all the places you hang out*
*They know your name and know what you're about*
*Whispers at the bus stop*
*I heard about nights out in the schoolyard*
*I found out about you*
*Streetlights blink on through the car window*
*I get the time too often on AM radio*
*You know it's all I think about*
*I write your name drive past your house*
*Your boyfriend's over, I watch your light go out*

*Whispers at the bus stop*
*I heard about nights out in the schoolyard*
*I found out about you*

As he read them, he could hear the song in his head. Jingle-jangle guitar. Soft, soulful voice. Melancholy tone. Yearning. Yes, the yearning. A yearning so deep inside him, aching for a future he would never have now, being here at the end of his life.

And he thought of her in that moment.

He remembered first seeing her, all those years ago. At church. She was so young and fresh. Dirty-blonde hair running down her shoulders in erratic curls. Fresh blue eyes. She had seemed so alive, and he knew she was the one for him. He had made up his mind to marry her. He had pursued her and finally convinced her to go out with him. She played hard to get, and he'd had to ask her several times. When they started dating, he had catered to her every need. He asked her what she wanted in life, and she told him. She wanted stability for a family, so he worked hard and built a foundation for their lives. Home. Career. College funds. She had wanted a large brick home, so he had bought it for her. She had wanted a faithful, dependable man, and he was home every night. He had fulfilled every wish she'd had. His now-past life he had achieved for her. He was the man he had been for her. Because of her. What type of man would he have been had he not met her? He would never know, but he knew she was the only woman he had ever loved, and the only woman he had ever wanted.

Where had that gone? How had that love died? Or did she just decide she wanted something different? Isn't it often the case that our needs change? Maybe it was inevitable.

The rain began to patter on the roof of his '78 Accord. It was all he could afford, and wouldn't last much longer. That was okay, after all. He wouldn't need it after today, and he doubted anybody would want it in the shape he was about to leave it. That thought made him chuckle dryly to himself.

For a moment he hoped his wife would be the one to find him—ex-wife in eight more weeks. Or in ten minutes. He hoped she would be the one to open the door, see the blood, see the empty stare in his eyes, smell the stench of decay and death. That would be his final words to her. He would show her what she had driven him to. His empty eyes would shout at her, *Look what you made me do!* The white mask of his dead face would be her final memory of him. Then she could listen to the song and read the words and perhaps understand his melancholy. Understand his loss. His yearning. Maybe.

He put everything back into this plastic box and clicked the lid into place. He put it on the seat next to him. He hoped they would have to wash his blood off of it.

He was parked down the street from his home. *Their home.* He could see Tony's Ford pickup in the driveway even from this distance. *As if a man like Tony needed a pickup. Compensating. Men with desk jobs don't need pickups.*

As he was about to turn the key, he saw a white-tailed kite against the brightening street light, turning left and right to coast on the updraft. He saw the beauty of the flight, alternating black and white markings as it swung from side to side. It was a perfect creature, ably suited for its purpose. Lean but strong, built to fly and hunt. He heard it whistle its cry, then flap hard and fly out of his sight. *I hope my soul will fly up with that bird,* he thought. *I want to be free of this world…I want to fly away from it…I'm done with this life.* He smiled at the thought.

He started the Accord and shifted. There was a hesitation and then the clunk as it dropped into gear. He pulled forward slowly, almost as if he would stop in front of each house along the way. Headlights off. The rain was picking up, so he turned on his wipers, though they did little but smear the grime on the windshield.

As he drew close to their home, he saw a white post with a For Sale sign, its crude base driven into his manicured grass. *They're moving?* He hadn't considered their plans. Where were they moving to? It wouldn't matter in a few moments.

He stopped by the mailbox, and he put it into park.

*So this is it. There is no turning back now.* He put the revolver on his lap…put his hand on the keys, but didn't turn them. He looked into his old house one last time. How he had loved that house. *They* had loved it together. She loved two-story homes and wanted a walk-in closet. He loved the large garage, with plenty of room to store tools and toys. He knew his Jet Ski was in that garage, and his bass boat was still parked on the side of the house. Bedroom set only a year old. New china in the hutch. So many things he had cared about once. He realized he had cared about them because *she* had cared about them. And yet when they bought that bedroom set, she must have already been having her affair with Tony. Did he purchase it for them? Had they made love in it while he was at work or church?

And they had put those things there in that house together. Every stick of furniture they bought together. Drapes. Stereo. Carpets. Tony was living in a house with his ghost, and Frank wondered how he could enjoy that. Perhaps that's why they were selling it. Perhaps he felt Frank's presence when he lay in his bed giving it to her. He was in another man's location. He was eating another man's lunch. Shitting in another man's toilet.

He could see movement through the sheer white drapery of the living room. Lights were on inside, but he could only see vague outlines. He wondered who it would be. Matthew? He wasn't sure from the outline. He hoped it would not be his children who would find him. His situation instantly became more complex. He didn't want his tall, slender son to open the door and see his blood splattered all over the interior. Perhaps he should wait until a bit later, to make sure the kids were in bed.

He shifted into drive and waited for it to drop again. He eased the car forward two houses. He needed to think. He checked his watch: 8:21. Maybe he should come back at about 10:00. He slid down in his seat and watched the house through his passenger side mirror. *Yes, waiting until later would be wise.*

And then he saw Tony in the porch light. The door was open, and he was talking to someone inside. He stepped back inside for a few seconds, and then out again. His old friend was dressed in acid-washed jeans and wore a down vest over a red flannel shirt. He thought the lumberjack look didn't mesh with denim. Tony stepped into the black F-150, started it, and then backed down the driveway.

Tony leaving gave him the best opportunity to ensure his wife would find him, which was what he wanted most of all. This would be the right time. She would be curious about the sound and go out herself. He wanted more than anything that she be the one to see him dead in that car in front of their house. *Shelly wouldn't send Matthew to investigate…she'd do it herself.*

As the Ford's headlights hit his rearview mirror, he put his hand on the shifter, intent on backing up and finishing what he came for. His other hand sought the heavy steel revolver on his lap.

Frank slid as far down as he could, waiting for the Ford to pass by. As it did, he found himself shifting into drive and not reverse. He kept the lights off, and pulled out to the street. It took him a few seconds to realize he was following the truck. *Just for a minute, I guess*, he thought.

The Ford moved through his old neighborhood. He kept a distance back, but could clearly see the white letters on the tailgate. Out of habit he waved to his neighbor Harry Mitchem, who was putting his garbage cans out on the curb.

The Ford wended through the narrow residential streets, then out to the main drag. Frank knew he would turn around at any moment and go back to do the work he planned for tonight. Yet he kept following. When the black pickup turned into the Raley's parking lot, he realized he had followed Tony to the grocery store. Probably buying a six-pack for the night. *Before he fucks my wife on my new bedroom set.*

Frank was about to drive past the entrance to Raley's when he caught a glimpse of a familiar face standing by a crimson Camaro. His hand cranked on the steering wheel before he processed the recognition, flicking on his lights.

*Red.*

Now dressed in more fitting attire—black jeans and a leather jacket—he was growing out his hair and Frank could see the beginning of curls and a scruffy, uneven beard. The pickup pulled next to the Camaro. Frank drove past them with his face turned away and drove toward the Raley's. In his rearview mirror, he saw Tony shake the other's hand as he stepped out of his truck.

As he pulled between two other cars, his eyes were locked on these two men. He saw them talking; Tony had one hand on Red's shoulder. They stood together, both facing toward the street, far enough away from lights so as to not be illuminated. Black jacket and red flannel in the shadows.

Frank was now moving involuntarily. He stepped out of the car, pushed the door closed, and slid the pistol into his belt at the small of his back. He looked over at the two men, letting the blood rise in him. Betrayal ripped his guts. Bile burned the back of his throat. Flashes of courtrooms and jail and divorce court and the I-Ball flew across his vision, rushed at him from all corners of his mind. A bad movie he couldn't un-remember. He felt his hands curl into fists, so tight his knuckles popped.

And then he walked. His heels hit the pavement, and the crunching sound was as steady as a ticking clock. Frank felt as if he were floating, but his legs pumped underneath him. His muscles were taut, and he felt as if his feet were gripping the blacktop below him. Crunching steps.

Rage. Burning. Seething.

He drew closer to them. Both thought something was funny, and both let out loud laughs. His footsteps sounded clamorous, but the two men were oblivious to his drawing presence. A semi was going by on the street, and its shifting low gears growled, minimizing the click of his heels. When he was within ten feet, his hand reached behind him, and the large silver pistol with black grips was out. He looked at it dumbly, there in his hand. Its cold steel. Its balanced heft. It was at his waist.

Still the clicking of the heels, the crunch of asphalt rocks.

*There's no turning back now.*

And then the pistol was stuck out in front of him, between him and the two men. He didn't will it to be so. Like so many events in his life lately, it just was. His hand squeezed the grip, and his knuckles turned white.

As the last few crunching steps sounded, Tony's head turned. He saw him but didn't see him. And then Red saw him. And then they both turned.

And then they saw the gun.

"Frank! Fuck!" Tony shouted. He threw his hands in front of his face.

Frank panned the gun between them. "On your knees…both of you," he commanded, teeth clenched. Tony instantly complied, but Red just looked back at him. Cold eyes. Frank sensed the man sizing him up. He leveled the gun at Red's face. "You want this? Should I give you what you deserve?"

Red looked at the gun dispassionately, but he slowly lowered himself down. Frank then turned the gun back to Tony.

"Don't do it, Frank...FRANK!" Tony began to shout.

"Do what? Shoot you?" He jabbed the gun forward, and heard a *thunk* when it hit the crown of Tony's head. Tony hunched over, hands on the ground in front of him, face to the blacktop, as if in Islamic prayer. "It's what you deserve, isn't it?" He swung the gun back at Red. "And you? You want this, Mr. Karrick? You want it?"

*There's no turning back now.*

The high, strangled tone in his voice scared him. His eyes swung wildly around. Time seemed slowed, as if he were moving faster than this event. That disjointed time gave their events a surreal quality. He could feel his heartbeat in his neck. The coursing adrenaline caused his muscles to twitch. Fight or flight. He wanted to fight.

"What're you gonna do, Joseph?" Karrick asked flatly. "You gonna shoot me or what?" His eyes were clear and even. Tony looked up from his crouch. He was now poised, muscles taut, and seemed to be coiling for a spring. Frank could feel their unspoken communication. Tony's face was up again, and on Frank's gun. A mad dash or physical attack seemed imminent.

Frank knew he had to regain control. He turned the gun toward his old friend. He cocked back the hammer with his thumb until it locked and then pointed it directly at Tony. He made his voice as deep as possible. "Go ahead, Tony...make a move...I want you to...I *want* to pull this trigger..." He forced his hand to be steady, his voice harsh and directive. Tony's face looked down to the hard surface under him; his will was broken. Frank felt him surrender. That settled, he then turned the gun back to Red, who now had open defiance in his eyes.

"Mr. Karrick, you look like you want to test me," he said, with the gun steady between them. He tried a wry smile, but knew he probably wasn't very convincing. "Do you think that's wise?"

"What do you want?" There was no fear, though Red was just a squeeze from death.

"What were you two up to?" The thoughts now began to take

shape. He began to understand, though that recognition was a bird chirping in the distance of his mind. Two men who testified against him in court were meeting in a parking lot. What could they be discussing? What had they planned? What had been on the agenda tonight?

"I think you know, don't you? I see in your eyes you understand," Red said. That was all the confirmation Frank needed. Red had no qualms confessing, which meant he felt no guilt. "Did you think a paper-pusher like you could really beat my ass in a fight?"

"Yeah, I know…I know you two worked together to try to get me put in prison. You thought I'd get locked away. Your friend wanted my wife, so you helped him." Flecked spittle flew from his mouth as he shouted. His voice was unearthly. Terror and rage both fought for control of his vocal chords.

"You're not as dumb as you look, Frank," and he now understood the game. Red was trying to unnerve him. Challenge his manhood. Emasculate the balls he would need to pull the trigger. But Red underestimated Frank in that moment. Frank's furor was rising in him now. His face burned. His hand tightened again on the rubber grip. His adrenaline flushed his muscles. The flight was gone, and only fight was left.

"Dumb? I was, wasn't I?" he now spoke confidently. He felt the power the gun afforded him. "Yeah, I trusted people. Guess that makes me an asshole. I trusted my best friend not to fuck me over." He coughed, then spat on Tony's back. "I trusted the police to investigate the cunt I see kneeling before me," and now he pressed the gun to Red's forehead, pushing just enough to sit Red back on his heels. "I trusted too much. Guess I *was* pretty dumb. I fix all that tonight. I fix that when I shoot you both and then everybody hears that my two accusers were in a parking lot together."

"You ain't gonna shoot me, Frank," Red said confidently. "You don't know me…or who my connections are."

"Oh, you're so wrong," and he pushed the barrel against his head again. "I've wanted to kill you since I saw you in the courtroom." That was a lie, but it sounded good.

Though the cold barrel was against his forehead, Red didn't flinch. "You're not going to kill me, Frank, because you don't have it in you. This isn't the first time I've had a gun pointed at me. I know lots of cops and lots of cons. I see in your eyes you aren't a killer, no matter how tough you're trying to act."

"Shut up, Randy!" Tony shouted from his nearly prone position.

"He's right, man," Frank growled back at him. "You should shut up."

Red just sneered at him. Frank turned the gun back to Tony. "Sit up, Tony," and he saw his friend jerk when he spoke to him. He lifted up slowly, pushing up with his hands on his thighs. Frank saw the fear that was absent from Red. "My old friend…here in the parking lot…shady deals at night…how deep does this go, Tony?" Tony didn't reply, but his eyes were raining. "This was all a setup, Tony? You did all this? You planned it? You couldn't just let Shelly file for divorce? You had to have everything?"

"You think he's just going to confess?" Red again, regaining control of the event. "You think this is somehow going to turn around for you, and everything will be erased?" Frank again swung the gun to Red. "The gun doesn't solve anything. Put it down and let's talk," he kept on, and now Frank knew Red was planning for action. He could see the mind behind the eyes working on the problem and knew it was seconds before Red made his move.

Thinking he could intimidate him into submission again, he inched the pistol back to Red's forehead, but Karrick was ready this time. With both fists, he punched at the pistol. With the hammer back, the strike forced Frank's finger to jerk just enough. The pistol erupted with a flash that both blinded and deafened him, firing into the asphalt next to Tony. Shards of tar flew up from the leaden impact. Frank almost dropped the pistol, and he swung it wildly to regain his control of it. As the pistol swung his way, Tony jumped back and rolled onto his butt, kicking up with hands and feet, as if he could kick the bullets he thought were coming his way. The loud crack had made their ears ring loudly, and each could hear his own breathing echoing in his head. Red was already ten yards from him, sprinting toward the cars to his right. Frank took aim between his pumping elbows, with the burn of gunpowder still stinging his nose. But he did not squeeze the trigger. He hesitated.

Red was between cars and then gone.

Frank swung the gun back to Tony, who continued kicking and clawing the air.

The intense ringing blanked all sound. The moment seemed unreal. Surely he wasn't a man in a parking lot with a gun. Surely his best friend wasn't engaged in a meeting with his accuser. This wasn't Frank's life. His life was family. Church. Hard work.

Inside, he yearned to run to his car and leave, but instead he refocused himself and smiled at Tony, who yelped when the barrel pointed at his face again.

"Your friend has more balls than you do," Frank chided. He spoke loudly above the ringing and heard his own voice as if underwater. "Are you going to jump and run? If you do, I'm ready this time." He saw the fear on Tony's face and his trembling hands out in front of him.

"Frank, please..." he cried, and tears were spilling down his cheeks.

"Why, Tony...why did you do it?"

"I never meant for that to happen," he shrieked.

Frank cocked back the hammer again. "Tell me why...*why, Tony...why did you have to fuck up my life?*"

"I wanted her, Frank...I wanted what you had..." Tony's eyes were pleading at Frank's.

"Why didn't you just have her file for divorce for fuck's sake?" He adjusted the gun in his hand, and was lining up the sights with Tony's forehead. He saw his old friend was losing his hair.

"She wouldn't do it...she wouldn't leave you...I just wanted to bring you down a notch...make her see you're not perfect..."

Frank's face again flushed hard. "So that's it...get me in a fight, get me in some trouble, then steal the woman you've been fucking from her oblivious husband." He was squeezing the grip so hard his forearm began to cramp.

"I...I never meant for you to lose your job...I never thought they'd fire you over a fight. I'm sorry, Frank...I love her!"

And the flashing memories again competed for his attention. The smell of beer and crashing glasses. The lockup. The whipping baton in the county jail. *All to bring me down a notch, so that my cheating wife would leave me.*

"Are you ready to die, Tony?" And he lessened his grip and stroked the trigger with his index finger.

*This is it. This is where it ends. There's no turning back now. I kill him, then kill myself. She can lose everything all in one moment. Let that bitch suffer. Maybe she knew all along. She must have.*

"No, Frank!" Tony shrieked. "No...NO!"

"The life you took from me was all I had!" Frank shouted, not just to be heard. "You took one hundred percent of everything...one hundred percent of who I was. Why shouldn't I kill you? Why should you live? Why should you win?"

"Please God..." he pleaded, and now his voice was weak. His energy gone. Resignation for the death that awaited him.

"We die today! Today, Tony! They're gonna bury us and all we were. We'll rot in the same cemetery. You like that, Tony? Are you ready to die? Just remember, *you* put us here. We die today because of you. You wanted what I had, and you killed us both, motherfucker!"

He would squeeze off four more rounds, and then use the last one on himself. It would all end neat and tidy. Crime of passion. Jealous ex seeking revenge. Let the cops and local papers sort out who did what. Maybe his family would learn about this meeting and put things together. Maybe enough would care to clear his name posthumously. Tony was bawling openly, preparing himself to die. Tony mouthed the word "No" but only croaking chokes came out.

An ammonia smell reached him, and Frank saw Tony had peed himself, and a large wet spot was on the ground beneath him. Acid washed jeans with a deep blue patch.

It would not occur to him until later, but it was the pee stain that changed his heart. His best friend, with whom he had shared so much of his life, was a small man covered in his own urine, rolling around in a parking lot. A little boy scared for his life. A sniveling runt who never thought he would pay for his actions. He looked like a dying cockroach, hands and feet busily working to block the inevitable copper-jacketed lead bullet that would crush his bone and muscle, ripping holes in his organs and letting the blood flow out of him.

Pity, it was. He hadn't lost empathy, no matter the injustice Tony had sent his way.

Frank stepped forward to build his nerve, the pistol in his hand leveled straight at Tony's forehead, arm stuck straight out, elbow locked, barrel just two feet away from its target. The pistol was the sharpened tip at the edge of a spear. Tony's hands and feet continued to kick and swing. He then turned his face to the side, eyes clinched tight, waiting for the explosion that would end his life.

Resignation and surrender.

And then Frank turned and ran back to his car.

# PART III: THE VALLEY OF THE SHADOW

# XI

Just north of Jasper County in the borderland straddling old and new worlds, a panel van with Mississippi plates pulled to the shoulder. A hulking man with thick, meaty hands and a grimy ball cap motioned him in. Frank threw his army surplus duffel bag onto the fast-food wrappers and then climbed in after it, wrapping his legs around the bag as he slammed the door. He tried not to shake off too much of the rain, so he sat dripping. He knew there was a towel at the top of his duffel, but underneath it was his pistol. Better to avoid that. He winced slightly at the acrid body odor of his host.

"Thanks for picking me up. Pretty wet out."

"Yeah, pretty nasty. How did you end up out here on the highway?" His voice was rough and deep, like an old diesel engine. The driver jerked the van into traffic.

"I'm hitching. Just wanted to see the countryside." He wanted to say something more introspective, but didn't have anything.

"Getting dark soon…you might've had to sleep out in this rain…"

"Yeah, glad you came along. Didn't see any overpasses up ahead."

He looked out at the long gray ribbon. It cut a four-lane path through the trees on either side. The storm obscured the outer edges of the horizon. Headlights hit the pools that collected at low points. The road humped and fell off as far as he could see.

"So where ya headed?" he asked with a slight twang now.

"East. Maybe Florida. Maybe up north. Not sure."

"Might be smart to head south until spring sets in."

"Yeah, I might do that. Dunno. Taking it one day at a time."

Frank felt the large man's gaze on him. An unblinking stare. He didn't turn to him and kept his eyes forward, as if he was studying the road.

"Well, I'm going to Jackson, Miz-sippi, but up through St. Louis first to get some parts. You can ride that far, if'n you want."

"Thanks. Yeah. That would be great." St. Louis sounded like a good city to work from, large enough he could stay anonymous and likely to have some shelters and cheap rooms.

"Name's Bill." No hand.

"Hey Bill. Fred Thompson."

"Nice to meet you, Fred."

"Likewise." He wondered if Bill's name was as fake as his own.

He felt the old van accelerate. He thought it was a bit fast, considering the rain, but didn't say anything. Suddenly, they jerked left, hard enough to make his head hit the window. He let out a "whoa" involuntarily.

Flashing lights lit up the cab. He turned and looked over his shoulder. A lifted pickup with chrome brush guard was inches from the back of the van. The headlights were directly aligned with the small windows on the back swing-out door. He could see the tools and car parts scattered haphazardly in back.

He looked at Bill, who was alternating between the road and his rearview mirror. The corner of his mouth was upturned. They were passing a row of semis, lined tightly on their right.

The lights flashed again. Frank could see the grease inside the windshield and the garbage piled on the center console. He could clearly see the hand grenade tattoo on Bill's neck, illuminated by the truck's lights.

He knew he shouldn't, but he asked anyway. "You gonna let him by?"

"Fuck that asshole."

Frank let out a nervous laugh.

Bill's eyes still flickered between his rearview mirror and then to the road ahead. "Assholes like that think they own the fucking highways. I have a right to be in whatever lane I want. If he doesn't like it, he can pass me."

"Ah...understand, Bill." He didn't really, but wanted to be on his side. He pulled in breath, though, when he noted him slowing down, foot off the accelerator. "What are you doing?"

"Gonna have some fun with this prick!" The needle slid left. The flickering lights behind him turned to high beams and stayed that way.

"Might be best to just let him by."

"Fuck that! I have every right to drive how I want. He doesn't own this fuckin' road."

Frank saw the *Slower Traffic Keep Right* sign and the speed limit listed as 70; they were going much slower than that. He heard horns behind and around him.

"Ready for some more fun?" Bill asked him.

"Yeah!" But he wasn't.

The semis to their right had been pulling ahead. The last truck in the line moved past them. The high beams behind him disappeared, and Frank could feel the pickup swinging to the right to pass them, lights now in the side mirror.

"Here we go!" Bill shouted with the gleeful voice of a child running out to recess. He floored the accelerator, and though old and slowed, the van jerked forward. Frank could see the large black Ford pulling past them on his side, but coming up quickly to the back of the last semi. "Yah! Look at that prick!" Bill shouted.

Frank saw the Ford's driver stick out his arm into the evening rain, and try to signal that he was going by. When the panel van moved forward, it cut off his path, and the large pickup had to slam on its brakes to avoid hitting the semi. The hand stuck out its middle finger as they went by. He heard the sharp crescendo and decrescendo of the Dopplered horn, at once before them, and then to the rear of them. He felt the large truck swing violently back behind them, and the high beams were again lighting the cab.

"Did you see the look on that prick's face?" Bill was gripping the grungy steering wheel with his meaty fists. He gave his thigh a good slap. "Man, I love showing pricks like that what I got!" His teeth were showing through the grizzled growth on his face. His eyes locked in the rearview mirror, and he was nodding to the driver behind him, acknowledging a game only one of them was playing.

"Dude...what if this guy runs us off the road?" Frank was gripping his knees tightly. His knuckles showed white.

"I'm not worried...you worried?"

"A little..."

"Don't be a fuckin' pussy...I ain't scared of no pricks...if he wants a fight, I'm ready..."

"Yeah, but I'm not."

Frank felt his driver's head turn to face him and saw a blank stare coming back at him.

The van then accelerated. Fast. Bill's foot was to the floor again. He looked forward and then back to Frank and then forward again. Blank eyes. Dead eyes. When he reached the front of the row of semis, he pulled over hard to the right until the tires screamed on the roadside grooves and then farther onto the shoulder. Frank saw the large black Ford fly by. The passenger window was partly open, and someone threw an empty beer can at them.

Frank felt the van grind to a jerking stop.

"Get the fuck out," Bill said, jerking his thumb to the door, eyes on the semis now powering by, tossing heavy sheets across the windshield.

Frank regarded the heavy downpour outside, and then looked back at Bill. He knew his pleading look would not evoke any sympathy.

"I said...get the fuck out, asshole!" Bill reached under his seat and produced a black semi-auto pistol. Frank popped open the door, grabbed his duffel, and was out into the rain, taking a few old burger wrappers with him. When he closed the door, the van peeled out and moved into traffic, cutting off a red Camry, which jerked hard, horn blaring. Frank watched the van drive away, a meaty forearm was out the driver's window waving a chunky middle finger. He didn't know if that was for him or the Toyota. Probably both.

He looked down both sides of the highway and didn't see an overpass in either direction. He considered the trees off the road. The trees would offer some shelter, but the ground around them was likely soaked and muddy.

"Fuck it," he mumbled. He slung the duffel over his right shoulder and started walking. He knew he needed to get off the highway before a cop picked him up. Even though he carried no identification, if fingerprinted he would be fed into a database of some kind. He was walking east.

As he reached a low point between hills, he felt the rain slacken a bit. A good sign. Perhaps he could cover some distance. The trees to his right were behind a fence line. Better to walk until he found unclaimed area. He felt his soaked shoes squishing under him. Water was down the back of his shirt, in his ears, and running over his eyelashes. This was going to be a miserable evening, even if the rain stopped.

Something made him stop his strides, something he heard or felt. He turned and behind him saw a large red and chrome Trailways bus, struggling up the small hill he had just summited. It was shifting gears and slowing down the semi behind it. Above the windshield he saw *Philadelphia* in bright amber letters. He stepped one foot into the road and held out his arm to it.

Though he couldn't see the driver inside, the bus swung away from him, tossing water from its wheel wells. Frank felt gritty rocks in the water as it washed over him.

But the bus then swung to the right and pulled over onto the shoulder ahead of him. Frank sprinted, duffel back tossing about on his shoulder, shoes making farting sounds as they squeezed out water and air. He reached the door as it opened.

The voice inside wasn't welcoming.

"What the hell, pal...I almost ran you over!"

"Sorry..." He stood there panting, and the bag slipped down to the ground.

"What are you doing out here? Trying to kill yerself?"

"No...I got dumped off out here...trying to get a lift. Somewhere."

He saw eyes inside peering down at him. Few passengers. His eyes adjusted, and he saw the driver's blue uniform lit by the dash, though he couldn't see his face in the darkness. He did his best to take on a needy countenance.

"Look...I can't pick up people...this is a Trailways bus. Going to Philly. These passengers are paying customers. Can I call a taxi for you or something? Do you need the police?"

"No...please don't." Frank stepped up on the first step, thankful for even the tiniest covering.

"You can't get on this bus, pal," the driver cautioned. But Frank didn't step down. "You gotta get off, and I gotta get these folks to Philly."

"Look, I'm all alone out here. I really need a lift bad. Just to the nearest town..." He again tried to look helpless, but was also unrelenting.

"I can't..."

"Please, sir...I could get killed out here. Someone tossed me out here...I got nobody to pick me up..."

He heard a woman's voice behind the driver say, "You can't leave him out here..."

"It's against company policy, ma'am. I can't give him a ride..." he said over his shoulder.

"Just to the next town..." the voice directed.

The driver looked at the voice in the rearview mirror, then down to Frank. He was shivering now, and it wasn't an act.

"Okay, listen...I take you as far as the next town. That's Springfield. I drop you off, and that's that, okay?"

"Yeah, thanks..."

"Okay, get on."

Frank scurried up the steps and took the first seat on the right side of the bus, just past the driver. Nobody was in this row. He looked over to his left and saw an older woman sitting under a blanket, three rows behind him. He smiled at her. She smiled back, leaned her head against the window, and closed her eyes.

"I'm serious...no farther than Springfield..." the driver reinforced as he pulled out into traffic.

"Yes, sir, I understand."

The hard shifts of the old bus made him lurch back and forth. He again regarded the road ahead of him.

The road took secrets. The road took desperate people. The road didn't judge. How many men, how many desperate men, had taken this road? How many had seen this same gray line, hoping to be free? Did their ghosts shamble up and down this highway? The road was egress and ingress. Sometimes it was a destination all its own. *There's no turning back now.* He wanted to roll past cities and over miles of highway. Feel the road rolling under him.

"How much is a bus ticket?" Frank asked, just audibly.

"Why?"

"Just curious…wondering what a ticket to Philly usually costs is all."

"Those who left Reno paid about a hundred fifty."

"How about if I bought a ticket?"

The driver looked up at him in the rearview mirror.

"Can't do it…you gotta go to a station and buy a ticket." The driver continued to regard him.

Frank looked over his shoulder and saw that the bus was sparsely populated. "Look, you're not filling this bus up. I'm just looking to get to Philly…"

The driver was still regarding him. He looked between Frank and the road a few times. He motioned Frank to him with a single finger. When Frank was next to him, he said in a low voice, "Three hundred."

"What?"

"Three hundred."

"Why so much?"

"Well, you look like someone on the run. No offense…" He downshifted up the next hill. "I figure you're running from the law. Three hundred keeps you on the bus and keeps me quiet."

Frank looked around. Nobody seemed to hear them. The woman under the blanket seemed to be sleeping. He nodded to the driver and went back to his bag. He opened the small pocket on the side of his duffel. He pulled out wet bills and counted them. Three hundred was almost all he had left. He looked out the window and could just see the outline of his face. But only darkness where his eyes were. Scraggly beard and shaggy hair. He stood up and handed the driver the wet bills. The driver put them in his shirt pocket, all the while scanning his passengers. Frank slid back to his seat.

"Just sit tight, sir. We have a rest stop in Columbia, then I'll be driving through the night."

He pulled out his wallet and took out the familiar picture. It was damp. The edges were worn. He looked at the smiling faces of his children. Proud, tall boys. Little Ruth's gap-toothed grin. He now regretted scratching out Shelly's face. This picture had caught a happy moment in his life. A moment only. That moment was now all he had to remember them. That moment might have been their last. It might be all his children had to remember him.

Distance. Longing. Emptiness. These spirits wrestled inside him. Fought for control.

He looked again at the road ahead of him, thumbing the photo. The rain picked up, and the red taillights around him would dissolve into the darkness, only to reappear in new shapes and sizes. He could just make out the profiles of those around him. A sea of profiles, like schools of swimming fish, all trying to get somewhere on this rainy night.

And these outlines, profiles, and red swimming lights were his new friends. He was now in love with the road ahead of him. His new path was his only endearment. Now he would be in love with the road itself, as it would never betray him. It would never lie to him. The road, after all, *is* truth. The path in front of him held no obfuscation and had no ulterior motive. It was a direction he could believe. It was a bare honesty that only made sense to him now, and it made the only real sense he could summon together at this moment. The road is verity and validity. Everyone knows its direction, and you could touch it and see it and believe it. It was all he had, and he would embrace it.

And there would be no turning back. No reverse. No U-turn. Forward. Along this gray and rolling artery. Mile after mile. He would point himself into the wind and drive for all he had. He put the still-damp picture in his wallet.

He felt the bus wheels bump over uneven road, road that was pitted and scarred. Seen from a distance, the road was a long, smooth gray strip. Up close it was filled with angry sores from weather and wear. Frank was the same.

When a bolt of lightning flashed in the distance, he again saw the outline of his face in the window beside him. It ended his reverie. He rested his head against the glass and fell asleep almost instantly.

# XII

The East. Old. Uneven. Tight narrow streets and five-way intersections. Confined. Pockmarked and blemished. The East is a man who lived too hard, was prematurely aged and diseased. Stately old cities of the East are young compared to Old World capitals, but they had grown and lived too quickly. Nearing death. Rheumy, decaying, waiting to give up the ghost.

As the bus lurched over the Schuylkill River on the 676, Frank took in the tall buildings and traffic of Philadelphia with the long shadows of the afternoon. The rain had subsided earlier as they cut through Delaware on the 95, and now the sun was shining through the clouds, stinging his eyes just a bit. Passing under the overpasses, he would go from dark to light, dark to light, and the sudden transition would startle his vision every time. He wished he had sunglasses.

Taking the Ben Franklin Parkway, the bus soon swung into the parking lot of the bus station. Frank saw the crowds of people moving into and out of buses. This was bad for him, as he was likely a wanted fugitive. He anticipated arrest warrants waiting for him, and perhaps they were even tracking him on this bus. He put on a ball cap, nodded to the driver on the way out the door, and stepped into the spring air of early afternoon.

He pointed himself toward the red-brick row houses, and started walking with a purpose. He slung the duffel over one shoulder and kept his face cast to the ground. When he reached the old homes and slid into the backstreets, he relaxed a bit. No shouts, no whistles, no sirens, no cops. Nobody knew he was here. Yet.

So then he walked, now more leisurely.

Where does one go when one has nothing to do? Frank hadn't lived without a purpose his entire adult life. He always had more things to do than time to do them. People had expectations of him. He had people counting on his actions. He was always expected to deliver on deadlines, and his calendar was packed with a full, active life. Now, he knew he had nowhere to go at all. He knew nobody would help him. He was alone and unneeded. People still wanted him, he was sure, but for different reasons. He had a small roll of cash, which wouldn't last long. He knew using banks and IDs would create a trail, so they would only be used in a pinch and only when he was ready to move on.

His shoes were still damp from the rain. His clothes had dried, but now sweat began to wet his shirt. So he walked. And kept walking. One foot in front of the other. Moving in a straight line, it didn't matter where. It felt good to be walking, and he stretched away the road stiffness.

When he came to a gas station, he stepped into the bathroom around the side. He fished out his pistol and stuck it into his pants at the small of his back, cinching his belt tighter. He turned to the mirror, and with his long shirt over it he could barely notice the bulge. He scratched at his scraggly beard, and he seemed like a different man. He pulled the duffel over his shoulders, which pressed the pistol against his tailbone. Still, he felt he would need it to protect himself here on the tough streets of Philly. He was right.

Philadelphia freedom, after all, was hard-fought and hard-won.

And so again he walked, turning down Arch Street. He moved through a small business district and then passed a few restaurants. The food smelled good and he was hungry, but he didn't want to show up on security cameras if he could avoid it. Just in case they came looking. Just in case there was an APB out for him. All he knew about justice he had seen on television shows, and he half expected squad cars to come screeching up at any moment.

He walked like he had a purpose. He walked as if he knew

exactly where he was going. He rolled his shoulders under the weight of the duffel, and avoided eye contact. He wanted to be sure people knew he wasn't to be fucked with, and the gun gave him the high hand in any altercation. He also knew that any sign of a gun would get him attention he didn't need, so it was only the very last line of defense.

He could smell the Delaware River as he approached it. He could see the docks and piers and knew this would be no place for him. He turned south on Front Street and kept walking. The sun was lowering, and he knew he would need a place to sleep.

As the sun neared the horizon, he came upon the Korean War Memorial Park. On his left, the smaller Spruce Street Harbor Park rolled out to the water. The trees near the water looked dark. *A good place to sleep for the night.*

He entered the park and passed through the trees. He saw a ship harbored to his right. It appeared to be an old warship. Just past it another ship was harbored, this one an old sailing ship. He was alone in the park. Alone with the sound of the water. Alone with the creak of ropes and wood under pressure. Alone with the soft breeze and the squirrels in the trees.

He walked to the water and sat down. He put the duffel behind him and sat cross-legged, looking out to the water. He had stayed busy to keep his thoughts at bay, but now he opened himself and surrendered to them. He let the swirling vortex of feelings and images compete for his attention, his mind whirling with these images. Tony's piss stain. Red's red Camaro. The courthouse. The judge's black robes. The meat-fisted van driver. Matthew, Mark, Luke, and Ruth. The smell of gunpowder and pistol oil. The hum of the highway. Rain on his window.

All these images contested and ran through him with blinding speed…but he wanted them out. He didn't want them in his mind's eye. He wanted to clear the slate. So he focused on the river. The blue river. Not muddy like the American River back home, but dark all the same. A timeless river. A historic river.

As he sat near the water, legs crossed, he took in the power of the river. He took in its strength. It could build cities, yes. Water was mighty. Its waters gave life to people and animals. The water was the giver of life. But it could also take life. How many ships rested at the bottom of these waters? How many were on the ocean floor? Water was weight. It was power. Yet it flowed and gave life and under its surface hid secrets. On its surface people had sailed and traded and migrated throughout history. Fish from this river fed the people of the city. The river, then, was as powerful as any god. Ancient peoples had worshipped river gods, lake gods, ocean gods. They knew then what he knew now.

And the river was as fluid as time. The river was cycle. A vast cycle. It was never the same at any point in time someone looked at it. The water he saw now flowed past him and was gone from his sight, replaced by other water. Rivers flowed to the sea. And oceans swelled. The water vaporized, turned to clouds. Clouds dumped water, which then flowed into rivers.

Were people the same? We dump our carcasses into the earth, which swallows us. Yet food pushes up from the earth from our decay. And humans eat that food. Earth, then, was like a river or an ocean. Earth and water. Consumption and growth and return.

A tree pushed up from the humus. It swayed in the breeze and tasted the air for the soil below it. A tree was the same as the hair on skin, moving and sensing and sending signals for what lies beneath. They push into the clouds, drawing from the soil and sending back to it. A send-and-receive vector for a spinning ball of rock hurtling through space.

Circles. Cycles. We were locked into them. Never free of them. Dependent on them, in fact. Any process that stopped ended all life around it. When the heat of summer dries up the pools of water on the African plains, all life ends. When the rain returns, it feeds the earth, and life flourishes. No matter man's growth and knowledge and technology, every person on the earth counted on these cycles wholly.

He felt at once as if the stars and history and life and water and earth filled him. His eyes were closed, and he was feeling the universe —all life—flowing into and through him. He was a piece of stardust on a ball of rock and water, flying through the vastness of space. And yet this speck of dust was interconnected with all around him in ever-widening circles. If he pushed out with his soul, he sent ripples through the galaxies. Across time. Through matter light and dark.

In each breath he inhaled particles from exploded stars. Each exhale sent reshaped molecules back out to the cycles and circles. He was consuming the universe with each breath and creating a new, changed universe with each exhalation. He ate life and returned death. He consumed plants and animals, and his leavings, his dead tissue, his excrement fed new life around him. His body would feed worms someday, and plants would grow from his rot.

He didn't know how long he had sat in his musings, but he felt a ripple in the space around him. Felt a presence. He jerked his head, and his hand found the pistol behind him.

He saw two older men in ragged clothes, both with packs and carrying plastic bags. They were seeking a place to sleep. They saw him, but they weren't approaching any closer than they needed to. Like all homeless, they knew that they had to set boundaries without ever challenging anybody around them. They were setting up their bedding near the tree closest to Frank. He now scanned the park, and saw other dark shapes moving about, setting up for the cool evening ahead of them. Some had blankets. Some had only plastic and newspapers. All had something, but piled in a mound together nothing worth more than a few dollars. It was like a post-apocalyptic movie…hungry, dirty scavengers sleeping in the open air, hoping bandits and predators left them alone for a while.

Frank knew this park was frequented by homeless for the same reason he chose it.

He looked back at the two old men near him. Both watched him with their peripheral vision. He reached into his duffel and found the blanket he had packed. He used the bag itself for a pillow. He pulled the blanket over him, and set the pistol on his stomach under the cover. He was more tired than he thought and fell asleep quickly.

# XIII

Frank found it important to stay moving. Too much staying put made him vulnerable to many things, especially theft and violence. He made use of public lockers and facilities when possible. YMCA showers. Lobby restrooms. Naps in a coffeehouse. Food was inconsistent, but the longer he was on the streets, the more places he knew to find it. He knew which restaurants tossed their uneaten food into dumpsters when they closed. He knew which churches offered food on which days. He kept a calendar in his head and knew where to be to stay fed and which parks were the safest. He was lean from the streets, and there were no signs of the paunch he had maintained in his early thirties. He was wiry and tanned. In other circumstances, he would have been considered in great shape.

Still, his hair and beard grew ever shaggier and unkempt. His clothes became ragged, and he needed layers of them, and those layers were filthy. Where he once wore Italian leather shoes, he now wore castoff sneakers he found in a dumpster. Instead of Hugo Boss, he wore layers of Goodwill shirts, with an army surplus jacket over the top. He began to smell, and he couldn't get the stench off. Not just body odor, but soot and mold smells. He got used to them, but he began to see the eyes of others look away hurriedly. Their noses turned when he was close. Businesses began to shoo him away. Children laughed and adults huffed and tsked. He was a shambling mound of rags, offending all around him.

So he kept moving and shunned contact.

On a warm summer day, he found himself downtown on Market Street. There were long lines of tourists, and the streets were crowded. He kept to the edges, trying to discern his location. He realized he was standing across a green field from Independence Hall.

He moved to a row of trees, and admired the brick façade and the white cupola crowning it. He moved across the expansive lawn. He approached warily, especially when he saw police near the entryway. This visit was fraught with peril, but he had nothing else to do. He remembered seeing photos of it as a child, and paintings of all those Founding Fathers signing a document that once meant so much to him. He had never found himself here and was impressed by its presence. He gazed at the statue of Washington, so stately and proud.

When he approached the side entrance into the rear courtyard, he fell in behind a family. Each person in front of him was emptying their pockets, opening their purses, and throwing out any bottled water.

The tired mother holding a blonde-haired little girl in front of him took no notice, but the child in her arms looked right at him. She was staring blankly with big green eyes. He looked back at her and smiled.

The girl shrieked, and buried her face in her mother's shoulder. Frank had forgotten the forming gaps in his mouth…bad diet and lack of care had quickly taken their toll. The mother turned around sharply, and gave him eye daggers. She looked him over and took in his filthy attire. She could smell his musty stench. She put herself between her delicate little child and the filthy man she saw behind her. She looked urgently to the man beside her.

"Ew, gross," she said to her husband, and ticked her head over in Frank's direction.

The husband took in Frank, and said, "Just ignore him, Cathy," as if he wasn't there. He put his arm on her shoulder, and moved her ahead of him, so he could shield her from Frank.

He felt that sting deep inside. *Ignore me? I didn't do anything to that rotten kid.* "Yeah, ignore me," he said too loudly.

Everybody stopped what they were doing and looked at him.

The family tried to pretend he wasn't there. They moved through the security line and then out into the park. When it was Frank's turn, he began to pull items out of his pockets. A large female guard stepped up to him. She wore gloves. He could see the expression of disgust as she ran her hands over his pockets, front and back.

"Go ahead, sir," she said, still with a lemon-sour expression

"Thank you," he said, again a little too loudly.

Out into the courtyard, he took in the beauty of the trees around him. There was a line to enter the hall, but he didn't have a ticket. Instead, he just wanted to appreciate the natural loveliness of the green leaves being moved by the faint breeze.

At the end of the entry line, he saw the family, and the woman and man were talking with some urgency. They watched him approach, though he tried to steer as far clear of them as possible. His path, though, would bring him close to them. They spoke loud enough for him to hear.

"Why would they let a disgusting animal like that in here? What about the children..." the woman began. The man answered with resignation, "Just look away from him," in an assumed long-suffering voice. Each was convinced they were better people than him, angelic in their tolerance of his existence.

Frank felt fury. Rage boiled inside him. He no longer tried to move slowly and away from them. He faced them and let his bile come forth. He stepped to just a few feet from them and let it out.

"I'm a human being, just like you!" he shouted, against his better judgment. "How dare you judge me?" The man stepped between Frank and his wife and threw protective arms out, as if Frank was exposing himself to them. He would tell friends that he saved his family from the vicious onslaught of a bedraggled savage. "Do you think you're better than me? You're not..."

He heard the movement. The running boots drew close to him. A rough hand took his arm.

"Okay, buddy, you need to leave," the voice commanded.

"I wasn't doing anything!" he shouted.

"Let's go," and now the arm was twisting his, and he was moving against his will back to the entryway. He looked over his shoulder and saw the smug satisfaction of the family.

He was pushed out to the street roughly.

"Independence Hall? That's a laugh!" he shouted at the guards, who motioned him to move away with dismissive flicks of their wrists. He had to cross to avoid an oncoming bus. After it passed, he shouted, "So much freedom in this country. I have as much right to be here as anybody else!" When his protests fell on deaf ears, he continued, still backing away. "Yeah! Well…go fuck yourselves then," he shouted and walked away, back to the green lawn in front of him.

# XIV

"Okay, folks, now let's bow our heads and give thanks for this meal." The pastor waited until all heads were down, though a few continued to spoon in food in this position. "Heavenly Father, we thank you for the opportunity to come serve those in need. We pray that this food will nourish their bodies…"

Frank stopped listening and sneaked a bite of cornbread. He was hungry, but the cornbread was too dry. He was weather-beaten today. He had panhandled in the bright, windy morning, but then the rain clouds blew in, and he fled to shelter. He had a few dollars in his pocket, though, and now this food would fill and warm him.

As the pastor droned on, he could feel someone sliding in next to him.

"…and we ask this in the name of our Savior, Jesus Christ." Pause. "Ah-men."

The bustle began, and people all around him began to push food into their mouths with vigor. Frank loved the food the First Presbyterian Church served on Saturdays, but he loathed the attempts at saving his lost soul. He thought of the line from the old song, "Salvation a la mode, and a cup of tea." Still, it was a chance to get off the streets, get his belly full, and take a few biscuits to snack on later. He hated being in a church. The sting of abandonment still ached, and he wasn't getting over it anytime soon. It made him feel phony.

He felt the person next to him squirming again. On the streets, he had learned to shun eye contact. Avoid looking around. Keep to yourself, eyes down, do your thing. But the figure next to him continued to squirm and twist.

He looked, and there sat a young boy, mixed race. Curls that were out of control. Dirty clothes and face, dark skin made darker with grime. Plum shirt, grimy jeans. The young boy smiled back at him.

"Hi, mister. I'm Perry. What's your name?" The boy's bright smile forced a smile back at him. The boy didn't react to his gap-toothed grin.

He immediately lost the street edginess. "Hi, Perry. Nice to meet you." He held out his hand to shake. "I'm Chris. Chris Jackson."

"Perry, leave that man alone and eat," the slender woman next to him scolded. Her knotted blonde hair ran down her back, covering most of her lavender blouse. She was pretty once, before the streets aged her. She still carried herself like a woman used to too much attention. He wondered if a woman ever lost that, once gained.

"It's okay, no worries," Frank reassured her. He wanted to say more, but didn't.

Perry dug into his meal, plastic fork scratching paper plate. Legs kicking randomly. After each bite, he would look up and smile at Frank. Frank watched him out of the corner of his eye. Being near a smiling, active child made him feel good.

He saw the pastor coming his way. A beefy man with blotched cheeks, he was nonetheless kind to Frank, and that meant a lot to him these days. No judgment, which is more than Frank would have given in his time. Others in the flock, though, annoyed Frank immensely.

"Hi, Chris," he said, sticking out his big, sweaty hand.

Frank took it. "Pastor Gloam. Good to see you again." They shook hands. The woman watched them both.

"Hi, I'm Perry," the little boy called out. Children don't know they're not the center of every conversation. The pastor shook his hand also.

"Well, hi, Perry. Nice to meet you. Is this your first time here?"

The mother interjected. "We were here before…'bout six months ago." Her pale cheeks flushed red.

"Well, you're welcome every Saturday. We want to share the good news of Jesus, but we're also happy to help people get a good, hot meal, no matter what you believe." Frank knew the pastor meant it. "Chris, you weren't here last Saturday. Was worried. Great to see you today."

"Yeah, I actually came, but I got here after you had shut down."

"You should have found me. We'd have made sure you got something to eat and some hot coffee." His East Coast came out, pronouncing it "kaw-fee." Jabbing consonants and twisting vowels.

"Nah, didn't want to be a burden." *If only Pastor Probst cared about me as much as this guy.* "Besides, I can usually scrounge something up somewhere." He didn't want to hurt the pastor's feelings by telling him he didn't eat last Saturday.

"Well, I'd better get back up front. Nice to see you again, Chris." Then he turned to the boy. "And it was a pleasure meeting you, young man."

"Nice to meet you too," the boy said with a mouthful of beans.

The pastor spoke to the mother, half over his shoulder. "I hope you'll join us often. Your little man is quite a character." And he was off before she could agree with him.

"He seems nice," the woman said in the direction of Frank. He heard just a bit of twang in her voice. Nice sounded like nah-ss. He felt her smiling.

"Yeah, he's great. He seems to genuinely care about those of us on the streets. I've been wrong before, though," he added. There wasn't a homeless person who hadn't felt betrayed by someone in their past, and he saw her nod her head. "Watch out for some of the others in this church, though. They'll show you *Jesus' love* by badgering you incessantly." He gave a dry chuckle. "But the pastor is a nice man."

She turned and faced him. She wet her lips, then said, "How do they feel about us taking some extra food on our way out, Chris?"

"They usually ask that we wait until three o'clock, just before they shut down. Then we can take whatever isn't eaten."

"What time is it now?"

Frank turned and faced her. Dark green eyes. "It's about two-thirty. Won't be long. Get another hot plate while you can." She pulled her hair behind her ear and smiled at him.

"Yeah, okay. Let's get some more, Perry." She took him to the serving trays, and they loaded up his plate with more beans and rice and biscuits. They returned to their same seats, but she sat a little closer to him. The boy ate, but she just looked at her plate. She ran her hand through her hair before she spoke again.

"I hope you don't mind my asking, Chris," she said, as Frank picked at his undercooked chicken. "You don't seem like someone from the streets."

"How so?" He had been working hard to fit in, and he knew he at least looked the part.

"Well, your accent isn't Philly."

"Neither is yours." He sounded a bit defensive, but she didn't respond to it.

"And you seem like someone…I don't know…who's had some education."

"I've had a bit of school here and there."

"Okay, you don't have to tell me." She smiled, but he could see she seemed bothered by it.

"Well, I'm glad to tell you anything," he started, "but perhaps we should get to know each other first. I don't even know your name."

"Sorry," she put her fork down, and stuck out her small hand. "I'm Mariah…Moer." Her hand was cool, but rough and dry.

"Hi, Mariah Moer," and he shook her hand. "And this little man is Perry Moer?"

"No, I'm Elbert Periwinkle Smith, *Junior*," he said with the loud voice of a child. His plate was empty, and he was starting to jerk and twitch again, looking around for something to do.

"I gave him his father's name," she said, almost apologizing.

"Where are you from, Mariah?"

"Originally from San Antonio, but I was actually born in Holland. My parents brought me to the States when I was a baby. How about you? Where are you from?"

"Las Vegas," he again lied. "Got tired of the heat."

"Well, I think about going south every winter, but then these summers are so beautiful, aren't they?" Her face was in her palm, elbow on the table.

"Yeah, they truly are," though he had only seen one. They looked at each other for a bit. "Hey, it's almost three. Let's get some takeaway."

On the way out, each carrying a plastic bag with biscuits and sweet rolls, Mariah and Frank paused, looking at each other. Frank felt something, but there were rules to follow. Protocols. Asking her where she lived directly might be considered a threat. Homeless rules. They stood in front of each other, eyes moving around, but not meeting the other's.

She broke the rules first. "Where are you sleeping? Do you have a good place?"

"I'm back at the Korean War Memorial. Not bad, but the cops roust us every once in a while."

"You don't like shelters?"

"Well, I haven't found a good one here. A few are really bad. I almost got stabbed in Union Center."

"Follow us, Chris. There's a decent one run by the city. Fifth Street Shelter. It's not bad. Place to get cleaned up. Bed to sleep on."

"You don't mind if I follow you?"

"No, I don't mind." She again smiled as she looked up and met his eyes. It had been a long time since a woman had smiled at him, and he liked how he felt when her smile reached him. A pretty woman can make a man feel better about himself, and he knew he wanted her.

She pulled her son to her side, the one away from Frank, and they walked. They started in silence. He could feel first the boy, then his mother sneaking peeks at him. Two blocks down, they stopped at the bus station, and she retrieved a large backpack from a locker, and she put their food in it. Frank's bag was in a bowling alley near the memorial. He knew better than to offer to carry her bag.

As they walked, Frank wanted to ask her so many things, but didn't want to make her feel awkward. So they just walked. When she finally spoke, it startled him.

"Chris, are you hiding out?" Her eyes were forward, non-threatening. "It's okay. Many of us are. Sorry to ask like that, but you know…"

He thought about it for a bit. He was sick of subterfuge. All the lies his wife had told him. Tony had told him. He wanted some truth, but doing so also made him vulnerable.

"Yeah."

"Okay. Don't worry…I won't say anything. Just wanted to know. I have my son to protect."

"I understand. It's nothing you should worry about."

"I sense that. But if shit goes down, don't involve us, okay?"

"You have my word."

"I believe you, Chris. I feel like you're not someone who would do that to someone. But on the streets it's easy to get burned."

"I know what you mean."

They trudged on, silent the rest of the way. But they were communicating with their proximity. They communicated mutual trust and support. That was a lot for them.

# XV

"Look, Mom! Look!" Perry jumped off the edge of the pool into the clear water. He made as large a splash as his skinny frame would allow. He popped up, wiping water from his face. "Did you see, Mom? Did you see?" he shouted.

"Yes, I saw, Perry! Why don't you try the slide?" Perry immediately trudged through the water toward the steps.

"Wouldn't you love to have all that energy?" Frank asked, in parent banter. He and Mariah both sat in the shade, leaned up against the wall of the shower room. All the chairs were taken.

"Oh my God, yes!" she replied, smiling back at him. He loved the deep green of her eyes in the shade. "I can't imagine I was ever that energetic." She saw Perry running to the slide. "Don't run, Perry!" she called out, but was ignored. He was at the top of the slide and then sent heels-over-head into the pool. He swam to the side and was at the slide again in seconds. "Thanks so much for taking us here, Chris. We don't get many fun days like these."

"It's my pleasure. I'm just so happy we had a sunny day." Frank was running his hand over his smooth face. He had shaven for the first time in a year, and the white skin underneath felt soft to his touch.

"Well, Perry would enjoy this pool even if it was snowing." She smiled at him. "And thanks for buying him a swimsuit."

"You don't have to thank me, Mariah." He saw Perry disappear under the water again.

"But I do, Chris. Nobody has been this kind to us since we've been on the streets."

"Well, you've helped me too. The shelter is much better than the park, believe me."

"I'm not used to people helping each other. I'm used to people trying to steal our stuff…or worse."

"Yeah." He knew what she meant and imagined it was far worse for a woman with a child than it was for him.

He looked over to her. As beautiful women do, she turned her head away to let him look. She was wearing shorts and had pulled her shirt into a halter. Her fair skin was already turning pink, even in the shade. He saw her many tattoos. None of them looked professional, except for the one on her belly, in a semi-circle above her navel:

# E. P. S.

He had marked her.

The rest of her tattoos looked homemade, or maybe they were prison tats.

"Anyway, I want you to know it's greatly appreciated. Since his dad left us, we've had it pretty rough."

"Do you know where he is?"

She looked at him for a second, gauging his intentions. "Hard to say. He's a musician…or thinks he is…guitar player. He's from Philly, which is how we ended up here. He might be around. He moves around a lot."

"Ah, guitar player…was he any good?" He really didn't want to know the answer.

"Honestly, he wasn't as good as he thought he was. He was pushing forty, and lived from girlfriend to girlfriend, letting each support him until she got tired and tossed him out. I was young and dumb, and I was pregnant when I finally figured out his *real* career was mooching off women. He turned me out, so he could stay at home, and he sold me dreams of his music making us wealthy. I was so stupid…"

"Sorry…that sucks."

"Do you know what you call a musician who breaks up with his girlfriend?"

"Um…no…"

"Homeless." She gave him a playful smile. "He spent his days faking injuries to avoid work, writing crappy songs nobody liked, and looking for his next victim. Plus, he was a heavy smoker, and his voice was trashed." He saw her eyes go distant. She was silent for a moment, and Frank wondered if she was remembering good times or bad. "When I hear his voice in my head now, I realize how dumb I was to think he would ever be a success. I was such an idiot."

"Do you ever think about going back to San Antonio?"

"When it snows I do."

"Not otherwise?"

"No." She shook her head. "My family never approved of me and his dad, him being black and all. Plus, they figured out he was a junkie, so they knew I'd end up right where I am. If I went back, I'd just validate their thoughts about me. I'd rather rot than let that happen."

"I hear you." He knew the price of being prideful. Only too well.

"What about you? Why not go back to Vegas? Probably more work there than here."

"Nah, nothing for me there." He left it out for consideration.

"You know, you don't have to hide anything from me, Chris. I know you were in some trouble. I know you're keeping things inside. It's okay, but I'd never tell anybody, if you're worried about that."

He turned to her again. Her green eyes sparkled with her smile. "Sorry. It's a lot. I'll tell you, but it's uglier than you might think."

"Well, nothing you will tell me will surprise me. I'm already filling in the blanks. I figure you're a spy on the run from the CIA, or a former member of the Manson Family."

"Wow!" He laughed so loud heads turned. "Well, I guess I'm going to disappoint you when I finally spill it."

"See? So don't worry about it."

"Okay. Just not today. Let's not ruin this perfect day."

Perry balanced himself again on the edge of the deep end, new purple swim trunks bright in the sun. "Mom, watch what I can do!" And he jumped into the water, making his best cannonball.

Frank let his mind wander. So many days in their backyard pool.

He'd be grilling burgers. The kids would be jumping and splashing. The dogs would be running around frantically barking at everybody. So many glorious California summers. So much sunshine and laughter. He thought those days would never end, but he was deceived by his own hubris. He had been convinced his strength and work ethic would protect his family from the harshest of realities.

Now he knew better. Perry and Mariah knew better also. They had seen all the horrors he had tried to save his family from. Yet here was the laughing, smiling boy making this summer day at the pool the best day of his life. He considered that all the people he knew in his past had no idea what life was like on the streets. They never would understand the things he had seen or the places he had been.

As his thoughts returned to the present, he looked over at Mariah. She smiled up at him. Though her teeth needed work, her smile was pretty. Bright. Her emerald eyes warmed him. He looked down at her slender figure. She tucked her feet up under her. He noted a long scar that ran along her left ankle, following the long bone of her leg. *A junk scar*. It was none of his business.

# XVI

He was carrying two five-gallon paint buckets. The twenty-pound industrial-sized paint containers weighed awkwardly, and with one in each hand, he grunted and walked with quick, flat steps. Any extra swing was extra work, sloshing the liquid inside. He was glad for the work, and he...*they*...could certainly use the cash. Still, he felt his age and knew he wasn't built for this type of work.

While in college, he had done much of the same type of work. Construction sites. Fencing. Installing sheetrock. It helped him pay for school. Even in his early twenties, this type of work had been too much for him. Now that he was pushing forty, he knew the years behind the desk had made him soft. He was toughening up quickly, but he would not last. He had to find a skill before his body began to fail. He could already feel it breaking down. Joints creaking and popping, blisters that were slow to heal.

"Jackson, get two more, then get the gas for the sprayer," his supervisor shouted. The foreman carried a clipboard; his hard hat was for show. His job was to make workers move just a little faster than they would on their own. Work in the margins.

Frank hauled the last two paint buckets and set them by the paint intake. He then retrieved the large gas can, opened the sprayer's fuel tank, and poured. His hands were wrecked, cracked and bleeding, so he had to overcompensate in his motions to be precise. Spilling fuel wouldn't get him invited back.

He had worked hard to get picked up on the work details. Early on in his time in the shelter, he had seen the construction supervisors come around looking for able-bodied non-addicts. When he sorted out whom they came to, Frank had begun to lobby for the work. Now that spring was turning to summer, the work was picking up, and he could count on thirty hours a week, all under the table. Anonymity was most important.

During their lunch break, Frank found some shade and drank water from an old milk jug. The water was as hot as tea, but he needed the fluids. He put his feet up, pulled his ball cap over his face, and closed his eyes. He felt Darryl slide into the shade next to him, propping himself against the wall. Frank could smell the tuna fish sandwich he was unwrapping.

"Thanks for getting me this gig, Chris," Darryl said.

"No problem. Glad to help." He had only recommended him, as they slept in bunks near each other and watched each other's things. Still, that was a close friendship for the shelter.

"It's the first nice thing anybody has done for me in a while. 'Preciate it."

Frank didn't look up. He was glad to help someone, if only a little bit. "I think we'll be able to get some good work in this summer. Let's both keep an eye out for each other, okay?"

"Yeah, I'd like that. Thanks again, Chris."

"Don't mention it."

"You and Mariah still doing good?"

"Yeah, doing good." He moved his hat off his face just for a second, and looked over at Darryl. The ratty army fatigue shirt he wore had far too many holes in it.

"I like Mariah…she's a good woman."

Frank was still looking up at him, wondering where this was going.

Darryl felt Frank's stare, and continued. "You just gotta be careful with girls on the street. In shelters."

He wanted Darryl to have a way out, before he became too personal. "Well, I guess we all have to be careful of each other, don't we?"

"Yeah…yeah, of course, Chris. I'm not judging her. It's just, you know…"

"Where ya goin' with this, Darryl?" And now it was serious.

"It's just that I've seen her type. She has the scatter of a pipe-hitter, but she's junk all the way. That junk gets in ya, there's no getting it out. Makes you make bad decisions. Like a bad boyfriend." He took a bite of his soggy sandwich.

"She's working on getting clean, Darryl. It's hard to kick."

"I know, I know. Just trying to warn you. Be careful. Hard to be in a relationship with someone who is already in a relationship with junk. I've tried before. Didn't end well."

"I know you mean well, Darryl. But don't presume too much, okay?"

Darryl looked down to Frank and saw the serious face. "Sorry, Chris. I'll butt out."

Frank managed to get a bit of sleep before the next shift started.

At the end of the day, the foreman put two twenties and a ten in his filthy hands and said, "You're a good worker, Chris. I'll be bringing you more work if you want it."

"Yeah, sounds good. But I don't want to work with Darryl anymore." He felt shitty for just a moment, but it passed.

"Oh, okay. Fine with me."

"Cool."

"But I could use a couple more…if you know anybody like you in that shelter, I'll take your recommendations."

Fifty was now a lot of money to him and the most he would get for under-the-table employment. He would have to accept what he could get. Still, the shelter was free, and with donated meals he was still up. He would take Mariah and Perry out this weekend, and maybe buy Perry a toy.

He held his ball cap and walked to the shelter with the sun on his face and felt like a man again. He was providing, if only a little. He appreciated the self-respect work gave him. And he was intrigued at how *honest* this hard work felt to him. In his previous position, he had always been covering his ass and protecting what he had. He had to always understand there were people lining up to take his livelihood from him…people who would do anything to have what he had. Every person on the chain of leadership below him wanted his job. They were all waiting for him to make a mistake so they could have his position.

And he had, ultimately, and everybody moved up a rung. They stomped over his broken carcass as they moved into their new positions. New offices. New paychecks. Everybody else got a little extra. Everybody fed from his failure.

The directness of his work this day pleased him. Nobody wanted his job. Nobody could take it from him as long as he did his job. That was a freeing feeling. He had never been this close to the edge before…he had always had a safety net. Yet he also had nothing to lose, and that was liberating.

He stopped in front of a sporting goods store and looked in. He saw the treadmills and punching bags. He remembered going to the gym, and working to stay fit. Fighting the middle-aged paunch. Now he was slender from hard work and inconsistent meals. He was tanned from being in the sun. It would have taken the old Frank months with a personal trainer to look like the Frank he saw reflected in the window.

He wondered for a moment how his children were doing. How were the boys eating? Were they playing baseball now that summer was here? Was little Ruth still doing gymnastics? He didn't know that they were thinking of him at the same moment.

He shook his head hard and walked away. It wouldn't do to start blubbering on the street. He kept his tears for the evenings, before he drifted off to sleep. He would let those tears wash out his eyes as he moved into slumber. He would dream of his slender sons and his smiling daughter. He would dream of them calling to him across the miles. He missed holding them. He missed seeing their homework, and helping with their projects. He missed playing catch with the boys and the smell of Ruth's hair as she sat in his lap reading a book. He knew he was missing wonderful things. Their smiles. Their energy. He missed hearing them play in the backyard and their laughs when they watched movies together. He knew someone else was in the home now. Did they call Tony Dad? Did Ruth sit in his lap while he read her a story?

How was Tony treating his children? He hoped well. He had seen Tony with his own children, and thought he was a good father.

But those were his own, and his wife had left him. Was he a good man to Shelly?

So many things he felt he would never know. But he would.

As he reached the door of the shelter, he waved to the front desk and was buzzed in. He mouthed *thank you* as he came in through the security door and heard it latch behind him. He signed in at the front counter and walked into the men's section. He needed a shower badly, but he wanted to see them before he cleaned up. The men's corridor was opposite the one for women and children. The somberness of the men's section was contrasted by the play and high spirits of the opposite. He threw his gear on his bed then walked to the women's doorway and stood there.

"Mariah, your man's here," someone called out. All eyes were on him, though he didn't notice it at first. He saw the blonde hair moving. Now that she was cleaning up and washing often, her hair was lustrous. He couldn't wait to hold her. He rolled up a twenty, which he would put in her pocket.

She was approaching slowly, but her head was down. He didn't notice her gait, but noticed the slumped shoulders. His internal alarms were already sounding when she drew near. He saw her black eye just as the smell of her cheap soap hit his nose. Her eye was so swollen, he could only see white on the other side.

"Mariah, what happened?" He grabbed her shoulders instinctively, and she winced under his grip, pulling back. He could just see the green and yellow bruising at the base of her neck. "Are you okay? Did you fall? Where's Perry?"

"Perry's fine. Debbie took him out for ice cream earlier...he's asleep now. He's a little traumatized, but he's feeling better."

"What happened?"

She only looked down.

"Mariah, what happened?"

"Chris, don't make a big thing of this, okay? We need this shelter." Her voice was defeated. Her face downcast.

"What happened?" His voice was direct. Demanding. He could feel his shoulders tensing. Fight or flight...he was all fight.

"If anything happens they'll throw us out of here."

"Why won't you tell me?" And now her face turned up. Her

emerald right eye looked into his.

"This is life on the streets. This isn't the first time."

He saw the movement of women and children behind, but they were hushed, hearing every word. Whispers and mouthed words flew around in volleys behind them. *They all know, and they're waiting for what will happen.*

"Mariah, we're not going to stay anywhere if you're going to be hurt."

"But I'm okay. I'll heal."

*"Mariah! For fuck's sake. What happened?"* His voice boomed out of him, and now behind them there was mute silence. Rows of eyes watching them, like they were a hit movie.

Face down again. "Darryl's friend. Dean…he pulled me into the bathroom. He…"

Frank knew the answer. He didn't need to hear it.

"Pack your shit. We're leaving."

"Chris, no…don't…" but he turned and walked across the hall.

Back in the men's section, he moved between bunks. He saw Dean, a heavyset, bearded man, sitting on the edge of his bunk. Their eyes didn't meet. Dean was in a position of readiness. Frank was in the role of vengeful boyfriend.

He took the key off the chain around his neck. He wouldn't need it soon. He knew his next actions would get him thrown out with prejudice; he would never be allowed to return. Nor would they.

He turned the key in the lock and pulled the door open. He opened his duffel and found the long-barreled pistol. He slipped it into his shirt and held it against his body with his elbow.

He saw movement. Several picked up on his body language. Others saw his quick motions. A few just got the vibe and moved away and out the door. The streets taught people to identify and flee trouble.

Frank straightened and walked back toward Dean, who still sat on the edge of his bed, with his back to him. As he drew closer, he pulled the pistol. The few who hadn't figured things out finally did, and several collided as they fled out the door.

But not Dean. He sat watching everybody flee, but didn't budge.

"Hey Chris," he said, back still to him.

"Turn around, Dean," Frank commanded, but he didn't move. "I said, turn around."

"What did Mariah tell you, Chris?" Dean asked, with just enough head turn that Frank could see his profile.

"Enough. Turn around."

"Not turning around. If you want to shoot me, you'll have to shoot me in the back."

"Okay, if that's how you want it."

Frank saw a flurry of activity out in the hall. He saw Mariah's golden hair, but she was too far to see clearly.

"Whatever she told you is a lie."

"Really?" He locked the hammer back. He had been there before.

"Yeah, really. We fucked in the bathroom. I paid her ten dollars. She wanted more, but I didn't have it."

"Is that why she has a black eye?"

"She started clawing at me, so I smacked her. Yeah."

"And how do you know that's not what she told me?"

"You're not the kind to pimp your woman. Everybody here knows that."

Frank pushed his thumb on the hammer and decocked it. He then stepped around the bed to Dean's side, standing next to him. Dean didn't look up. Frank swung the pistol violently. The first hit was on the crown of his head, and blood splattered the wall and Frank's face. Dean slumped sideways as the blood flowed quickly down his forehead and into his eyes and moustache. His eyes were rolled back. But the violence in Frank wasn't sated. He wanted to mark him, like she was marked. He wanted him to always remember this beating. He swung his arm down several times more, splitting skin with each strike. Blood splattered them both, and it was in Frank's eyes and mouth.

And then a moment of clarity. It came so quickly, during the last few strikes. He realized he wasn't striking out to defend her. He was striking this man he didn't know for a reckoning. For all that had happened to him. For Tony. For Shelly. For Red. He was smashing their faces. He was smashing their bodies and marking them. They all had it coming, but Dean was paying the price for them. *He's their own personal Jesus Fucking Christ*, he thought.

"Chris!" he heard Mariah shout. "They're calling the cops."

He looked down to see a mask of blood and beard; Dean was limp and pouring blood from several open wounds. He could see bone on Dean's forehead. Red spray covered the pillow and the wall. His hand was filthy with skin and hair and crimson.

He wiped the slick, bloody gun on Dean's shirt. He did the same with his hands. He walked to his locker, grabbed his duffel, slung it, and walked to the hallway. The pistol was in the small of his back. Mariah and Perry were waiting at the front door for him, the young boy rubbing his heavy eyelids.

They stepped out into the dusky light. They walked quickly, though they knew cops responded slowly to this part of town. They kept a brisk pace all the same. They turned down as many narrow streets as possible. Cops would avoid narrow, dim streets, especially when there were reports of a gun.

As they had put some distance away from the shelter, she said, "Wait, Frank," and she was fishing in her bag. She produced a hand towel. His hands were still slick and bloody. He wiped them as they walked briskly, then tossed the towel into an open dumpster.

Down a few streets, they found a multi-floor parking garage next to an office complex.

"This will keep helicopters from spotting us," Frank said. They moved through the garage. As they were getting ready to exit out the other side, Mariah pointed to a row of panel vans. Frank nodded, and they moved over to them. They were fleet vehicles, each marked *Ling's Dry Cleaning*. They chose the middle one.

Frank dug through his duffel and found a wire hangar. He shaped it, and dug it into the passenger side window, under the rubber seal. After some fishing, he pulled up, and he saw the lock lift up through the glass. Outside he could hear fast cars, and he knew they would be the police coming in force.

He lifted Perry in, then followed Mariah. He pulled the door closed.

The van was filled with dry cleaning, and they moved around the hanging plastic like swimming in a translucent sea. They pushed away a clear spot in the middle and pulled their things together. They stretched out and made pillows of their packs.

"Thank you, Frank," Mariah said, still shaking from the rush.

"You're not mad I got us kicked out of that shelter?"

"No. I liked it and all, but it means a lot that you would fight for me. For us. Nobody has done that in a while."

"No problem."

"I won't forget it."

He felt her soft, cool hand on his, and he held it.

Outside, they heard the blare of police sirens. It was moving fast: the tone rose and then fell in seconds. The sirens faded until they couldn't hear them any longer.

"Momma?" they heard Perry say softly, near a whisper.

"Yeah, baby boy?" she said as softly.

"I'm scared."

"Don't worry…everything will be okay."

After a bit, Frank heard him sliding around until he was on the other side of her. Mariah was between them, and Frank rolled over until his head was on her shoulder. Then Perry spoke again. "Could you read me a story?" he asked again in just above a whisper.

"It's too dark, sweetie," she said. "I can't see."

Frank pulled open his duffel, stuck his hand in, and rummaged until he found a slim flashlight. He put it in her hand.

"Won't it give us away?" she asked, face to him.

He thought for a second. "I think we're surrounded by enough plastic that it won't show through."

She twisted it on to just enough to see. Perry already had a blue book in his hand. She opened it and began reading, just above a whisper.

*The sun did not shine. It was too wet to play.*
*So we sat in the house, all that cold, cold, wet day.*
*I sat there with Sally. We sat there, we two.*
*And I said, "How I wish we had something to do!"*

Her soft voice made Frank relax, and like a child himself he drifted off to sleep. That night he dreamed. Vividly. He dreamed of his children, his tall, fair-haired sons and curly-haired daughter. They looked at him with their blue eyes. Four sets of eyes regarding him with expectation. Looking to him for an answer. They asked him questions he could not understand, and their eyes turned downcast when he could not respond. He knew they were pleading…pleading for his reply. But he could only hold open his hands to them, and no words escaped his lips.

And then the eyes faded, blue to gray to ghostly white to clear. Then they were gone. And then the only eyes that regarded him were his own. He was looking at himself, and judging what he saw. His judgment was harsh.

# XVII

The Fairview Motel sat on the end of Marshall Avenue in Lancaster, where it ran into an abandoned construction site. It had long ago lost its highway charm and no longer lured late drivers and truckers. It was now the flophouse of choice for street folk who came into a bit of cash, and hourly room rates guaranteed a steady stream of hookers and johns. Garbage reeked. Cement walkways were slick with mold and urine. Hustlers and thugs stalked around its edges, just out of reach of the decreasing lights. Cops came only in heavy numbers, and many pursuits stopped when reaching the edge of its gravity. The black hole of the Fairview was the refuge of those who most needed it.

Frank puffed the last few drags of his cigarette, and he tasted the filter. He was jonesing badly now, and his hands were shaking. The cigarette offered little solace. The flop sweat felt clammy on his face. He was already starting to get the jerking muscle spasms. The itch under his skin was intensifying.

"You okay, Chris?" the man asked.

"Yeah," he lied. "Just needing."

"Yeah, me too. How soon will she be back?" He was picking at a scab on the back of his hand. Mike had been using for years, and Frank could see how collapsed all his veins were. Scars lined his arms and hands. "I don't know how long I can take the itch. Gotta get something fast."

"She'll be back soon," and he peeked out the window, hoping she'd be there.

"Don't forget, you guys owe me a dime."

"We pay our debts, Mike," Frank said, eyes narrowed. "You know that."

"Yeah...sorry...the need talking..." Mike said, but was only partially sincere. Frank understood that the need drove them all. They would all do whatever it took to fulfill it. He could already see Mike's eyes skittering around the room, looking for something worth selling. Even a few bucks could get him a hit, and that would take away the pain...for the moment at least.

"She'll be back before you know it, and we'll get fixed up."

"Yeah."

Frank heard Perry flush in the bathroom, and he came out holding a book. Frank put down a cigarette he was about to light, then looked over to him and smiled. Perry was wearing a pomegranate shirt and jeans they had just bought from the thrift store. Frank noted that his face was dirty. He needed a bath. He would try to remember to give him one after he shot up, but he also knew he'd probably forget and fall asleep instead. That's probably why Perry was dirty now.

"Will you read this to me?" Perry said, approaching cautiously. He was holding *The Wind in the Willows*, a book Frank had bought for him a few weeks before.

"Sure, little man, in just a minute, okay?" His weak smile was all he had to offer.

"Okay," and Perry found his Superman toy and began to play with it.

Mike continued scratching at his neck and scraggly beard. Loose hairs fell out on his jacket. "Maybe we should go pull a quick job, in case she doesn't get back." Frank could see Mike was in a worse state than he was. "We could get out, hit a quick stickup, and then be back in twenty minutes."

"I can't leave Perry, Mike...he's only seven."

Mike's eyes shot to the boy, almost accusingly. He was dope sick, and everything around him aggravated him.

"She'll be back. I promise. Besides, I'm not comfortable with stickups. Too much risk. Too many chances to get caught."

"Not if you do it right. Hit hard and smack any fucker who gets in the way." He knew Mike had a .38 snub-nose in his pants pocket, and he saw him slide his hand over it. He was jerking and twitching now, and Frank could see violence in his eyes.

He tried to talk him down. "I try to avoid it...hurting people and all...sometimes it's better to be patient..."

*"Fuck patient!* I'm dying here." He was rubbing his nails across his shoulder and chest, digging at the biting, angry nerves just under his skin like so many crawling bugs. "I don't care about others... that's their problem. It's tough on the streets...gotta do what you gotta do. You take a hundred bucks from most people, and they just go to the ATM and get more. I don't give a fuck if they feel scared for five minutes...I'm scared every day of my life. They built the system, and I'm just trying to stay alive in it."

"I don't consider junk staying alive..."

"I do! It's the only part of the streets I still enjoy." Frank knew it was a lie. Junkies reached a point with heroin where it took a lot just to feel normal, and Mike had crossed that bridge years ago. The amount it would take to get him truly high would probably kill him.

"Well, hurting someone for my own bad habit isn't how I want to go out. Besides, if you hurt someone, the cops look extra hard for you. I'd rather just keep on as we are." He shuddered, remembering the county lockup.

"She won't be able to turn tricks forever, Frank...you gotta think long term."

He felt the momentary sting, and Mike's eyes on him. The knowledge he fought to bury pushed to the surface. "I know that. And you know I've pulled a couple robberies in my time. They're perilous, though...you get caught with a loaded weapon and the wrong cop, you're six-feet under."

"Better to go out in a blaze of glory than to die like a rat."

"You'd rather get shot than jones for a while?"

"We all gotta die...just a matter of when...today is as good a day as any. Every death seems like a tragedy at the time, but later it's just a footnote."

"I'm no footnote..."

"Aren't you? Remember the Titanic? At the time, it was such a tragic event, all those people drowning. But now all the survivors are dead anyway. Go out one hundred years and we're all dead and buried. So it really doesn't matter much...today, tomorrow, next week...we're all dead."

He could hear Mariah stomping the snow off. He jumped up and opened the door. "Momma!" Perry shouted, and ran to her, slamming his face into her side. Frank saw her fishnets had a run, and her stilettos were still covered in snow.

"There's my good boy," she said. She handed two small balloons to Frank with a nod. He in turn handed one to Mike. "I'm good, I'm fixed," she said to Frank's questioning eyes.

"Okay, we gotta fix up now," Frank said with a bit of desperation in his expression.

She took Perry's hand, and led him to the bathroom. Both Frank and Mike had their kits out already. Folded spoon. Candle. Frank popped open the plastic wrap of a new needle he had gotten that morning from the needle exchange at the methadone clinic downtown.

Mike began to pick through his skin looking for an area he hadn't ravaged yet. He dug through scars, smacked skin, hoping to raise a vein. Frank, though, was only just now getting his first scars, so he had plenty of places to choose from. Mike watched Frank get right to work.

Frank put the small grains of powder on the spoon, then took an eyedropper and squeezed in a small amount of water to mix. He used the tip of the needle to stir. As it heated above the candle, he took a vial of clean saline and drew in a small amount. As his mixture bubbled, he watched it eagerly. He was ready to shoot up before Mike removed his shoe and started picking spots on his feet.

Frank was still infatuated with smack, like a new girlfriend. Buzzing with anticipation, he knew the warmth was coming. The high was nigh. He found the vein at the crook of his left arm was still healthy and could take a few more shots before it began to collapse and scar. He moved up his bicep just a bit and chose the spot. He took the rubber tie-off, wrapped it, and held it in place with his teeth.

The vein quickly jumped up for him. It swelled, as if proud.

Blue, going straight to the heart to get pumped back out again. Blue, the color of the lips of a dead junkie. Blue, the darkest night, and the sleep of death. Blue for lamentation and loss. The blue note.

He drew the sweet opiate mixture into the bindle. He then dropped the cotton square onto the spoon to sift up the film. He wanted every bit. *Every grain in the brain.* He saw Mike was preparing to inject between his toes. He shook the needle, then pushed the plunger to clear out the air bubble.

Frank aimed the needle at the big blue vein and found the mark, going in shallow so as not to come out the other side. He drew in deftly and saw the wisp of blood mix into the fluid. Almost there. His blood and the water and the junk blended together.

So near. The final inhale before ejaculation. The last breath of a dying man.

He slammed home the plunger, and he could feel the warmth of the mix enter his bloodstream. His arm felt warm instantly. He could feel it pump through him. Each beat spread the warmth. To the heart and then the pleasure radiating out with each heartbeat. He felt it climb up his neck and down his arms. Down his torso to his crotch.

A momentary fog and then the feeling of the most intense orgasm he had ever had. Warmth circulating through him, tingling every nerve ending in his body. Each heart pump sent the soothing bliss through his body. Each pulse like the rhythm of a climax. His fibers drank in the opiate pleasure and gave him waves of heavenly ecstasy in return. He felt the tingling moving through him. So smooth and warm and welcome. The pain was gone, a thousand miles away.

Instantly, his eyelids were as heavy as lead, and his tongue became puffy, his mouth slack. Warmth ran through him like a tropical rain shower. He felt a post-coital weakness take him, and he gladly surrendered to it. He looked through hazy eyes at Mike, who watched him enjoy his high with an upturned smile.

He knew he would be out soon. He could hear Mariah starting the bathwater. He stood up, holding the chair for balance. He had to get horizontal. He aimed for the bed and fell onto it.

Instantly he felt the junkie's falling feeling. As if he were flying, but with his nose pointed to the ground. Swooping like an eagle.

Rush and descent. Then he was sinking into the bed and then into the floor. He was disappearing into his warm high. Melting. Ice cream on a hot summer day. Wax from a hot wick. Dissolving into the earth, which embraced him.

He woke with a sudden jerk. It was almost morning. On the bed next to his, Perry lay curled up under the covers. He rolled over and realized he had pissed himself. It was cold and he was shaking. He heard the sobbing. He saw Mariah sitting at the small table, where his fixings were still in their same positions. Mike's side of the table was empty.

"Mariah..."

"Frank, goddamnit..." she said softly between sobs.

"How long was I..." he began.

"Mike's gone, Frank. He took all our junk. Everything. Even our needles. He went through my purse and took all our cash. Your wallet is empty on the floor." He looked at the pile of junk in the room, and his wallet lay twisted on top of it.

"Mike took it?"

"He took everything, Frank. How could you fall asleep with him in the room? What were you thinking?"

He was shaking off the cobwebs and trying to recollect. He vaguely remembered shooting up. Mariah had been giving Perry a bath.

"It's almost daylight now, and I need some, Frank. You let Mike take it all, and I have nothing. I had to turn three tricks yesterday to buy that shit and to pay him back. Now he took it all and we've got nothing."

Frank felt the surge of anxiety pushing through the fog of his waning high. He hopped up onto unsteady legs and moved to the heater vent. He jerked it open and pulled out his pistol. He stood up as if to go out into the streets.

"Frank, wait...you can't go out...you're covered in piss...Mike's long gone..."

"I can't just let him get away with this." He looked down and saw his piss-stained jeans.

"Trust me…you'll never see him again, Frank. He's a junkie…he'll take all that and be good for a few weeks. He'll just start again in another part of town. Guys like him have been on the streets so long they just rotate around town."

Frank sat down on the bed. He could smell his wet crotch and it was sticking to him. He set the gun next to him and slid his pants off.

"Frank, you can't make mistakes like this around junkies. They'll cut their own mothers' throats to score." He looked around for clean pants, but there were none. "You have to pay more attention. Perry and I were in the bathroom…things could have been much worse."

Frank just stared at the corner of the room, still trying to make sense of things. He said flatly, "How much was in your purse?"

"About a hundred and fifty. The rent for this room for a few days and our next highs."

"Fuck."

"Yeah."

He looked at her now. "Don't worry, Mariah…I'll take care of it."

"How? I can't go back out until tonight."

"No, I'll take care of it this time."

"Frank, don't do anything stu—"

"I'm not going to have you turning extra tricks for my mistake! I'll get us some money. I just need to figure out how."

"Frank, for fuck's sake…just relax. I'll be fine. I'm just feeling my jones right now."

"I'm sorry. It was my fault. Won't happen again."

"I know, I know…I forget sometimes that you're not from the streets. You're too innocent sometimes."

He looked back at her, and his expression gave her confidence. She saw resolve, and she knew he would find a way to take care of things.

Frank got up and went into the bathroom. He washed his crotch with an old brown hand towel. He looked in the mirror and scratched at his ragged beard. He opened his mouth. The gaps allowed his teeth to interlock. When he drew them apart, his maw was both fearsome and ghoulish. He cupped his hand under the faucet and got a quick drink.

He saw the scab on his arm and started to pick at it. Junkies and tweakers can never leave their flesh alone, as if picking the nerve endings until they bled would get rid of that incessant crawling-bug feeling. Junkies always have infected sores at injection points, partly due to repeated use of dirty needles and partly from the constant picking. Needles grew dull with repeated use, and no needle-exchange could keep up with their rapacious need.

Most junkies weren't honest with themselves, but Frank was. He knew exactly why he was a junkie.

*I have memories I'd rather not have.*

He looked at himself in the mirror and then looked away.

He pulled the car to a jerking stop around the side of the motel and honked. He saw the door open and Mariah and Perry moved out, bags in hand. Perry had a sleep-rumpled look. He felt the exposed wires rubbing his pant leg, so he tucked them up under the dash. The car was old, and he hoped nobody would be looking for it anytime soon. At least for today.

Frank's heart was racing. He knew what had to be done. Daylight robberies, though, were dangerous. Too much foot traffic. Too many bystanders. But he was not going to leave her in her current condition. He knew the ache. He knew the cramps and sweating. He also lived with the knowledge that she had been prostituting to support their habits, and he had let her. She had given her *everything* for him, so he had to do the same in her hour of need.

Perry climbed into the back, and Mariah slid in next to him, moving close across the bench seat. She still smelled of heavy perfume from her work the night before. "Frank, are you sure you want to do this?"

"Yeah, it's fine."

"It's dangerous. Let's wait for tonight, and I'll go back out."

"No, not tonight." He kissed her quickly. "I put us here, and I'm going to fix it."

"I'm worried, Frank," she continued. "What about me and

Perry?"

"Don't worry, it's all figured out. Everything will be fine," and he tried his best to feel confident. He would assume all the risk, and they would walk free no matter what. "I think I know a place. I got it all sorted out." She knew he was lying but settled back into the seat. They each lived with many lies between them. She was nervous but was also feeling the sickness so she couldn't protest too much. Frank said, "Buckle up, Perry," before shifting into drive and pulling out.

He was reminded of *The Grapes of Wrath*. The entire family loading up in the jalopy and heading west, hoping for new opportunities. *The West*. He thought of it fondly in that moment. Wide open. New. Warm. While the East is old and bleary, the West is drumskin-tight, ready to bang loudly with new rhythms. Rebel against its parents. Aspire to the ideals the East surrendered years ago. Traveling west was traveling to the new.

As he drove through the frozen streets of Lancaster, he passed through the old town, and took in its red-brick row houses. He sensed this would be the last time, though he didn't know why. Perhaps because the West was where he was from. Rebirth and renewal awaited him.

And that was it, he reasoned. He was in a rut and wanted newness. But he also knew that his old life sat waiting just beyond the horizon. West.

He found the 7-11 just as he had seen it a few weeks ago. It was on the edge of an industrial park and was in a neighborhood where people didn't question. Exactly the type of neighborhood he needed. This wouldn't net them much, but enough to get going, get out of Lancaster, and point to the setting sun. And, most importantly, get them a bit of junk for the trip.

He circled around the block twice. Saw the empty homes nearby. Saw the industrial park was closed. Things were still; nobody was out.

"Is it a holiday today, Mariah?" he asked.

She laughed. "It's New Year's Day, dummy!" she chided. She was pale, but gave him a wan smile. She was already trembling and scratching.

"Wow," he said, "…1998." How had he lost track of these days? Most people were home nursing hangovers. That would be better, especially in these early hours. He didn't see anybody on the streets to challenge him.

The orange, red, and green stripes ran along the side of the store, and he pulled past it and parked a half-block down. He turned to Mariah.

He was jittery with adrenaline and the comedown, so he spoke quickly. "Okay, here's the deal. I'm going to go up and do my thing. You stay here. If you hear *anything,* you take off. Don't look back. Got it? If anybody stops you, you say that you didn't know what I was going to do and that I asked you to drop me off."

"Frank…"

"It's okay," he smiled. "I'll be in and out in five minutes. Just don't take any chances. Any questions, you bail and drive off."

She looked up at him, then put her head to his chest. "Be careful, okay?"

"Yeah."

He kissed her hair, opened the door, and slid out. She moved over and took the wheel. As he closed the door, he said, "Don't shut it off…it was slow to start."

She nodded and rolled up the window against the cold. He slid the revolver into the small of his back and pulled his shirt and jacket over it. It was a still morning and briskly cold. He turned to the store and began to trudge through the packed, icy, sooty snow on the ground. He did his best to appear nonchalant, but his heart was thumping in his ears. He could feel the flush. His breath came out in clouds.

But he tried to stay steady. He knew what he wanted to do. Had to do. This wasn't his first robbery, and despite his apprehensions, he knew he would be fine. Walk in, demand the cash, and get out quickly. Most of these 7-11s were staffed by college students who didn't care about the till.

*There's no turning back now.*

As he entered the store, he heard the jingle of the passive sensor. He made a couple steps up toward the counter, when he saw a man stand up suddenly behind it. "Hallo frien," the man said, with a thick European accent. "Happy New Year!"

"Yeah, Happy New Year," he said.

The surprise of someone standing up so quickly unnerved him, so he turned and walked toward the refrigerators. He felt his hand trembling as he grabbed the sliding door, which seemed incredibly heavy as he pushed it open. He grabbed a bottle of Pepsi and turned back toward the front counter. There was suspicion in the man's eyes immediately. He saw anticipation. Frank knew he was sending vibes, and he had picked up on them. *Fuck it! I just have to do it. There's no turning back now.* He walked back toward the counter.

Their eyes met as he came forward. The man behind the counter was probably in his early thirties. His dark, wavy hair was cut short. His dark eyes regarded Frank as he continued to amble forward. The counter seemed so far away, and his legs felt heavier with every step.

Frank saw the cigarette rack behind the counter as he approached. He put the Pepsi on the counter and said, "Let me have a pack of Winstons." The clerk looked at him and knew he had no choice. He hesitated with a blank stare, then turned to the cigarettes. Frank jerked out the pistol and it was pointed at the clerk before he turned back around. He didn't see surprise in his eyes—he saw *I knew it!*

"Sorry, man, need all your cash in the register." The clerk looked first at him, then the gun, then stepped to the register with jaw muscles flexing. He pushed two buttons, and the cash drawer slid open. He took the bills out and stacked them on the counter. Frank only saw a few twenties, a couple tens, and some ones. "The coin rolls too," he said with urgency in his voice. With a slow, deliberate pace he put two rolls of quarters, a roll of dimes, and two rolls of nickels on the counter.

"You vant pennies too?" Their eyes met.

"Nah, just the silver."

Frank stepped forward, pulling the pistol back just a bit, should the storekeeper lunge. He used his left hand to stuff the bills in his pants pocket and the coins in his jacket pocket. He kept a careful eye on the clerk. The man's nametag said *Hadur.*

Frank grabbed the Pepsi, and kept the gun leveled at the clerk. He then turned to move toward the door. All he needed was a few quick steps and he would be out the door and around the corner to the car, and then they'd be off.

But within the first two steps, he heard fast movement and then the heavy *clack-clack* of metal against metal.

"Stop, muthafucka!" he heard the clerk shout. He turned to see the pump-action shotgun leveled at him. Immediately he jerked down into a crouch.

The first booming report sounded like a thunderclap, and next to him one of the two swinging doors shattered, the glass blasting out onto the sidewalk. Small shards sprayed him, like glittering snowflakes. He heard another loud *clack-clack* and then a second boom, and small-bag potato chips that were stacked on a display flew in a thousand directions. He could feel the hot burn of pellets on his left arm, like bee stings, and black liquid streamed out of the Pepsi in his hand. These happened so fast that Frank didn't see the cashier or the store. His eyes swung wildly about, and his arms flew up in front of his face, as if to protect himself. His legs turned to rubber underneath him.

A third *clack-clack*, only this time he swung his pistol toward the counter while the other hand still covered his face. He jerked the trigger hard and heard his own loud report. The .357 nearly jumped out of his trembling hands. He didn't hear the shotgun blast, so he again jerked off a round, while sliding back toward the door. The recoil made him stumble backward.

Now his feet found purchase, and flight took over. He dove against the glassless-swinging door, and was out. His feet skittered on the shards on the sidewalk and he went down to one knee. His left hand hit the glass, and the Pepsi gushed out the last of its contents. He pushed with his hand, and he was up on his feet and flying with all his will. His neck instinctively pulled down, and his shoulders came up, waiting for the blast he was sure would sound any second.

He was around the corner, and in the distance he could see the car pulling forward, moving away from him.

"Wait! STOP!" he shrieked, terror in his voice. He saw the brake lights, and the car stopped. Steam vented out from the exhaust pipe.

His legs were pumping involuntarily, and he couldn't feel his feet hitting the asphalt. He could only see the old car in front of him, could only hear his wheezing breaths and footfalls. All else was the silence of death. His mind was pure flight, and he was at the passenger side throwing open the door in seconds, not even looking back to the store. He went in headfirst and shrieked, "Drive, drive!" before he could get the door closed. All he wanted was to be away, far away from where he was.

The car leapt forward, and they were around the corner.

# XVIII

The drive home was the worst part for him. He could feel the last of his energy drain away from him, and he was as empty as he had felt that night. Each shift, each press of the pedal, each turn of the wheel took incredible effort. He was as weak as a baby. He just wanted to get home and relax. Put his feet up on his recliner. He knew he had to plan…yes, he definitely needed a plan. But now his choices seemed very limited.

And, of course, he would have to deal with her. He would have to tell her at some point what was going on. But not today…today he just needed to relax. That *conversation* would have to wait until he could consider alternatives and gird himself for the ensuing battle.

As he drove he watched the movie of events in his mind. He remembered them all sitting around the conference table in the downtown union office. Betrayal. An old friend had betrayed him. There was no other way to look at it. How could he? They had known each other for years. Why would he turn on him like that?

*I guess he's bucking for lieutenant. Why else would he Judas me like that?*

They had sat around that large, polished wood table. Clear plastic pitchers of ice water. Sipping glasses. Stacks of papers. Rolling cart with VCR. It had all been carefully orchestrated. He knew they had planned this just to destroy him and take away his life and livelihood. And the betrayal was the final stroke…the last blade to his innards, and it came from a friend.

*You also, Aldis?*

He winced when he ran through the DA's recitation. "Deputy Jensen, we have reviewed your sworn statement, dated September 7th, 1994. You offered a very specific account of the events of the evening of September 5th, 1994. In Section Five, you stated, 'I entered the cell to help Mr. Joseph, as he seemed to be very upset. It's not uncommon for a person to feel this way their first time in jail. When I entered, he attacked me. I used my baton to fend him off, but he continued to attack.'"

His union team had fought very hard for him. They had filed multiple procedural requests. They had maneuvered through the collective bargaining agreement and filed countless protests and grievances on his behalf. It had taken these last two years to reach the point of this hearing. But now, at this most critical moment, they were mute. They had seen the evidentiary tape that was about to be played. They knew its contents. They knew the eventual outcome. There were no more maneuvers to play.

And then the television was turned on, and the tape slid in. Everybody turned to watch the segment except Sergeant Franklin, now with a few white curls and a few more pounds, who looked straight at Jensen as the gray images danced across the screen. Jensen could only watch himself.

The camera was positioned above and just outside the cell door. They all saw Frank Joseph slapping the glass with the flat of his hand with a *whap whap whap*. Deputy Jensen moved to the security door and stood there. The angle did not permit a clear view of their faces, but Frank was speaking, demanding a phone call in a croaky, exasperated voice.

Then Deputy Jensen extended the keys from his belt loop, and turned the large metal key in the lock. Frank Joseph stepped back from the door, and it was easy to see a relieved look on his face. Jensen entered the room, and the door closed behind him. Then the baton was out.

Franklin's eyes were still on Jensen, but Jensen was wincing with each stroke of the baton. Strikes to the leg, body. Grunts and cries. But the hard strikes to the forearm, which clearly distended it, were the most gruesome. It had all seemed so different there in that room. It had all seemed like something that had to be done. *Lies…these are lies. They must have edited the tape. My enemies are upon me. They have all the power.*

As Franklin and the other deputy rushed into the room, Jensen turned toward the camera, and his slack face told the entire story. That was where the DA paused the tape. His ghostlike visage stayed frozen on the screen, with Joseph's prostrate body behind him, right hand holding his broken left forearm.

*The video doesn't tell the story*, Jensen thought. *I'm being railroaded. They doctored it. They went right to the end…there was much more. They are setting me up and making me a scapegoat.*

Sheriff's Captain Rob Smythe sat next to Franklin. He was the first to speak.

"Deputy Jensen, the actions on that tape show behaviors we cannot support. You have a history of excessive force, which is why you were transferred away from patrol in the first place. Clearly, you have issues, and you have refused the multiple offers of counseling and other support." Jensen looked to Franklin, who was still watching him. He knew his old friend had made that point. "I have no choice but to place you on indefinite, unpaid suspension."

The DA added, "We encourage you to seek trial counsel, Deputy Jensen. We are gathering evidence, and will present it to a grand jury in two weeks."

Franklin thought, *Nobody has even mentioned Mr. Joseph in all this.*

Jensen never said a word. He stoically suffered the arrows in his back from his former compatriots. He let his enemies feast upon him. *They'll get theirs.* But the betrayal of his friend was the most hurtful. The most crippling. They had attended the same academy class. They had worked the streets of Sacramento together. He knew with full certainty that Franklin had turned on him to get close to the captain, and that's what had now happened. It was confirmed when he saw Franklin lean over to the captain and whisper to him. He didn't know that Franklin was asking about his victim; he was certain of more devious intentions.

But Jensen knew something they didn't know: he knew

retribution would come. A final judgment. He knew he would be vindicated someday. He knew his enemies would fall at his feet. Question him? Challenge him? How dare they? He knew these evil men would fall to evil purposes. Jensen had prayed with his pastor, who had promised him that God's good works never go unrecognized. That Jesus was the final judge. Jensen knew he would be judged as a good man, no matter what he saw on the tape. Either now or in the next life. Someday he would sit with his Creator and look down upon these low men and their low purposes. Maybe Jesus would let him cast them into the Lake of Fire. That would give him incredible satisfaction.

He pulled up to his house just as the rain began to fall. A soft patter hit his windshield as he parked on his driveway. His garage door opener was busted, and he didn't have the money to fix it. He edged his pickup close to the door, then turned off the ignition. He sat there for a moment; he hoped he wouldn't face one of Crystal's bad days. He hoped she would be in a good mood, or at least let him rest first. He was tired and wanted to have his feet up. Needed to.

As he came through the front door, he saw suitcases aligned in a row near the fireplace.

"Crystal?" he called out. No answer.

He could hear her moving in the bedroom. He walked slowly to the opened door.

Crystal Jensen was packing her last suitcase. She was carefully arranging her clothes, and making sure her jewelry was tucked away safely. Next to her suitcase, her makeup case was open, and her last few bottles of Lancôme were to be placed in their neat rows. She didn't look up and kept to her work.

"Crystal, what's going on?" He honestly knew better than to ask, but it came out of him anyway.

She continued packing while she spoke. "You know what I'm doing. I heard what happened today. Cindy Franklin told me. I'm not going to stick around while we lose everything."

So. Aldis' final betrayal. *I guess he wants to destroy my entire life.*

She moved past him and into the bathroom, returning with her hair dryer. She coiled the cord around it and placed it neatly in the corner of her case. Her pace was frenetic.

"So just like that you're gone?"

And then she looked up at him. She was grinding her teeth, and her jaw muscles were knotted. "Why should I stay? Why would I possibly stick around a loser like you? You've already made me live like a peasant." He could see storms in her dark eyes. "I have had to work like a slave because you're too lazy to get a good job and take care of me. All my friends laugh at me for being with a weak man."

*That's because you tell them you have a weak man,* he thought. He didn't dare say it.

She placed the final vials of makeup in the case and closed it. Zipping her Louis Vuitton suitcase, she again turned to him, eyes still ablaze.

"All these years I've wasted on you. I worked. I cleaned. I cooked. I took care of you, even though you're cheap and lazy. I gave you children. I should have left you long ago!" She grabbed her cases and used them as battering rams to push past him, stomping her feet as she went by. She took them to the front room and carefully placed them next to her other cases.

"Where are the kids?" he asked numbly.

"They're with my sister. I'll be staying there while I get a lawyer. I probably won't get a single penny from this fucking marriage, so I have to start a new life, living like a pauper with my sister. She'll be here any minute to pick me up."

"Okay, I understand."

It was all clear now. The kids were gone. Perfect.

She was right, after all. There was no money to be had. Nothing but credit card debt and a second mortgage. Neither of them was winning on this deal. Neither of them would be able to rub two pennies together after it was over. They were flat busted, and soon he would be unemployed and unemployable.

So Peter Jensen took the steps he knew to be most logical. He took the cards fate had dealt him. It would be for the best, after all.

He went into the bedroom and took off his gun belt. The holster was empty, as he had turned in his issued pistol and badge. He loosened the collar of his shirt and pulled off his necktie. He laid that flat on the bed. He took off his uniform shirt, folded it, and laid it next to his tie and empty gun belt. He opened his nightstand and took out his .38 revolver. He pushed the release and flicked open the chamber to ensure it was loaded.

*There's no turning back now.*

He walked out into the living room. Crystal stood there, petulantly turned away from him with folded arms, watching out the front window with impatient foot tapping. He followed her gaze and saw her sister's Honda drive up and slide into the driveway next to his truck. Crystal exhaled and moved to grab her suitcases.

As she straightened with a case in each hand, Peter Jensen fired the first shot into her ear. Blood exploded out from the exit wound, spraying across the fireplace mantel, while the bullet shattered their wedding picture, which fell to the ground. She dropped with a hard thud to her knees, and her torso pushed over her row of cases. The sharp crack made his ears ring loudly. He wiped the blood spray from his face with his left hand and wiped it on his duty pants.

He stepped over her twitching legs and looked down at her. Her eyes were vacant. Grayed out. Her legs jerked with their final, involuntary motions. Though he knew she was dead, he wanted to be sure. He fired two more rounds into her head, which turned to mush. Brain and skull oozed out onto her expensive suitcases. He smiled at that thought.

Though his ears were ringing, and he was mostly deafened, he could just hear the pounding of Crystal's sister at the door. He thought for a moment about opening the door and shooting her as well, but decided against it. He knew Meredith would take good care of his children.

*There's no turning back now.*

He put the pistol to his temple and pulled the trigger. His body fell on top of his wife. One final grapple to end their lives together.

# PART IV: PHOENIX

# XIX

Frank twisted open a beer and settled into the wrought-iron chair. His skin was grimy with sweat and soot, and he could smell his own stink. He took a long drink and enjoyed it sliding down his throat. It had been a long, hot day, and he was wasted from the heat. Welding was hot work even on an average day, but Arizona summers could suck the life right out of you, and this day had been a scorcher. He needed to take in as many fluids as possible, and the comforting buzz felt good after a long shift.

"So you made this chair today?" she asked.

"Yeah, it looks pretty good, doesn't it?" he said with a sense of pride. He adjusted from side to side so she could see his handiwork, too tired to stand up. The twisted iron bars and meshed seat looked professionally made.

"I'm very impressed." She winked at him. She sat on the brick planter, nursing a beer herself, book face down and open next to her. "Will you make me one too?" She put on a girlish smile.

"Well, I'm guessing when we're done here, this one will stay. But sure, we can leave two instead of one. I guess it's only fair we leave something behind."

"It would be nice for nights like this." She took the last drink, stood up, opened the trashcan, and dropped it in. She opened another and was back on the planter. She looked straight up. "Oh, I love these desert summers, Frank." She winced, then mouthed *sorry*.

"But look at the moon, Chris," she said, face up again. "I love the moon."

"Yeah, it's nice."

"The moon is my favorite. I hate the hot red sun. So ugly, so angry. Especially here. The beautiful moon has always drawn me. She's changing, like a sensual woman. She can be bright or dark. She can move through the sky and alter her shape. Transform. She is never the same."

"So does that make the sun a man?" he asked with a laugh.

"Of course!" she smiled at him, then continued, "It's a big showoff, the same blazing hot ball every day. Boring. Predictable. Just like a man," and now they were both laughing.

"Okay, girl, okay..." he said. "So what's the book you're reading?"

She picked it up and showed it to him. *Poems of Love*. "It's a collection of romantic poems. I don't read books much, but I love the words in this one. I borrowed it from the counselor this morning... she had it in her office, and she loaned it to me."

"What's your favorite?"

"They're all good, but the one I was reading earlier really touched me."

"Why don't you read me a little?"

She picked up the book, and read, careful to say each word correctly.

*The years shall run like rabbits,*
*For in my arms I hold*
*The Flower of the Ages,*
*And the first love of the world.*

*But all the clocks in the city*
*Began to whirr and chime:*
*'O let not Time deceive you,*
*You cannot conquer Time.*

She pulled the book down and looked at him. He was looking out into the distance. He let the words settle into him. He pictured them, lined up in a row. Letters outlined in leafs of gold, then flickering flames.

"You okay?" She was looking at him with her head tilted.

"Yeah…yeah," he said, breaking his reflection. "That was deep. What was it?"

"It's a poem by W.H. Auden, called *As I Walked Out One Evening*."

He took another drink of his beer. He could feel the words working on him, touching places he kept hidden. Locked closets and bolted chests. The words of the poem knocked on those places. He let those words move around. *Cannot conquer time. Goddamned right.*

They were quiet and listened to the evening sounds. Buzzing bugs. Cats in the bushes. Frank enjoyed his beer, and he felt worlds better as it filled and cooled him. They were both lost in thought.

Frank ran his tongue over his implants. They felt funny in his mouth, but were better than the jagged gaps. Hard work had tightened him and darkened his skin. He saw the small cuts on his hands and the twisted veins now more pronounced. And still those words ran through him.

"I got a call from Perry today," she said, breaking the spell. He turned to look at her. She nodded at his questioning look. "Yeah, his foster family called and said he wanted to speak with me."

"That's very kind of them."

"Yeah…yeah…" and she turned, so he wouldn't see her eyes mist. "It was so great to talk to him. He sounded great. He told me he was praying that he would turn into Superman."

"Superman?"

"Yeah. He said he wanted to fly to me and rescue me, like Superman does in the cartoons."

"That's so sweet."

"He seems to be thriving with this family. They have him enrolled in school, and he's going to church. He just started the fifth grade today."

"Wow! Fifth grade." The thought of his own children had been far off, but now moved closer.

"Yeah, and he's very excited about his teacher…said she's very nice to him."

"That's fantastic…I'm so happy you got to speak to him." He tried to mask his own sadness. Ruth was probably in the same grade. Matthew should have already graduated high school. He wished he could talk to them, but knew it was out of the question.

"I'm hoping we can visit him when we finish up here."

"Yeah, I think that would be great. We have three more weeks in the program, and then you can ask the court for visitation and then custody once we're settled."

She changed the subject. "So tell me about the chair. I didn't realize you were making this much progress."

"Yeah, I'm really enjoying welding. It's more fun than I would have thought. Today they showed me how to use the torch to make the wrought iron hot and then how to bend these bars. Then I would connect the ends by beveling them with a grinder…"

"Beveling?"

"Slope the edge. It gives the angle you need, so the weld has a place to go and fill in. The MIG torch does such a nice job that I could get a very clean surface. Here, look at the weld on the armrest," he said, pointing to a thin, beaded line.

"Is that good? I'm sorry, I don't understand anything about welding…"

He laughed. "Yeah, I understand. I wouldn't have known a few months ago. My boss at the shop said I have an eye for it. It's funny…in my old career I collected certificates and credentials and hung them like trophies on my wall. All those credentials told me and the people around me who and what I was. Degrees. Certifications. I had many, but it's all lost, and I have nothing to show for it. Now I'm getting real skills, and they're all in my head and hands. Bending iron. Using a torch. I'm building skills that are self-contained; I don't need a diploma hanging on my wall to prove I can do it, and they go with me wherever I go."

She watched his reverie. "Fantastic."

He smiled back at her, not noticing her inner turmoil. "Yeah, and Charlie said he's going to talk to the owner about hiring me on after the program."

"That's great…Chris," she said. "Would be great if you had a job coming out."

"Yeah, it would," he smiled. "Would give us something to work with."

"Us...that's nice to hear."

"Of course, Mary," he said. That name felt odd to say. "Us." He caught her green eyes, and she squinted against the porch light of the house. "What were you thinking?"

"Well, just worried is all."

"Worried?"

"Well, of course."

"Why would you be worried?"

"Well, I'm extra baggage. You have recovered so quickly, and I'm an old junkie with a kid. You have your own kids to worry about." She again turned her head. She was ready to say what she hadn't yet been able to tell him.

"What's up?"

"I...I just wouldn't blame you if you left when we finished rehab. I wouldn't blame you at all."

"Why would you think that? You know I love you." He paused for a bit. "And Perry. I love you both."

"You can do better."

"What do you mean?"

"I mean...you're a man with skills, and you're successful. You quit junk in a couple weeks, and I'm still fighting a few months later. You're getting skills and I'm still dope sick. You should go off on your own and rebuild your life. You don't need us holding you back, dragging you down. Perry's probably better off with that foster family than with me." And now her head was turned completely, but she couldn't hide the tears from the porch light; they dropped one by one off her cheek.

Frank stood and walked over to her and put his hand on her chin. She wouldn't turn though.

He knelt down beside her. "Mariah," he said softly. "Please don't talk this way. I love you. I made a commitment to you. We're cleaning up. You were on it longer, so it's taking you longer...but we're getting clean. We'll get out of this program, and we'll get a place of our own. Then we'll get Perry back. If we stay clean, we can have a good life."

"Goddamnit, Frank. You don't get it...I'm hurting. I miss my son, but I miss skag too. I miss shooting up. I'm not over it. You should just move on. I don't think I can stay quit. I think I'll always fall back to it." Her hands were rubbing the lines on her face.

He put his arm around her, and she settled her head against his shoulder. He spoke softly. "Mariah, I will stay by you. If you fall, I'll catch you and help you. You'll get cleaned up. I know you will. Perry needs you, and you'll do it for him."

"I'm weak, Frank...weak. I always fall. I want to fall, I think. It's easier than fighting. I'm no good at this..."

"Then let's be strong together. You're just having a bad day...I have them too. Let's work together. We can do it for ourselves and for Perry. We can get our lives together and succeed. I believe in you...in us."

"I can't help how I feel. This is what's inside me."

"You're letting weakness and fear control you...you have to be strong...for us...for Perry."

In her heart, she felt a sting, as if he was using her son to manipulate her. She couldn't help feeling resentment, though she also knew he was right.

He took her hand in his and pulled gently. She stood up, eyes still averted. He walked her into the house, leading her by the hand. They moved to their room. Mariah was still spilling tears. Frank pulled her to the bed, then locked the door. He slid the bolt into place. He moved to her and kissed her. She kissed him in return, but tears splashed their lips.

He tugged her blouse over her head and kissed her bare breasts. As his lips kissed her skin, more tears dropped to his head and ears. He saw the junk scars on her sides, and he kissed the tattoo on her stomach.

Mariah relaxed to his kisses. She welcomed the physical contact. She welcomed his body on hers. His penetrations warmed her and soothed her. She pulled him to her and let his heat move into and through her. She closed her eyes and dreamed of the warm opiate filling her veins, the way he filled her now. She wished his ejaculation was her lover, H, and that its sweet conjoining would heal the ache in her bones and quiet the storm in her mind.

# X X

Frank hadn't ever thought he would be voluntarily sitting in a lawyer's office ever again. And yet here he was. He looked around at the diplomas and certificates on the wall. He saw the usual: pre-law at Chapel Hill, JD from Harvard, multiple certifications. Trophies on the wall for Sarah Renn, Attorney-At-Law. She was a professional because her diplomas showed she was. The frames on the walls told you all you needed to know about her.

She sat across from him in her crisp black pinstripe suit. Legs crossed tightly. It seemed so familiar for him to assume the same posture: back straight, legs crossed, hands folded in his lap, though his shoes were not Italian and his polo shirt was business casual. Now that he was clean and shaven, though, he could easily have just stepped into work from a day off, or come in after a golf outing. He reassumed the visage he wore for so many years, and it felt comfortable...familiar.

She looked at her notes. "So I have worked out a deal with the Sacramento DA. He is more than eager to clear the books of your case."

"I still can't believe all that happened."

"Well, after you gave me the whole narrative, I'm honestly not too surprised that his life imploded. It's tragic how it all came out in the end, but violent people usually can't shut it off. It's just a shame you didn't find this out four years ago...must've been hard living under the shadow of this…case."

"Yeah, hard to sleep when you keep waiting for the police to kick down the door. Every time a dog barked or a car door slammed, I would just about shit myself." *All that worry for all these years.* Waiting for some inevitable reckoning that would never happen. Afraid some cop would run his ID for a speeding ticket. Afraid someone would recognize him at a mall. He could feel a calming exhalation, going out long and slow. An unclenching of his jaw. He took one long blink, savoring that cleansing breath. Worry slipped from him. *All those years. Wasted years of worry. Always anticipating… dreading.* He let out a dry chuckle to himself, shaking his head.

He opened his eyes and looked again at the copied article from the Sacramento Bee. *Disgraced Sac Deputy Murders Wife, Kills Self.* He looked at the faces. Her photo, obviously a glamour shot, with heavy hairspray, opera gloves, and feathered boa. His stern and serious official photo, in full dress uniform. He looked at the face closely. It was familiar, yet only distantly so. In his mind's eye, the deputy had grown into a fanged ghoul with a mile-long baton. Haunting his nightmares, ready to open the glass door and do damage. To see the troubled man himself, in a uniform he was proud to wear, made him…human. He hadn't expected that. *No mention of the victim in all of this, either.*

"So what's the deal?" He slid the paper back to her.

"In exchange for clearing the parole violation they want a statement from you eschewing future lawsuits against the county for the actions of Deputy Jensen. Both slates are wiped clean. Warrants cleared, files closed."

"And you're sure there's nothing from Karrick and Santos?"

"Nothing. Sounds like they didn't want anybody to know. And with Karrick serving time in Chino, I don't think there's anything he could do for a couple of more years, at the earliest."

"But I'll still have the battery conviction?"

"Yeah…no clearing that. It was a jury case. You could ask for a retrial, and my guess is some of the witnesses might not show up. Still, retrials are hard to work and generally take years." She saw Frank's hesitation. "All in all, it's probably the best you could hope to get, Frank. And you'll get your name back. You can move forward with your life."

"Yeah." He looked up. "I guess it's a good deal, all things considered."

"And, most importantly, you're free to pursue your business license."

"Right...right."

"You don't seem very excited about this."

"Sorry, Sarah," he smiled. "It's just that there might be one more issue out there."

"Really?"

"Yeah."

She got up from her desk and walked around it. She pulled up a chair and sat next to him. He remembered another time in another office.

"Okay, Frank. Have you committed another crime you're worried about?"

*So many...*he thought. "Well, potentially. Would you please contact Pennsylvania...quietly?"

"Any particular cities?"

"Philadelphia and Lancaster, primarily."

"Primarily?"

"Yeah...better check Harrisburg and Mechanicsburg while you're at it."

"Christ, Frank!" she teased. "You were a naughty boy, weren't you?" He didn't smile back.

"I don't know if there are any charges pending. But I just want to be sure.

"Okay, I will check. Will call you as soon as I find out anything."

"Thanks, Sarah."

"You're gonna stop these shenanigans now, right, Frank?" She took the countenance of a scolding mother, though it was her business to work with people who didn't listen to authority.

"Yeah, I'm all clean now. If I don't have any pending cases then I'll be even better off. Meantime, make that deal with Sac County."

He drove home feeling positive for the first time in a while. *So long...so many years living under the threat of prison. Years of worry.*

*Wasted years.* He turned off his air conditioner and opened the window. He let the oven-like breeze blow in on him. He wanted the wind. He wanted it to wash over him and purify his breath. He wanted to let go of all the old demons. He wanted to release the fear completely.

As he drove, the road slid under him. He was feeling a taste of freedom he hadn't felt for some time. He thought of the deputy and could still see the eyes, see his sweat, and feel the sickening strikes of the baton. Jensen went too far that night and would have had to pay for it. Rather than face his consequences, he ended his life. He took his wife with him. Someone with so many problems in his life had been handed a badge, a gun, and the right to wield deadly force; Frank was just the match that lit his flame that night, all those years ago. Now, he could put that in his past and roll over it like this road. The road cleansed him. The road was freedom. And now he *was* free.

He pulled up to the simple ranch house they were renting. He saw Perry sitting on the front porch. Perry waved at him as he pulled the car into the garage. Perry was at the door as he opened it.

"Hi, Frank!" he shouted.

"Hey Perry! What are you doing outside in the heat?"

"Waiting for you to get home. Wanna play catch?"

"Sure, in a sec. Let me get changed. Is your mom home?"

"Yeah, she's inside."

"Okay."

He found her in the bedroom. As he changed into jeans, he told her the news.

"That's fantastic, Frank," she said. "So I don't have to call you Chris anymore?"

He laughed. "No, I think we're good. Let's see what she hears about Pennsylvania, but I think we're in the clear."

"That's wonderful news, Frank." She sat down on the bed. "So what now?"

"Now? Well, once I know for sure about P-A, I will file for a business license and start our own company. It'll be a bit tight while I build our client base, but once I have enough steady work, we should be doing fine. I've always had a head for business."

"I'm so proud of you, Frank. You've really done well."

"Thanks, baby," he said. "I'm gonna play catch with Perry now."

She smiled from the living room, watching Perry and Frank throw the ball back and forth. He was exactly the type of man she needed…and she knew it. He had accepted Perry as his own son. He was providing well for them. She had everything she needed. They were living in the best house she had ever lived in. Perry was in a good school and wearing clean clothes. He had friends to play with. Things could not be any better for them, and for the first time in years she could count on things…count on food, a home, and security. This was new to her.

She went back to the bedroom and pulled the box from the back of the closet. She produced a small envelope of brown heroin and put some grains in the pewter pestle. Grinding it carefully, she then blended in the small amount of water to make it a paste. She sprinkled in milk powder, which absorbed the fluid and scraped away the powder leaving thin beads of paste. She leaned over and snorted the mixture.

She carefully put the kit away and went back to the kitchen and started making dinner. As she cooked, she felt the warm euphoria move through her. Tingling. A gentle wave of warmth. A confidence in her life in this moment.

She relaxed and enjoyed the buzz, a dreamlike smile on her lips.

# XXI

"Right this way, sir," the young officer said, opening the half-door and holding it for him. "We just have a few forms you need to complete."

"Thanks," he said. He stepped through.

He was pointed to a chair next to a desk. He sat and was handed a clipboard, with several forms stacked, then handed a pen with too little ink. He scratched out his name, her name, their address, and all the particulars.

A tall sergeant moved into the room and sat in the chair at the desk as Frank completed the forms. He looked up as he sat, then back to his forms. He saw the sergeant wanted to talk to him.

"You the husband?" the sergeant asked, hands on the arms of his chair.

Frank looked up. "Yeah."

"Okay."

Frank looked at the tall, slender sergeant for a second, waiting for another comment. There wasn't one, so he returned to his forms. He could feel that the sergeant wanted to say more. The uniformed man leaned back in his chair and was watching him. Frank looked back up and returned his gaze.

"Is there something you want to tell me, sergeant?" He did his best to appear nonchalant. In his head, he knew what the point of the conversation would be. It wasn't going to be the first time.

"I'm just wondering how a man who seems to be doing well can have a wife out buying heroin in the park." His brown eyes looked into Frank's, and he had the confidence only someone in power can have, knowing there would be no retribution for arrogance when you had a gun strapped to your hip and a badge on your chest. Frank knew that all too well.

He knew he shouldn't reply, but he did. "That's our business, not yours." He looked back down to his forms. He started shaking the pen to get more ink to the tip.

"You should keep an eye on her. Wouldn't want this in your neighborhood."

He again looked up and this time put the pen down. "*This?* What do you mean by *this?*"

"You live in a good neighborhood, Mr. Joseph. I'm sure your neighbors wouldn't like knowing they have a junkie living next door to them."

"Well, that's none of their business, is it?" He could feel the tension building, and now their eyes were locked on each other's. They were in a mental contest…a test of wills.

"In some neighborhoods, I'd say it's not. In yours it is."

"What difference does it make where we live, sergeant?"

"It makes all the difference…we watch out for our good communities."

Though he again knew better, he could feel his blood coursing furiously. "I thought your job was to watch out for *all* communities."

The lean sergeant stood up. "Listen, Mr. Joseph…wise up. You got a junkie for a wife, and you live in a well-heeled neighborhood. Get her off the smack, or there will be problems."

He couldn't hold back his response, though he knew he was being obstinate…dangerously so. "You listen, sergeant. I don't care who the *fuck* you think you are. I pay my taxes. I work hard and provide value to the community. You think that badge gives you the right to tell me what to do with my life? Well, sorry to tell you, it doesn't. Who the fuck do you think you are?" His volume was increasing; his ears were flushing. "Your job is to enforce the laws. That's it. You're not the judge; you're not the jury. So why don't you butt the fuck out of our business, let me fill out your fucking forms, and get my wife out of here, okay?" He half expected the sergeant to pull out his baton and attack him, but his blood was up.

"Hold on, man, I don't know who the fuck you think you are..."

Both men turned when a door opened suddenly, and a gray-haired captain stepped out. The sergeant looked at the captain, and his head dropped. No words were spoken, but the sergeant walked unbidden to the captain's office. When he entered, the door closed.

Frank completed the forms, scratching angrily at the paper, and handed them to the young officer, who now looked a bit blanched.

"Sorry, sir..." the young officer said.

Frank smiled at him, still shaking from adrenaline. "Not your fault."

As he sat in the waiting room, he caught sight of the sergeant leaving the captain's office and going back to his desk; he sat silently and began to fill out paperwork.

He heard another door open, and Mariah was brought out to him. A female officer held her upper arm with a latex-gloved hand.

"Frank, thank God," she said. She walked quickly and wrapped her arms around him.

"Thank you, officer," Frank said through her hair. "Are we free to go?"

"Yes. Be sure to answer the summons."

"Will do," he smiled. He turned and led her to the front door of the station. He could feel her hand shaking as he used his free one to pull open the door.

"You okay, Mariah?" he asked.

"Yeah, I'm just jonesing...I gotta get a hit, Frank...I'm aching all over."

"Do you have any at home?"

"No, I'm out...that's why I was scoring." He opened the car door, and she slid in. "Can we go get some? I know a place."

"Mariah, you just got released..." He closed the door and came around, sliding into the driver seat.

"Frank, I need a hit...badly...you gotta take me somewhere. I'm itching all over..."

He thought for a moment. Getting caught buying smack after

bailing her out wouldn't be the smartest thing he'd ever done. He looked over to her, and he could see her face twitching and body jerking. "Okay, but let's make sure it's in another part of town...we can't get picked up by the same cops."

"I know a place...get on the highway..."

# XXII

"We'll take two hotdogs," Frank called out. He nodded to the people in his row as they passed hotdogs in one direction and money in the other. He handed one to Perry.

"Thanks."

"Yeah, sure," he said with a smile.

It was a blistering July day, and he was glad the stadium was covered and air-conditioned. They chomped their hotdogs and sipped their drinks.

"Well, I think the D-backs aren't going to win today, buddy," Frank said. The score was 8-2, and they were into the ninth inning.

"It's okay," Perry said. "Still fun to see a game."

"Yeah," and he looked at Perry, who smiled back at him. Perry had gone through a recent growth spurt and he was quickly approaching six feet, now just an inch shorter than Frank. "Let's try to see a couple more games before the end of the season. Once you start high school, you'll have a lot less time for these things."

"Yeah, that'd be great."

As they watched, the Diamondbacks came up to bat at the bottom of the ninth.

"I miss my mom, Frank." Perry didn't look at him.

"I know you do, buddy. I miss her too."

"How long before she comes back home?"

"I can't say. She just started on her program. I think she'll be there at least a few weeks, if not longer."

"Okay," he said.

They heard a loud cheer as the first batter hit a blooper to right field and got on first base. Frank and Perry weren't cheering.

"I hope you know, this is the best thing she can be doing."

"I know. She needs to quit before it kills her. She told me that the day you took her to the clinic. I just miss her being home."

"Yeah."

A loud groan went up when the next batter hit the first pitch into a double play.

"When they let her have visitors, we'll go and see her, okay?"

"I'd like that. Thanks, Frank."

On the way home, they stopped by the shop. *Joseph's Welding* was a bustling business during the week, but on this hot Sunday only two welders were finishing up detail work. Frank and Perry walked through the open shop and waved to the metal-masked men, being careful not to look at the blinding arc.

The weekend supervisor came out of the office and greeted Frank. "We're almost done here, boss. I was just finishing up the invoices for the pipe…"

"Don't worry, Lamont…I'm just here to pick up a few things. Not checking on you."

The supervisor looked relieved. "Hot today…" he said, then turned back to the front desk.

"Yeah, very hot," Frank said.

On their way to the staircase that led to Frank's office, Perry admired an extended chromed-out motorcycle they walked past.

"You're making choppers now?"

"Yeah, there's good money in custom choppers."

"It's beautiful," he said, putting his hands on the handlebars. Frank could see his eyes sparkling.

"Yeah, we buy these S&S motors pretty cheap, then the rest is just the pipe we already have. We build it, then take it apart to get chromed and powder-coated. Costs us about two thousand in labor and parts, and we sell them for twenty or more. Real money makers."

Perry was still gawking at the chrome. "Wow. Will you make me one?"

"Your mother would kill me. Those things are death traps."

At the bottom of the stairs, Perry stopped again and looked at a car being assembled. Frank was proud to see Perry interested in his work.

"You like that one?"

"Yeah."

"That one there is a '69 'Cuda. My first car. I think I might keep this one, but not sure."

"It's gorgeous, but why that awful green?"

"That was the stock color, but we mixed metallic flakes into the paint to make it a bit more modern."

"It really is nice…but would look better in red."

"Maybe when you're ready to drive we can make something for you. I'd feel better with you on four wheels instead of two."

"When are you going to let me do some welding?"

"Well, if you're ready we can start soon."

"I'd like that…I want to make my own chopper!"

"Okay, slow down," he said with a chuckle. "You gotta learn the basics first. It takes a while to get to that level of skill."

As they reached the office, Frank put together some papers and notes he needed to complete that night. As he sat on his chair, Perry took the one across the desk from him. Perry didn't see Frank look at their picture on his desk. They had only taken the picture a few months before. Perry's large smile was offset by the tired smiles of Mariah and Frank. He noticed today how pale Mariah looked in the photo. In the corner of the frame, he had wedged in the photo of his family in Sacramento. The picture was spotted, stained, and torn. He looked at his sons and wondered if they were as tall as Perry. Or taller. Matthew and Mark were probably taller. Both would be adults now. He wondered if they thought of him. He hoped they were both in college.

He collected the papers he needed and was ready to go when his phone rang. He picked it up when he recognized the number.

"Hello?"

"Hi, Frank, this is Warden Ford…how are you?"

"Hi, warden, how are things at the penitentiary?"

"Great, thanks. Sorry to call you on a Sunday. I was talking with the governor last night over dinner. He was asking me about the type of programs we have here at the federal pen to help parolees transition. I described the few programs we have, and I mentioned yours."

"Well, it's small, isn't it? We've only taken four guys. Not much of a program."

"Yeah, but all four of them have successfully transitioned. Don't underestimate the success of four men leaving prison and not returning."

"Well, glad to help. Do you have another person you want me to work with?"

"No, that's not why I'm calling." He paused. "The governor wants to highlight your program's success and get it a bit of media attention."

"Why? I don't understand. Four people…"

"And you also give those great talks to new inmates. Those are immensely helpful. Right now, he's taking some heat for the sheriff in Maricopa and his tent-city jail. He feels showing the work we're doing with parolees might help offset some of the negative media."

"Ah, I see. Still, it's small potatoes."

"I know what you're saying, but little things like this make a big difference. He was hoping to get the local ABC affiliate to run a story on it. He has a friend at the station. Maybe also show one of the talks you give…if you have time."

"Well, I don't know. I'll have to think about it, I guess."

"Understand. Do think about it, Frank. Keep this in mind: if you save even one person from a life in prison by giving him a skill, you've made a huge impact in that one person's life. Don't we all need a hand up once in a while?"

"Yeah, we all do."

"Okay, so will you give me an answer by Wednesday?"

"Sure, will do."

Frank was lost in thought as they drove home. Perry was reading a comic in the seat next to him. Frank knew what the warden had meant, and he knew himself that he had relied on help from so many people. That was his motivation for working with parolees and helping to train them; he wanted to help others who were down on their luck. And he had been successful.

But he had also spent a lot of time keeping a low profile. Too much attention wasn't a good thing, considering Mariah's struggle with addiction...and his own. Still, some goodwill from the community couldn't hurt, and perhaps it would open some other doors for him. If he could get into the state and federal contracts honeypot, he could expand his business even more. It was growing quickly, but he had managed much larger operations in other jobs, and envisioned similar success with his own company. Now that he was the owner, he was truly building something to leave behind...his legacy.

When they got home, he went to his room. It was dark and quiet. He stepped into his bedroom and sat on the bed. He thought of Mariah—he missed her smile.

He also thought about the picture on his desk at work. He thought of his tall sons. He thought of his old family. He wondered how they were. Matthew should be nearly finished with college, and Mark should be just starting. He hoped they went to college.

He pulled out his wallet. Next to his few dollars, he found a slip of paper he'd had for some time. It was aging too, like the photo on his desk. It was wrinkled and the corner torn, but he could clearly see the logo of Sarah Renn, Esquire. He had scribbled a note on it once. But he could see the original message clearly:

*Tony and Michelle Santos 310-294-4643*

Frank looked at it as he had many times before. He moved to put it back into his wallet, as he had many times before.

And then he grabbed the phone from the nightstand. He began to dial and then hung up. He put the phone back. He was going to walk out of the room, but then found himself holding the phone again.

"Hello?" He knew Shelly's voice immediately.

"Hello, may I speak to Matthew Joseph?" He felt ridiculous for changing his voice. It just happened. He knew she would probably recognize him anyway.

"He's not here now. May I ask who's calling?"

Frank hung up the phone.

# XXIII

"Hi, baby boy," she said, unfocused eyes trying to smile at him. "Come here and hug Momma." She put her arms out, her cigarette a quivering stub between her fingers. Perry slid into her arms. She had a slowed affect from heavy doses of medications, and she trembled weakly.

"I missed you, Momma," Perry said into her gown.

"I miss my big boy too."

Perry pulled away. They took seats around an outside table. Frank couldn't help but examine the quality of the wrought-iron table and chairs. The large umbrella staved off some of the heat, but it was still very warm.

"How are they treating you, Mariah?" Frank asked.

She was pale. Blanched. She reacted to his question, but slowly, as if she was on a delay. Long distance. "Well, it's hard…I miss you guys." Her blinks stopped halfway down.

"Yeah, we understand. We miss you too, don't we, Perry?" Perry nodded.

Perry reached into the paper sack next to him. He pulled out a small wrapped box. "This is for you, Momma," he said proudly.

Again, slow to react. "Ah, that's my baby boy…" and Frank could hear a bit of slur in her speech. He had been where she was. He had kicked. He knew the medicines they used to bring a junkie down. He now knew what others had seen in him.

"Go ahead, Mariah. Open it," he encouraged.

She gave an anemic smile and bared her yellowed teeth. She stubbed out her cigarette, even though it had been to the filter for a while. "Oh, this is such a pretty wrapper," she cooed. She picked up the box, but her hands worked against her as she tried to open it. Perry looked at Frank, and Frank just nodded back to him.

"Let me help you, Momma," Perry said. While she held it, Perry made the first couple of tears in the wrapper. Frank remembered doing the same for little Ruth on her first Christmas.

Mariah ripped the rest of the paper. A small box was underneath. She struggled to lift the lid, so Perry held the bottom. "Oh my gaw, it's so beautiful," she said, voice croaking. She pulled the necklace from the case. She held the heart in her jerking hands.

"It's a locket, Momma. Open it."

Mariah struggled again, so Perry reached over and pushed the release. Inside was a picture of her on one side and Perry on the other.

"Oh, I love these pictures," she said.

"Let me help you with it." Frank stood up and came around behind her. He took the locket and draped it around her. He then moved to clip it around her neck.

"Excuse me!" someone shouted. "Excuse me!" Frank looked up. "No necklaces allowed!" Frank saw a nurse moving toward them; she was scolding him with her waving finger.

Frank help up a flat hand to her. "Okay, sorry," he called out. He put it back in the box.

"I'm still on suicide watch," Mariah said, wan smile on her lips. She wished she hadn't said that in front of Perry.

He put the box down in front of her. "I'll hold this until you get out."

"Thanks, Frank. It's beautiful. Thank you both," and her lips were too dry. She fumbled for her cigarettes. Frank pulled one out for her, and after she put it in her mouth, he lit it.

"Momma, when are you gonna come home?" Perry asked.

"Soon, baby. Soon," she said, but she knew it wouldn't be.

"I have some good news for you, honey," Frank said. Mariah was looking off into the distance. "Mariah?" She turned slowly to him. "I have some good news for you."

"Oh? Good news?"

"Yeah, a television crew came by the shop."

"Yeah, Momma...I was on TV!" Perry said proudly.

"You were?"

"Yes, he was. They were doing a story about the work we've done with parolees. The governor has a contact at Channel 5. So they did a report on our program and interviewed some of our crew. They filmed Perry welding the frame for the chopper he's working on." She smiled at her son. "I taped it, and I'll show it to you when you get out." It was warming up, and Frank was beginning to sweat. "Anyway, I've been asked to speak at the prison more regularly and perhaps teach that class monthly. Figured it would be good to give back some, you know?"

Mariah's eyes were distant and lost again.

"Momma, are you okay?"

She came back more slowly this time. She smiled, this time not at anybody in particular.

"Mariah, would you like to walk around a little?"

She looked up at Frank slowly. He could tell her medications were coming on hard, and she was beginning to disappear into them. Walking would get her blood flowing. Without any acknowledgment, he stood up and the grating of iron on cement made her eyes focus. He helped her up, stuffing the necklace case into his pocket.

They began to walk down the path in the grassy recreation area. She was off balance, so Frank held her hand on one side and Perry the other.

"Oh, it's so nice to be with my men," she said in a faint, far-off voice.

"We're here for you, Mariah."

The heat in the sun was beginning to spike, and he could feel sweat running down his neck. He looked at Mariah, and she was as dry as a stone. Her skin was yellowed. She was probably dry from vomiting...part of kicking.

"We'd better walk her back, Perry. She probably needs to rest."

Perry didn't say anything, but didn't protest as they turned around.

When they neared the shaded visiting area, Mariah leaned close to him and whispered, "Frank, you need to get me out of here. I'm dying."

He spoke softly back to her, "Mariah, it's for the best…"

"Frank, I need to be home. I will die here." He could feel her body trembling against his. He looked down to her, and through the fog in her eyes, he saw she was serious.

"You're just dope sick, Mariah, you've gone through this…"

"It's different this time. I'm not getting over it. I'm not kicking. I can feel myself dying."

He tried to keep his voice low. "Have you talked to the doctors?"

"Frank, you know they won't listen. I have to get out of here. *You* have to get me out."

"But you'll go back to using…"

"Frank, if I don't leave here, I'll be dead. I need out."

He looked down at her again. She had the stink of pharmaceuticals. Her lips were chalky. Her tattoos looked faded, like crayon drawings on yellowing paper.

"I'll see what I can do…" and he gave her a soft smile.

"Promise me, Frank. Promise me."

And he did.

# XXIV

The news anchor's plastic hair and smile moved in unison as he turned to the new camera angle. "And finally tonight, a former homeless drug addict's dramatic turnaround and how he's helping others. For more we go out to Nicole Garcia, joining us from Phoenix, Arizona."

From the split screen, young, dark-haired Nicole held the microphone just below her chin, ensuring the NBC logo was visible. "Thanks, Henry. Tonight we're sharing the story of Frank Joseph. He is owner of *Joseph's Welding*, a Phoenix shop that does custom welding, as well as building motorcycles and cars." The camera panned back, and the shop was in clear view. "Mr. Joseph is a former homeless heroin addict. He was financially destitute, so he turned to theft to feed his growing habit. Now, he's the owner of a successful welding company, and he's giving back by helping parolees get new skills. We'll speak to him in a moment, but we want to show some footage first. We followed Mr. Joseph to the Arizona Federal Penitentiary today, where he spoke to a group of inmates."

The camera cut to pre-recorded and voice-overed footage.

Michelle Santos was cooking dinner when she saw Frank's face on her small kitchen-counter television. She moved closer to it and watched as Frank spoke to the room of men in denim. He had aged, and his hair was grayer. He looked twenty pounds lighter, but had a lean hardness to him. His teeth looked whiter. He had regained the confident smile she remembered. The smile he had courted her with so long ago.

"Mr. Joseph recounted the years of homelessness and addiction."

The footage rolled, and she saw a close-up. She couldn't look away. "Those days on the street were tough. I had lost everything. My family. My work. I had given up hope. I lived on the streets for several years. Hopelessness led me to try heroin for the first time. It took away the pain and loss for just a few hours, but those few hours were more than I had had for a few years. It felt like it washed away my memories, so I kept at it."

"Shelly, shut those fucking kids up, will ya?" she heard her husband shout. "I'm trying to watch the fuckin' game."

She switched off the TV. She moved down the hallway, to the closed doors of her children's bedroom. Ruth and Luke were on their bunk beds, laughing at a show playing on the small TV in their room. The room was small, and there was room for little else.

"Hi, Mom," Luke said, but his smile faded when he saw her face.

"I told you guys, keep the television down," she hissed. "You know Dad gets angry when it's too loud."

She jerked the remote from Ruth's hand and pushed the volume button down until neither could hear the show. Shelly threw the remote onto Luke's bed, then stormed out. Ruth began to sob softly.

Shelly was back in the kitchen, and checked if she could hear her children. She could not. Mark hadn't come home after school, and she knew he was getting ready to drop out of the community college he attended. She was worried Tony would have another of his rages. Tony seemed to have taken a dislike to Mark lately, so Mark avoided him, which only made it worse.

The small townhouse in San Pedro was cramped and the kitchen small. They had sold their last townhouse now that Tony wasn't working. Since they were on assistance and renting, they were all on top of each other.

"Dinner will be ready in about five minutes," she called out. Tony didn't reply.

She turned the television back on, but a sitcom was now

playing, so she turned it off again.

"Shelly, get me a beer," Tony called out.

She opened the cramped fridge and saw there were only two left. She had better run to the market. She took him the beer and grabbed two empties from the coffee table. Tony never broke eye contact with the television. He was paunchier now, and with his feet up on the ottoman she thought he looked very old, like her father.

She was back in the kitchen, but her mind was on the images she saw on the television. So many years, so many memories. She knew every inch of that face, every movement of that body.

She set the small table for two, as only two could sit at it. She served a plate for Tony, then went to tell him dinner was ready. He was asleep on the chair, head slumped forward to his chest.

And she remembered. She remembered her life so long ago. Her happy family. Children playing in the pool. Their beautiful brick home. All that they had, all that they were. She was somebody then, and her circle of friends was extensive.

She went back into the kitchen, sat at the table, and wept.

The noise from the next apartment was incessant. The constant boom of the bass drum thundered day and night, and as these were basement apartments the sound had nowhere else to go. He always kept the television up high, and the deafening racket made him angry. He would yell sometimes, shriek others. The neighbors responded by turning up the bass even more.

The room was small, the furniture old. Stacks of newspapers and empty beer cans were on every flat surface. Empty pizza boxes and microwave dinner trays were underfoot.

Tonight was a bad night. Tonight was the type of night he had often lately. He had struggled to put on his mechanical arm; the harness was difficult to work with one hand. He had wanted to go out and get a hot meal. Without his arm, he would not leave. He had shrieked and cursed and cried, but he could not get the straps tight. He had thrown it down in disgust, and a strap lock had broken off. He would be without his arm until he could get it fixed.

So he had opened another beer and sat with hot, angry tears in his eyes. He looked at the stump, moving it to shake off the tingling, the ghost of the arm he lost so long ago. He cursed in Hungarian and drank the beer too quickly. It was the ache in his heart that would not go away. He couldn't drown it, but he tried.

He had lost everything that day. He had lost his manhood. He had lost his business. He had incurred expenses he couldn't cover. All in one moment. All consuming.

When his girlfriend came to visit him in the hospital, the burning loss of manhood hit him just as that bullet had. He had seen her look at his bandaged stump, and he saw what he knew he would. He was less of a man. Though she would have never said it, he knew the look in her eyes and it affirmed his own feelings.

He had sent her away in tears and told her never to return. In his mind, he knew he could never be with a woman who wouldn't view him as a man.

The ache of the amputation was more than he could have imagined. The heavy opiates he was given made him dopey. But he needed them. Badly.

He had been so proud of that store. He had worked so hard to save the money for the down payment. When he had purchased it, he remembered the pride he felt the first time he received a shipment. He loved stocking the shelves and filling the coolers. He loved that everything he made had been his own. He never minded working long shifts and only reluctantly hired help. That day, that long distant day, his morning help had called in sick; he wasn't even supposed to be there. Bad luck had put him in the path of ruin.

His father had never known the satisfied feeling of building something on his own. His father had been a civil servant back home and had fled with his family when he could. When he arrived in America, he simply took a desk job and was happy with a steady check, though secretly he yearned to be home and never fully adjusted to life in the US.

Hadur wanted more. He wanted the American Dream. He sweated and worked and saved every penny until he could afford his own store. His own. He knew someday he would own two, three, or even four stores. He knew his hard work would make him a success.

He loved to work, to build. He wanted to craft his own future and hand his sons an empire, leave them with something more than his father could give him.

And then that New Year's morning, it had all changed so quickly.

When the news came on that night, he was half-asleep from his oxy and beer. Though his tolerance was up, they still made him logy. Street oxy didn't match pharmaceutical-grade, so he always had to take extra.

And then the news had come on, and he was close to turning it off. He was tired and would take another oxy and drift off to sleep.

Then he saw that face. There it was…clean-shaven now, but with the same eyes. Eyes that had grown terrible in his nightmares. There was no mistaking it. A face he would never forget. A face that haunted him. A nameless face, nameless no more.

He began to shriek. There weren't words for what he felt. These were the sounds of the black places in his soul.

# PART V: CINDERS AND SEEDLINGS

# XXV

Frank was in his office when his phone rang.

"Yeah?"

"Hi, Frank, it's Claire at the desk. There's someone here to see you."

He sensed something in her voice. "Who is it?"

"She won't give me her name."

He thought for a bit. "Does she look like trouble?"

"No, I don't think so."

"Okay, be right down."

Since the television show, he'd had a few stray visitors. Fame makes people crazy. People just want to meet someone famous, or they're bored with anonymity. Or they think famous people know something they don't. Some came just to meet him. Others came asking for something. He would shake their hands and answer their flurry of questions. *No, I don't know anybody at the station who could get you a job. No, I don't need any new people. No, I don't have any connections in television. Thank you for coming by.*

From his office, he walked out onto the floor, sweat quickly forming from the heat. He saw the bright arcs of the welding. Cars and motorcycles were being tacked and assembled. He loved the smell of the ions and crackle and blinding sparks. Loved to hear the sizzle and zap. He had twelve teams working on different projects. Business was good. He paused a second to see Perry and two others sliding the engine onto the frame of his chopper. It was shaping up nicely. Perry's skills were growing quickly.

He turned and moved into the office.

From the other side of the counter, she smiled at him. "Hi, Frank," she said, smile too wide.

"Fuck!" he said under his breath. He tensed. Though he didn't want to, he immediately took her in with his eyes and recognized everything about her. She had put back on the weight she had lost the last time he had seen her and some extra on top of that. She was still wearing too much makeup, now covering up more than before. Her dress didn't fit her well, and her dye job was a single color... *out of the bottle*. Her eyes were grayer.

Claire looked up at him. "You okay, Frank?"

He smiled back in her direction. "Yeah, fine, Claire."

He came around to the front of the counter, and Shelly turned to face him expectantly, like a prom date waiting to be taken to the dance. Everybody pretended to be working, but all eyes were riveted on them.

He stepped up to her. "Hi, Shelly."

She cleared her throat. "You're in the welding business now?"

"Yeah." He could feel the weight of the stares in the office. "Let's step outside." He walked to the door, and pulled it open for her. She stepped out, and he pulled it closed behind him. She wore new perfume now, but he knew her movements and recognized every swing of her arms, every sway of her hips. Though he would have hated to admit it, he felt the familiarity in her proximity. Almost comforting.

They walked for a bit...he wanted to get some distance from the prying ears. He walked out to the parking lot and then past the handicapped spots. He stopped when they neared his truck. The sign said *Reserved, Owner*. He slid his elbow onto the tailgate.

"Is this your truck, Frank?"

"Yeah."

"Tony used to have a black pickup like this."

"His was an F-150. This is an F-350. Both Fords, though."

"Well, you know I don't know anything about trucks."

His eyes flashed at her. He remembered Tony's truck clearly

and the last time he saw it. "You're not here to talk about trucks, are you, Shelly?" He shoved his fingers through his hair.

"No," and her eyes went down to their feet. Through her heavy makeup, he could see she was blushing, and her ears were red.

After a pause, he asked, "Then why are you here?" His voice was direct, with a hint of acid. More than a hint.

"I saw you on television. It was nice to see you after all these years. I thought I would come see you."

"Does Tony know you're here?"

"No, Frank. He doesn't." Eyes still down to the ground.

"Shelly, I don't have all day. I have a job. What do you want?" He faced her directly and shoved his hands into his pockets. He jangled his keys and coins.

"I just wanted to see you again, Frank. You're my ex-husband. The father of our children. Is that so bad?"

"Shelly, you fucked my best friend and dumped me when I lost my job. You left me without anything. You took the kids, and I haven't heard from them in years."

"You can call them any time you want, Frank."

"Call?"

"Yes."

"Yeah…I have to call my kids. Nice." His hands were now on his hips, as if he were scolding a wayward child. But he hadn't called his kids and felt the shame of that self-admission.

"Frank, please don't be angry."

He took a deep breath and looked away. "Why are you here?"

She looked up at him, and their eyes met. She looked back down again, away from the steel in his gaze. "I wanted to talk to you." Her voice was soft, just above a whisper. She took a half-step closer to him. "I wanted to see you again and talk to you." Her hand went out to touch him, but his disapproving look made her pull it back.

"Talk about what?"

"Talk about the kids…talk about…us." She looked up again, and then her gaze went back down.

"What about the kids? Are they okay?"

"Yes, they're fine," she lied instinctively. "They're good."

"You're all down in LA?"

"Yes."

"In Tony's house in Hermosa Beach?"

"No, we moved to San Pedro." Her face flushed again. She knew he was drawing conclusions from every word she said, and there were places she didn't want to go. She wanted to take back the conversation. "I'm very happy you've landed on your feet, Frank. You seem to have come through quite well. I somehow always knew you would…you're too smart…you were always too smart to let anything defeat you…"

"Thank you," but it was cold.

"I was thinking that since you have put your life back together…I thought…" and her voice trailed off.

"You thought what?"

"I thought that if I could just see you again that we…" and she again let it hang.

"You thought *we* what, Shelly?"

"This is hard, Frank."

He waited. He knew what she had to say, but he wanted her to say it. To commit to it. He wanted to spurn her as she had spurned him all those years ago. "Just come out with it. Tell me why you came to Phoenix."

"I thought maybe you and I could give it another try. I thought we could try to start over."

"You what?" He was purposely incredulous.

And her eyes rose up again and saw the bitter coldness in his. "You loved me once, Frank. Maybe you still do. I know I still love you. I thought I didn't. I was wrong. I was just mad that you had let that happen to you that night."

"Let that happen? You mean get beat up in a bar fight protecting my best friend who was fucking my wife and then beat up by a sheriff who killed himself and his wife?"

"I didn't understand all that, Frank. I didn't know what had happened. Nobody knew."

"You were my wife…you were supposed to stand by me *no matter what. In sickness and in health…for richer or for poorer.* But rather than do that, you jumped out. Jumped out with a man you had been fucking behind my back for at least two years. Longer, probably."

"I was worried…about the kids…"

"You had been fucking Tony for a long while…I just gave you a reason to bail completely."

"I had to think about the kids…" Her voice was pleading now.

"The kids? Don't act like sleeping with my best friend and then leaving me for him was somehow noble, Shelly. You don't get to have nobility out of that." He had squared up toward her again. His shoulders were rolled forward, and his hands pulled into angry fists. "You can't pretend to be a good person for doing what you did."

"I'm not saying that, Frank…but I felt…compelled at the time."

"Did Tony tell you?"

"Tell me what?"

Had he told her? For a moment, Frank thought he would tell her…tell her the truth about her husband. The gun. The parking lot. *Your husband set me up and pissed himself when I pointed a gun at him.* He wanted to crush the last of her little world. But the words didn't come out.

He changed the subject. "So you thought that after wiping me out and taking the kids, you could just fly here, and I'd take you back?"

"We have four children together, Frank. We're not just two people with a past. We have a family."

"Had."

"*Have.* Those children are yours forever."

"I haven't heard from them in years." It stung him to say those words.

"We didn't know how to get ahold of you, Frank."

"Did you ever look?"

She changed the subject. "We can rebuild, Frank. We can start anew. Our love was so strong once; we can have it all again. We can go back to church. The Lord will help us, if we let Him."

"The Lord?"

"Let's go back to God, and let Him…"

"God?" he scoffed. "The woman who fucked my best friend and

ran off with him wants to talk to me about God. That's nice, Shelly. Very *fucking* nice." His volume was steadily increasing.

"Frank, only the Lord can heal us now. Only the Lord can heal these wounds."

"You think you put on a mask and I won't recognize you?"

"Recognize me? Frank, I..."

"I know the real you...I saw her in divorce court. You are great at wearing the mask of whoever you want to be or wish you were, but peel it off, and you're ugly and hollow. I saw you...I saw you..." He squinted against the afternoon sun.

"Frank, please don't say things like that..." and though her voice trembled, her eyes were dry. Frank looked at her and felt nothing. Worse than nothing. Rage. Disgust. In the darkest corners of his mind he wanted to put a fist into her mouth. She had destroyed him financially, and he wanted to destroy her physically. *Payback*. But he knew he could never do that.

But he wanted her to know. Wanted her to understand she was dead to him. With a cool heart, he leveled his eyes and said, "I am with somebody else now, Shelly. Somebody I love more than I ever loved you. I have a new family now. And you're married to my former best friend. You deserve each other...go home to him." And those words cleansed his soul. In his eyes now she looked small, a lost child who needed someone to find her.

She grabbed his right hand with both of hers. "Take me back, Frank. We can make all this work again. We can put all the bad things behind us. We can go back to church and rebuild our lives." Her eyes were still dry, but red and imploring.

Frank yanked his hand free, more fiercely than she was ready for. She winced, as if she saw a blow coming. Instead, his words came with hot jet fuel; his eyes threw blades. "Take you back? Take *you* back?" he knew he was far too loud, nearly yelling. No doubt everybody in the office was listening now. "You're a careless woman, Shelly. You expect someone to take care of you, and when you thought I couldn't do the job, you ran off with your lover. Now that he's obviously failing," he bitterly pointed to her cheap dress, "then you want to run back to me.

"You and Tony destroyed my life. You laughed at me when you

took everything I had in my entire life. My home. My children. I almost swallowed a bullet over it. Now you want me to take you back?

"Nobody can replace you, Frank. You were always a *good* man. The most dependable man. The *right* man…"

"You should have thought of that before you opened your legs to my best friend. I was all those things once, but while I was providing for you, you and Tony were fucking behind my back. He then fucked over my life to win you, and now you're stuck with him. Get used to it."

"Frank…it wasn't like that…"

"No, you listen to me, Shelly." His finger was like a pistol in her face. "I have finally started to rebuild my life. I've started to build something I can be proud of. Something I own completely. You're my past. A *painful* past. I'm moving on to a new life, and you're not in it. There's no going back now."

"Frank…"

"No!" and now his voice was booming, "You leave now, Shelly, you horrible fucking bitch! Get in your car," he waved his hand toward the rows of cars, "and get the fuck out of here. I've worn my masks. I'm done. I'm not changing who I am anymore. I am going to be me, and you're not part of me. I'm going back inside to *my* business, and if you come back in, I'll call the police. Imagine explaining that to Tony!"

He spun on the heel of his work boot, and stomped back to the front door. In the glass, just above his company logo, he saw her reflection, still standing where he had left her. He entered and ignored the stares of his employees.

"Claire, if she comes back in, call 9-1-1."

"Will do, Frank."

He moved past the counter, and then out to the shop floor. He threw on some coveralls, and grabbed a mask and torch. "Perry, you need a hand with that chopper?"

# XXVI

"I can't believe how much deeper your voice is, my son." He was wiping tears and swallowing hard.

"It's been a decade, hasn't it?" *Brusque.*

"I'm so sorry I've missed these years, Matt. I'm so glad you landed on your feet."

"It wasn't easy. I could have used you there."

"I'm so sorry. I have no excuse."

"So what do you want now, after all this time?"

"I want to help. I have gotten myself together. I was in a dark place before, but now I'm doing better."

"Congratulations." There was the snide.

"What I mean is, I want to help you with grad school."

"I don't need your help, Frank."

*Frank?* "Matt, I don't blame you for being upset…"

"I don't go by Matt anymore. I'm Matthew. You'd know that had you been here."

He was trying to sift through the bile, looking for gems that weren't there. "I deserve that, I guess. But I'm back now…"

"Look, you want to help, Frank? Call Mark. He's getting in trouble. Since Mom and Tony split, he's been running with the wrong crowd. He's on his way to jail if he doesn't turn around. He'll end up fucked-up if things don't change…fucked-up like you."

He knew it was pointless now. "Okay, I'll try to reach him."

"Good."

One last try. "Do you need any help with college? Is there anything I can do to help you?"

"No. Full ride, and I present my thesis this May. Good thing, too…both of my fathers are worthless to me."

"Okay, but…"

"Bye, Frank," and the line went dead.

He put the phone on the receiver and put his face into his hands, feeling his warm breath. He knew he deserved it. He knew everything his son said was right. He had left them. He had run off. No matter the reasons, his son went through his teenage years without him. He felt bad that he took satisfaction that Tony, apparently, hadn't been there for him either. No matter who didn't do what, his son was angry and hurt and deserved his feelings. Frank could only blame himself.

He stood up, feeling exhausted. Legs jittery. He heard Perry in the front yard, practicing his free throws on the hoop he had installed on the garage. It was too quiet inside.

"Mariah?" he called out. "Mariah?" He went up the stairs. He could still smell the glue from the new carpeting. "You up there, babe?" he called. No reply. He climbed the stairs. "Honey?"

When he opened the bedroom door, he heard her shallow breaths. Pants. She was lying on the bed, arm still tied off, empty needle next to her. Arm bleeding onto the white duvet.

He knew the routine and all too well. He untied her arm, wiped the blood with a warm washcloth, and laid her on her side. He watched her for a second, to be sure her breaths were steady. Her color was good…not too white. Lips had color, if light.

He put her fixings in the cigar box. He took the needle into the bathroom and rinsed it. He worked the plunger to push out the last of her blood. He put the cap on it, put it in the box, and put the box in the closet.

He heard the front door open. "Mom? Dad?"

He didn't want to shout over her, so he moved to the top of the stairs. "Up here, Perry. Down in a second."

"There're a couple men here to see you."

"Oh?" He took a couple of steps down the stairs, but didn't go farther.

"Yeah."

"Okay, tell them I'll be right there."

"Okay."

He went back to the bedroom. He grabbed the fixings kit out of the closet. He took the folded paper that contained the heroin, along with a balloon that contained more. He flushed them down the toilet. He cursed under his breath; in their new neighborhood it was harder to maintain anonymity.

He came down the stairs and saw the two men in suits at the door on the other side of the screen. The slender suit mumbled something to the larger man as Frank approached. Frank knew they were cops immediately. As he approached, the slender man opened his jacket and slid it open with his hand, putting his hand on his hip. His shiny badge was on full display now, as was his smirk.

"Everything okay, Dad?" Perry asked. His face showed worry.

"Yeah, I'm sure it is," Frank smiled at him, patting him on the shoulder. He stepped up to the screen. "Good afternoon, gentlemen." He donned the mask of a man with nothing to hide.

"Good afternoon, Mr. Joseph. Sorry to disturb you." He flipped open a thin leather wallet and displayed his badge and ID. "I'm Officer Michael Morrison of the Lancaster PD, and this is Deputy Marshal Bill Lawrence. May we come in?"

"What's this about, officer?" Frank knew that inviting an officer in was often considered granting a consent to search. "Lancaster PD?"

"Yes, sir. We're here investigating a cold case, a robbery and shooting dating back eight years or so. We'd like to come inside and ask you a few questions about it."

"Why me?" Frank's mind flashed images of breaking glass and an exploding Pepsi bottle.

"Well, sir, I'd like to come in and talk with you about it, if you don't mind."

There it was. A decision point. Send them away and call a lawyer, or see what information they had. "Sure, okay. Sorry." He opened and pushed the screen door and let them in. He walked them to the dining room table. He could see the panic on Perry's face. "Perry, why don't you go check on your mother?"

No reply, but hurried movements up the steps.

As the men pulled up chairs, Morrison began speaking. "Thank you for letting us speak with you, Mr. Joseph. We have to do our due diligence in these cases. On the morning of January 1st, 1998, there was an armed robbery at the 7-11 on the corner of Manlove and Grand in Lancaster. The owner, *Hadur Fadrusz*," he pronounced the name slowly, "an immigrant from Hungary, was wounded and lost his arm."

*Lost his arm?* Frank looked back and forth between the men. Officer Morrison had a practiced, disarming smile. Deputy Marshal Lawrence was a small, slender man who gave off tension.

The deputy marshal spoke. "We have video of the event if you're interested."

Frank put on a crooked smile. "I'm sorry, gentlemen. I don't know what this has to do with me." He thought he was a better actor than he was, and the officers saw through his mask.

"We'll get there in a second," Lawrence continued. He began unzipping a black case and produced a portable DVD player. He had hard eyes, and Frank knew he would be Bad Cop. "First, we'd like to show you the video."

"Okay." A part of him was curious about it. Another part of him knew he should not watch it. He also knew they were going to gauge his reaction and measure his response, so he resolved to be dispassionate. What he didn't know was that he was already convicted.

Marshal Lawrence turned the screen toward Frank. Grainy surveillance video, broken into four quadrants with each showing a different area of the store, began to play. On that small screen, it was difficult to see details...at first. He could see the date imprint, and the time showed 8:03 am.

In the upper left corner, he saw his ambling, shoddily dressed image push through the swinging two-sided glass door. Though his hair was shaggy, he recognized himself immediately. Junkie Frank. Homeless Frank. Skinny, filthy, wearing rags. Still buzzing and slack from his last high. Missing teeth. At the time he thought he was acting cool, but now he saw how jittery and twitchy he was. When the man behind the counter stood up and greeted him, he saw his jerked response. His ghostly gray image turned a hard left and walked over to the drink coolers, and he passed through two other quadrants of the screen, past snacks and then to the drink coolers in the back. Facing one screen quadrant, his back to another. He saw his hand shaking as he struggled with the door and grabbed a drink. At the cooler, he turned and looked right into a camera. There was no mistaking him. This was the only close-up image. Jagged teeth, greasy hair, ragged clothes, junkie shakes, but definitely him. The rest were from a distance. The turn to the cooler marked him and put him at the scene.

*There is no turning back now.*

"Stop it please," Frank asked.

"We're not finished yet." He saw Lawrence wore a leering smile. He was the predator, and Frank was the prey.

"Please, just stop it." He felt sick, worse than any dope sick he had felt.

But they didn't stop it. He watched as the curly-haired man turned to get the cigarettes. He saw himself pull his .357 from behind his back and, with a trembling hand, point it at the owner. He watched Junkie Frank stuffing wads of dollars and rolled coins into his pockets with his left hand. As he turned to the door, he saw Fadrusz reach under the counter and produce a pump-action shotgun. There was no sound, but he saw him shout. Frank's eyes were riveted as Junkie Frank hunched over and moved for the door, then covered his face as glass exploded all around him. A second blast sent potato chips flying. Frank turned and fired blindly, gun jerking hard from the recoil. He saw Hadur drop from that first shot. Junkie Frank fired again, then ran out the door, sliding to four points on broken glass, leaving the Pepsi bottle behind among the shards.

And then the wreckage. The ashes. After a moment, he saw Hadur stand up, shirt covered in black blood, arm hanging limp. He staggered over to his phone and picked it up. He dialed quickly and then fell again.

"The paramedics found him unconscious," Lawrence said, clicking off the video. "He had lost a lot of blood, and the area behind the counter was filled with it…and chunks of his bone." Frank looked down at his hands. "When they got him to the hospital, the brachial artery was beyond repair, and the tissue had gone necrotic already. They took his arm just below the armpit. He barely pulled through."

Frank felt the heat in his eyes. He could feel the tissues swell. He felt burning in his throat.

The officers exchanged glances. Morrison spoke next, in a deep, soothing voice. Fatherly almost. "Mr. Joseph, we understand your predicament here. You're a successful businessman now. You have a family. I understand how this is tough for you." Officer Morrison was Good Cop. "We know that it isn't easy to face some stupid thing you did in the past, and I'm sure any judge will consider what you've done since that time."

Frank looked up and smiled at Bad Cop, who didn't smile back. "My whole life is a series of stupid things from my past, officer. My whole life." He paused for a minute. Morrison and Lawrence knew the confession was close. Their eyes told each other so. "So how did you find me after all this time?"

Officer Morrison smiled again, leaning back in the chair. Shirt buttons strained against his large belly. *Almost there,* he thought. "Mr. Fadrusz saw you on television. He had remembered your face."

"After all this time?"

"Well, you have to understand that this was a major turning point for him…life changing. He also had a copy of the video, which he says he watched now and then." A pause. *Keep talking. Let conversation flow.* "At the time we could never place the face. We had APBs out for you, but you fled town and cleaned up. No new arrests, so nothing to trace. After a while, the trail grew cold. We never thought to check California where you had a record. Or Arizona."

"So it was just a matter of time, probably."

"Yeah, we like to think so. We had your fingerprints on the Pepsi bottle. Your blood on the scene. Eventually something would have hit on a database somewhere."

"I wonder why it didn't before."

"Well, unfortunately we have a harder time when we cross states. It's getting better, but it's not there yet. Plus, you stayed clean…we count on most criminals to reoffend."

Frank sat back and looked down to his hands again. He looked at the hand that carried the gun and pulled the trigger. All those years ago.

His mind's eye showed the images. Deep in his thoughts he saw the shooting from his own perspective. The gun leaping in his hand. The flash and crash of broken glass. The boom of the shotgun.

"Mr. Joseph?"

The images came to him disjointed, out of order. The gun. The cooler. Mariah in the car. All scattered about and disorganized, but all there. He wasn't going to escape those memories now. They had stayed locked in their compartment for a long time, but now they were with him and they were going to stay with him. He knew the next stage of his life would involve these images, and they would haunt his sleep. The men he worked with in the Arizona penitentiary told him that. *You spend your nights reliving what put you there...it's like a bad movie you can't stop watching.*

"Mr. Joseph?"

He looked away and spoke softly to himself. "Another juke..."

"Sorry?"

He looked up and smiled at the large officer. "Another juke... life gave me another one..."

Morrison put his elbows on the table and leaned toward him. Maybe it was time for a second Bad Cop. "I don't follow..." with a more commanding tone.

"Juke...football..." He remembered a game, so long ago. "When a player fakes out another one...they call it a juke. A fake from the hip. A sudden twist with the shoulders, and then they're past you." So long ago, it was. "A juke."

The two officers looked to each other. Lawrence tipped his head and mouthed *now*, but Frank turned to him and smiled. "Life made a juke again, Marshal Lawrence. It faked me. I thought I had it lined up this time. Getting all of it, *finally*. Hitting it for all I was worth. Time after time, life has faked me out. *Every fucking time*. This is just one more fucking juke. Whenever I put myself together, life fakes left, and I miss it. I was so close this time. So close. A juke. And then I fall to the ground, empty-handed."

He thought for a moment. "Life's the matador, and I'm the blind, enraged bull, chasing a phantom...a red cloth waved in front of my face." He knew what was waiting for him. He knew all too well. State penitentiary. He knew the men that lived inside it…he had worked with some of them. He was under no illusions. He knew horror awaited him.

Morrison put his hand on his shoulder. "Mr. Joseph, I understand…but we're here…"

"I know why you're here. I know. Don't worry. You'll get what you want. You want a confession?" The two officers looked at each other, and Frank watched their eye contact. "You'll have it…don't worry. I'm ready. I was never meant for a life like others. I was never meant to have a good life…a regular life. Life was a big *fuck you…thanks for playing*, and I'm done with it."

"No offense, Mr. Joseph," Marshal Lawrence said with narrowed eyes, "but how do you think Mr. Fadrusz feels? I'd say his juke was worse than yours. What say you?"

"Thanks. I needed more, marshal." There was no pity in Lawrence's eyes. "This isn't hard enough already."

*There is no turning back now.*

Frank looked out the window and saw a red-crested cardinal in the tree in his front yard. It quickly flitted from branch to branch, and then flew off suddenly. Frank smiled, then looked to Morrison. He was Good Cop, after all. He would at least feign sympathy. "Give me your forms…I know that's what you need. It's all about paperwork, right? I'll give you what you want."

# XXVII

The Super 8 in Harrisburg was weather-beaten these days. The stucco was beginning to crumble. It was to be his last stop as a free man, and it would have to do. He spent his last night of freedom eating soggy pizza. Few words were said. He hadn't slept and instead read the stains and crawling bugs on the ceiling. Now that it was near noon, he was bracing himself for the surrender. He was giving his life for his sins and the sins of some others. He was taking the burden on himself and accepting the penalty.

He sat on a chair, and she sat weeping on the bed, face in her hands. The door was open, and officers stood near it. Frank looked at her distant eyes. He saw the locket around her neck. She was losing herself in the moment, but he couldn't blame her. He never had…he fully understood her.

"Frank, what are we going to do when you're inside?" She was looking at the complete reshuffling of her life. Everything that was before was no more. All their dreams. All their plans. Most of all, she knew the score…she was an aging junkie without someone to support her habit. She would have few options in a short period of time.

"You're going to have to be careful, Mariah. You have to think about Perry. You have to stay clean, or only use a little. You have to take care of him."

"I've tried to stay clean, but I can't…you know that."

"Mr. Joseph, you have ten minutes," the sheriff called out,

nodded, then turned back to his fellow officers. Several badges were standing at the doorway, talking and drinking his motel coffee. Ten minutes and then the descent into Hell.

"Okay, thank you," he called back.

"Frank, I don't think I can hold it together. I can't quit…"

"Look, the house in Phoenix is paid off. When you get back, you have a house waiting for you, and Perry is in school. You have a bank account with enough cash to last you a long time," then quietly adding, "but junk will eat it up if you aren't careful. If you use carefully, you'll be fine."

"It's not enough, Frank. It'll only last me a little while."

"It'll have to do…I had to leave some to my kids…"

"I know, but they don't know you anymore. I'm here now…" and she regretted it as soon as she said it. "I'm sorry…"

"It's okay, baby…I know you're hurting…" but it did sting. "Look, we've been over this…you have to make the money stretch. You only need to pay the utilities and buy food. You have a hundred grand in the bank…that can last a long time if you limit your intake as much as possible."

He felt bad for wishing he had her problems, but he knew he was facing something much darker…much deadlier…and much sooner.

Perry came out of the bathroom. He had a hard stare on his face.

"It's okay, Perry. Don't worry." Frank smiled at him. "Everything's okay." Perry didn't respond. He stood next to his mother, eyes like iron on Frank.

"It's not okay, Frank…it's not." She collapsed down to the bed and put her arms over her face. "We can't make it out here without you, Frank. *I* won't make it."

Perry put his hand on her shoulder. He gave Frank a harder stare, throwing daggers. He saw blame in those dark eyes. Gone was the little boy who couldn't sit still. Now he was a young man, tall and straight, with a man's mind. A young man who wanted to protect his mother.

She looked up again, eyes lidded but tears still pouring out. "Frank, you accepted a plea for fifteen years. Fifteen years. How can we make it that long, Frank?"

She was waiting for his plan, but he had none. "I know, Mariah. I know." He felt the weight of it. Fifteen years. It was a heavy load. He understood why she wouldn't wait, but the thought burned in him. "I know you'll need to move on. I don't blame you," though a part of him did. *I stood by you through all our street madness.* But he also understood she was a junkie, and that would require attention and energy.

"Okay, Mr .Joseph, time's up. Let's go," the round-bellied sheriff commanded.

Dutifully, Frank stood up, though Mariah grabbed his arm. He smiled at her, unwrapped her fingers gently and stepped away. Her head went down to the bed again. "Bye, guys," he said, looking at Perry this time. Perry didn't answer. He stepped toward the officers at the door. "I'm ready, sir."

"For your safety and ours we have to search and cuff you," the baritone directed.

"I understand." He assumed the position against the opened door, and felt the rough hands on him. He put his hands to the small of his back and the metal cuffs were clicked around his wrists. The metal bit into his bone. He winced. *I'd better get used to that feeling*, he thought. *Going to feel that for some time.*

The officers led him out to the awaiting car. The officer pushed his head down and he slid in. The door shut behind him. He looked back to the room, hoping to see them one more time, but they didn't come out.

He thought back to that night, now nearly a decade ago. Frank remembered the indignation at being put in a cop car. He remembered the flashing lights and his Miranda rights, all those years ago. He had wondered how someone like him could be treated in such a way. Now he knew he was exactly the kind of person who should be treated that way. He belonged in that car. He was a dangerous felon, and the cuffs protected the police officers from his violence. Once, he had wondered why anybody would become a violent criminal, but now he understood precisely.

He was no different than any vicious felon, and the old Frank would have wanted someone like him rotting in a jail cell somewhere.

He couldn't argue with the logic. He wondered, though, if every felon felt this way on his way to prison, felt that he was the one exception to the rule...the one person who didn't really deserve the predicament he found himself in. Did every trip to prison come with indignation? A sense of betrayal? He guessed he wasn't alone in feeling this way.

He was on his way to a new life. One that would require all the danger he had in him. *The Big House.* Pennsylvania State Pen. Home to the most hardened men in the state. He would be one of them. No cushy white-collar prison. No. He had earned a ticket to the maximum-security prison. He was guilty of a crime so heinous that he could have received a life sentence. The words in the charges they had filed sounded so unlike what he felt inside: *Attempted murder. Reckless endangerment. Unlawful discharge of a firearm. Armed robbery.* The plea bargain had saved him a decade of jail time and the state a lot of money.

At the sentencing, he had repeated the word "guilty" as each charge was read. He had listened to the drone of words, this time convinced of his guilt, instead of angered about his innocence. The sense of himself was gone, along with his sense of entitlement. He accepted each charge and signed forms without protest.

What he hadn't expected was to see Hadur Fadrusz in person. When the judge asked for impact statements, the doors were opened, and he was shown in. Frank could only stare in awe as the now paunchy, graying man entered the court, carrying the burden of a mechanical arm and years of torturous demons. The heavy arm was strapped over his shoulder. Hadur tried to show pride on his face, but Frank could only see the pain in his eyes. He stood in front of the judge and read his statement with a thick accent. He never looked at Frank, who looked at him, taking in every inch of his face. *This man deserves to hate me. I deserve to be punished for this.*

"Frank Joseph, I stand before you a broken man. A half-man. That New Year's Day took everything from me. *You* took everything from me. I lost all I had. When you pointed that gun at me, I thought you would murder me. When you shot me, you took away my manhood. I can't work. I can't love. My girlfriend left me. I am all alone. I live in a tiny apartment, on disability. You crippled my body and my soul. I will never recover from what you did to me. I hate everything you are, and I wish you had died that day. You'll have a chance to live when you get out of prison. I never will again." Frank heard the timber of sorrow in his voice. Heard the years of unanswered agony.

Fadrusz then took two steps forward and spit as hard and as far as he could. Frank didn't recoil when it hit him in the face. The bailiff grabbed the man and escorted him out of the room, now shouting "You deserve to die! You deserve to die!" Frank didn't even wipe it off for a minute; he felt it was the least he could do for the man he maimed. *Let him have that victory. It's not enough, but it's all I can give him.*

He had, after all, seen the arm. He had heard the pain in his voice. He knew the spit was nothing compared to a bullet destroying part of your body. And your life. Whatever would happen to Frank would be miniscule compared to the damage his victim had suffered.

He was given a date to report to prison. It gave Frank time to sell his business and set up trusts. He set aside a hundred thousand dollars for Hadur Fadrusz, even though he hadn't been fined. He had his lawyer arrange the transfer of funds to him. He then put all that was left in bank accounts for Mariah and Perry, plus trusts for his children. He didn't realize he had signed Mariah's death warrant.

# XXVIII

As bad as Frank had anticipated prison would be, it quickly became far worse. Immediately, he was identified as new meat, and he was set upon by the predators. Most men who made it to the penitentiary were hardened criminals, the worst of the worst, with numerous, progressive convictions for violent offenses. Frank had lived on the streets, but only by running and avoiding danger. He had been a mouse, and now he was surrounded by lions. At every meal he had to fight to keep the food on his tray. Every corner unseen by guards was an opportunity for someone to threaten or strike him.

"New bitch, you owe me," said a black man he had never met.

"Why do I owe you?" he stupidly asked.

"You owe me so I don't pound the fuck out of you," and his hard punch to the solar plexus sent Frank to his knees.

Each terrifying day brought new enemies. They knew he wasn't *prison hard* and saw a plum target. Rather than be beaten, he accepted the grabs at his food. Whatever he had in his cell was taken by others. As he hadn't had any money credited, he had to perform services for other inmates: washing clothes, running errands. Every day brought new demands from dangerous men.

The day he knew would come came when he wasn't expecting it. After a shower, he was walking, wet towel in hand, past another cell when he was bum-rushed in by three other inmates. He felt his pants ripped down, and hard punches pushed out his air. A viselike hand on the back of his neck held his face to the floor as each man took turns raping him. Screams brought jeers and laughter. Movement brought hard blows. Acquiescence gave him semen in his torn anus. Blood was a poor lubricant, but all he was afforded.

"That was good, honey pants," the bull inmate Harley had whispered in his ear. "Your ass is nice and tight. I'm gonna tap that ass from time to time, and you're gonna be my bitch. Got it?" They left him there bleeding, covered in semen and his own filth. He'd had to tie his shower towel around him like a diaper, and still blood and feces ran down his legs.

After the infirmary, the stitches on his anus itched and burned, and his short-stepped walk brought catcalls from other inmates: "Did Harley pop your cherry?" "Can I be next, honey?" "Don't worry…I'll be gentle, sugar!" He was a mark, and this violation only exposed that more. Now others eyed him, and he knew there would be more attacks, more rapes.

He realized the score all too well. Fight or flight, and there was nowhere to run.

"You're going to have to make a stand," his cellmate, Jesse, told him. "You're not fighting back, so they'll just keep taking more."

"I'm scared, Jesse," he said. "I'm not ready for this." He saw the scars on the other's face and wondered if they came from inside.

"You'd better get ready. Once those stitches come out, you're going to get it again."

And he knew he was right. Frank, though, had a problem. Though he was plenty brave with his .357 in hand, he hadn't physically fought anybody for years and only then because he knew the worst reprisal was a beating. He was now thinking of how to fight someone much more dangerous, someone who might kill him.

But there was no choice. There were no options. If he went snitch, he would be a pariah and take beatings from everybody. Nobody in prison could survive as a snitch. He had to man up and take what was coming. He had to set his course in his new life inside. Jesse had told him, "Man up or bitch up…make a choice."

*There's no turning back now.*

He spent the afternoon honing the end of his plastic toothbrush until it was sharp. He needed a target. He walked the long aisle toward the showers, a bar of soap and towel in his hand, waiting for someone to move into range. He held the toothbrush in his right fist, under the towel. He walked slowly, hoping it would invite an aggressor.

Near the showers he saw Harley talking with three friends. Harley was prison tough, made large from hours pumping weights in the yard. Tats and muscles and violence. Frank was glad it was going to be him…Harley had it coming. Even if Frank died today, at least he'd give him some of what he deserved.

As they saw Frank walking, the men started whistling. "Here's our girl!" one of them said. As he drew closer still, Harley said, "Good, honey, go wash that ass up now. I might want a little more tonight." Frank hung his head abjectly, trying to wear the affect of the passive. The bitch. As he drew even with Harley, the large man blew a loud kiss at him, face pushed forward with exaggerated pucker. Frank drove with all his strength, and shoved the sharpened toothbrush into Harley's eye. Clear fluid, tears, and blood squirted out onto Frank's face and arm. Immediately he was set upon by the others, who rained down punches and kicks on him.

Not Harley though. He fell to the floor bellowing, and held the remaining chunks of his left eye in his hand. Above the grunts and kicks and punches he received, he could hear Harley screaming like a maddened elephant. Blood poured into his ears. "My eye! My fucking eye! I'm blind! Kill that motherfucker!"

Harley's compatriots redoubled their efforts, and Frank realized how strong they were as he received the beating they gave. Through it, he took pleasure in hearing the wails of his rapist, even as he saw stars and his vision and hearing went.

The guards saved Frank from being beaten to death, but the beating was savage all the same. He was taken by stretcher to the prison hospital, where he spent three nights. The two broken ribs, three broken fingers, and twenty-five stitches were a small price to pay, all things considered. *Better than stitches in my asshole*, he thought. He was fortunate Harley was taken to an emergency room outside prison, or that night might have been his last.

Frank accepted the year addition to his sentence gladly. He knew it was necessary. Part of being in prison—get hard or get dead.

Harley was transferred to another prison for health reasons. It would not be the last time he would need to commit violence, but it gave him some breathing room and a bit of respectful distance from those who wished to do him harm. Nobody would ever consider him an easy mark again.

So Frank grew hard. He adapted to this life as he had adapted to all his others. He took on the countenance of those around him. He sharpened his mind and built his body. He started with pushups in his cell...mean mugging those who were too near to him. When confronted, he threw fists and kicks like a savage. He shadow boxed in his cell and pumped weights when he was returned to outdoor privileges. Within a year, though middle-aged, he was in the best physical shape of his life. Lean and powerful. He projected danger, and others learned to keep a healthy distance. His glare meant violence.

He killed his kindness. He snuffed out his heart. He became like all others inside: deadly. Ill-tempered. He tried to carve out a spot in his heart for kindness, to remember that there was love in the world. But when he sat down to write letters to his children, he knew he was faking the love he professed to them. His insides were black and dead. And as every day passed, the world outside became more distant...a phantom, a shadow. All that mattered was the now. That minute. Inside. There was nothing else that was of consequence.

So it was with a heart of stone that he read a letter from his lawyer, not even a year after he began his sentence. Ex-lawyer, he assumed, as he had no more money to pay him.

*Dear Frank,*

*I'm sorry, I wanted you to know. Mariah was found dead in a hotel room in Phoenix. Her son, Elbert, is in foster care. Apparently she had spent all the money you left them.*

*I'm so sorry for your loss.*

He tore up the letter and flushed it down his cell's toilet.

Months later, he was walking across the yard when he was approached by a member of the Aryan Brotherhood. He knew he had to respect the most violent gang inside. If he ignored them, it was a slight he would pay for. Politics in prison is truly a blood sport.

"You gotta get with your race, Frank. The colored savages in this place ain't gonna stay away forever. You woke people up, but they're still out there, and you will get hit. You pledge with the AB and we'll be your shield. Nobody fucks with us."

Frank tried to be non-committal. Gangs both created and solved problems inside, and he had hoped to avoid them. "I'll think about it, Ned...I need to lay low for now. I just had a year added."

The man's smile didn't hide his serious eyes. "That's okay, Frank...we got this shit wired tight. Something happens, we never rat on a brother. We protect each other and help each other out. Someone attacks you, they die. Someone steals from you, they die. Nobody fucks with us...not even the guards. We run the church services too, and Brother Weezer is the pastor...you go to church now and then, and that looks good for parole. Weezer writes a letter to the parole board saying you've had perfect attendance and are a changed man...well, that's something positive the board can consider. You'll probably do *less* time because you're with us." Frank smiled for a second and wondered if he could sit through a church service again, even if he knew it was for show. "And one more thing you'd better consider...Harley's crew isn't finished with you. I hear they're saying 'eye for an eye' to people they know."

"Okay," Frank said, "let me think about it for a bit."

"You think about it," he repeated, his face serious and eyes narrow, "but don't think too long. You need to back your race in here. Don't let the niggers and spics turn you into a piñata. You join the Brotherhood, and your enemies become our enemies." He turned the back of his hand to Frank, folded over the middle finger, and flashed the three-fingered sign of the Aryan Brotherhood. Frank saw the black Nazi cross tattoo on that hand. He walked away.

Frank thought, *Yeah, and your enemies become my enemies.*

He knew he'd have to declare for the Aryan Brotherhood, and he knew he'd have to commit a stabbing to join. *Blood in, blood out.* That would be more time added to his sentence. A second stabbing would probably add multiple years. But gangs were a fact of prison life, and he knew he was either with them, or they'd be against him. He hated those toothless twitchy bastards, but he also wanted to live. Survival was the first need he had to fulfill.

As Frank walked the yard that day, he reflected on the Frank he was before. So long ago. Sacramento Frank. He pondered that man, who now seemed light-years away.

Sacramento Frank was naïve: a good man with a good heart, but innocent to the ways of the world. He lived in a world of rules. There were responsibilities and proper consequences. Societal norms to conform to, and structure to the events of the world. Go to college. Pay taxes. Tithe at your church. You don't lie, cheat, and you certainly don't steal. Hard work was its own reward, but the harder you worked the more the paychecks came. God sat in judgment in the end.

He didn't understand that these rules weren't set by some cosmic order. He didn't understand chaos and entropy. He didn't understand other forces could align against him no matter how he lived his life. When he was hit by the storm, his roots weren't deep enough to keep him upright, and he buckled, cleaving his home and his life. Shallow-rooted Frank was a disaster waiting to happen; it was just a matter of time before something knocked him down. Without that strength of character, he didn't have the wherewithal to pick himself up. When presented with his first real fight-or-flight test, he had fled, and now found himself in a prison yard, surrounded by men who meant to do him harm.

That evening, he pledged to the Aryan Brotherhood, and was given a shank to stab a Mexican of his choice. *Blood in, blood out.* A week later, he sported his first swastika tattoo.

# XXIX

He slid his hand into his navy sport coat's pocket. Frank instinctively tensed, though he knew no weapon would come out. He produced a small torn and spotted picture. He put it on the table and slid it toward him. "I saved this for you. The one of us got lost somewhere in my first foster home."

Frank knew the picture very well. Being in the center of it, his face was the most pronounced. He was so much younger then and wore a tailored suit. Full head of hair, styled. Smiling, unfettered eyes. Sacramento Frank. The edges of the photograph were twisted and split. Water spots. The face of his wife completely unrecognizable, scraped off in a moment of pain. Matthew and Mark were barely visible through the stains and small tears. Little Ruth, though, was smiling up at him, as was Luke. He looked down and regarded it. Feigned bravado was his first response.

"Yeah?" He looked at him with dead eyes.

"I thought you should have it back."

"I don't know those people."

"They're you, Frank…your family…"

"I know who they were….and I know I'm not that person. That person is a stranger to me. Those people are all foreigners. A life I don't remember. The person I was then…I've mostly forgotten him. He had a skewed sense of the world. He smiled through his well-cared for teeth, and wore Armani. He put money in bank accounts and investments, planning for a life that wasn't going to be there. A fantasy future. He thought his life was secure and that he had built something that would last forever, like the Pyramids of Egypt or something. Such an asshole..." He looked away from the photo as if it was ugly to him. "Tomorrow knows the lies we tell today. All of them."

Perry considered the man in front of him. Frank continued, face still turned away. He was gritting his teeth, and his jaw muscles were flexed hard.

"There's a price for what we do, Perry. There's a penalty. If you sit in your home and never go out, you're fine. If you venture out, you're building up friction. You cut someone off in traffic, or you give a cop a dirty look. Friction. You grate against others. You grind out your existence. Abrasive existence. That scraping will make a spark and start a fire. I found that out the hard way. I worked hard. I loved my family. I didn't cheat...didn't smoke...drank a couple beers a year. I worked sixty hours a week. I saved. I invested. I paid my taxes, and I tithed from every paycheck. And look what happened to me!"

His raised voice drew the attention of the guards, so he softened it, though his lowered voice contained more menace. "I left my home one night with a friend and never got back. Life stuck a knife in my back...my best friend held the blade, but it was bigger than him. The giant, unrelenting, and unforgiving force of the universe took a shit on me. I left my home that night with a full life...a life I was proud of. I came back the next day, and I was human wreckage. Societal offal, to be cast off with the rest of the trash. Life grinds people up. Your mother once told me, 'you cannot conquer time.' I found that out...found it out the hard way. Everything I've done in my life I've paid for and then some."

"I don't buy that, Frank, and neither should you. This place can fuck you up...screw up your perspective. *Generally speaking*, life gives you good things if you are good. Good brings better, bad brings worse. It's just that sometimes bad things happen to good people."

His eyes leveled at him. "That's just it though...bad things *do* happen to good people, and good things happen to bad people." He kept his voice measured. "People rape and murder innocent victims every day. Every…single…fucking…day. I'm in here with many of the perpetrators. You're just a minute away from disaster. At any moment, someone like me could pull a gun and change you forever. I know, because I've been on both sides of it. Everybody in this place committed a crime against someone like you. Found an easy victim and hurt him. For money, or drugs, or excitement. Out of sheer boredom. And yet some thieving politician rakes in millions, robbing the people he's supposed to serve, and nothing bad happens to him.

"Nobody wakes up thinking it's going to happen to them. Nobody gets up in the morning thinking it's their turn for tragedy… or worse. Nobody in a plane crash ever imagined they would die that day. Nobody who is raped or murdered thinks it'll be their turn. But I know…I know too well…it can be your turn at any moment, and there's not a goddamned thing you can do about it. Someone is going to be murdered today. Someone is going to be raped today. Someone is going to be robbed or stabbed or shot or hurt today, and there's little they can do about it. I shared a cell with a guy who raped and murdered an eighteen-year-old girl, and every day he told me he wished he could have killed fifty more young girls.

"And just look at me! I lost my family, my career, my best friend…everything I had worked for…poof! Gone in an instant! Everybody involved in that night ended up in calamity. I'm sitting in prison after a long series of bad events, but I was backed into a corner. I'm paying for my own sins, sure…but also for the sins of others. When I hit back…when I fought against the forces aligned against me…I ended up caged like a rabid dog. The funny thing is that I was not dangerous before. I was a good man, if imperfect. Now…living here…I'm dangerous. Very dangerous."

Perry was used to swagger from men inside and wasn't taken aback by it. He knew it to be a defense, a wall against the pain. He tried to break through that fortress. "But you've done a lot of good things in your life, Frank. You've made a difference in the lives of many people. Bad things happen to everybody, and we all make mistakes and hurt other people, whether a little or a lot."

"It's a pretty idea to think about…that I somehow did something good in my life. But it's all ashes. My son…my second son…Mark…he's in jail. I got a letter from my oldest. Mark was busted for drug trafficking. A half-pound of coke. How did I make a difference? Mark and I used to go to Boy Scout camps together. Now he will be in Folsom Prison for the next few years. Reality caught up to my family. I was good until I wasn't, but none of that good got transferred to them. Only the bad. My baby girl, Ruth, is living with some guy, and they have a kid together. They're living on food stamps. My children are all damaged. All struggling with having me for a father. I left behind a legacy of ruin. I'm worse than nothing...I have done more harm than good."

"You made a difference in my life, Frank. That's why I'm here."

Frank looked at him flatly. "Did I?" It was almost a challenge. "Your mother died, and you went to foster care."

"I'm here because you made *all* the difference. For me."

Frank looked up at him again. In that moment, he saw the teenager he had left. Saw him from afar. And he remembered the small skinny, dirty young boy he had met all those years ago.

"It's true, Frank. My mother's gone, and I can't bring her back. When the police found her in the motel room in Phoenix, she was already cold and stiff. I had run away when she sold the house...I knew all that money would go in her veins. They found me sleeping in a park. And I was angry...so angry." Frank winced with the imagery. "I slept in the police station the night they picked me up. The next day they took me to a foster home. I stayed there awhile. Then I was given to another family and then another. I was a handful...I had some things to work out."

Frank was looking down at his hands. He was rubbing a scar across the middle knuckle of his right hand. He had busted it on the head of another inmate in a fight over cigarettes.

*Another child I left damaged. Another child I left to the vagaries of the world.*

"But through all of that, Frank, I thought of you. I never knew my real father. I only saw a couple of old torn and stained photos. But you, Frank, showed me, I guess, *man things*. How to be a man, I suppose. You can't protect people from the world...all you can do is help prepare them. Teach them. And you did teach me."

"What did I teach you?"

"Welding, for one. And more. Demeanor. The drive to succeed, to provide. To care for others."

"You're a welder?" He looked at him down and then up. He didn't look like a welder. His hands weren't scarred and pitted. His clothes were clean and expensive.

"I was. Now I own a welding company." He reached into his jacket pocket. Pulled out a business card. Slid it over to him, next to the family photo.

*Perry Smith*
*Owner and CEO*
*Royal Welding*
*Phoenix, Arizona*

He read it over twice, then fingered the raised plum letters. He put the card down in front of him and looked away. His eyes went across a candy machine, but he wasn't really looking at it. He felt familiar feelings, though they were far away and gray. A distant sunrise. He felt the memories. Picked them up and examined them. The years. The pain. The loss. That's really what churned inside him. *All that I've lost. My life is wreckage…rusted red hulks on the side of a highway. Grass growing through the floorboards.*

He felt a hot lump in his throat. His eyes burned.

"Frank, I owe my success to you." He heard those words across a great distance.

And then he was standing on the edge of a canyon. One promontory, looking down into the vastness. Across the canyon, he could just make out the many images of his former selves. He could see Sacramento Frank, dressed in a black suit. That Frank was innocent and ignorant, and didn't know the betrayal in his own home. On another foreland he saw Philly Frank, a skinny, shaking junkie. Philly Frank was out of control. A slave to a white, powdery master.

And then he saw Arizona Frank. Hard-working. More worldly. Caring for a woman and her son. Building a new future and helping others. He liked Arizona Frank, though he knew that man was to be short-lived…he had a cancer he couldn't see.

Frank turned again to Perry.

"You don't have to…" Frank began.

209

"Thank you? I really do feel gratitude. You taught me how to weld. You showed me how you did business. How to work with people. You were, for those years, a father and mentor. *That's* what I want to thank you for. But I am also thankful for the role model you are...or were." He paused for a second. "Sorry, that came out wrong."

"No, I understand. Not much of a role model wearing numbers."

"Well...but yeah, I was a young boy who had only lived in homeless shelters and on the streets. Mom was too busy scoring junk to give me much, though I know she loved me and tried her best."

"She did try."

"Believe me, I worked through all that. I have seen what addictions can do. Addictions of all kinds bring people down. Even you." Again, leveled eyes. "I also know that you can still make a difference, if your mind and heart are in the right place. Just the time we spent together, with you giving me a trade, showing me your books...it gave me something...a set of skills that when I decided to, I could build on. And I did, but that was up to me."

"You've done very well."

"I'm doing okay. I owe a lot of that to you, and I do my best to share it out to others, like you did."

"Share what?"

"That's why I'm here. I'm not just here to thank you. I'm here to talk to you and consider you. Evaluate you. I always remembered how you used to take people on parole...people in need...and you gave them a chance. Many didn't want it...a few failed...but you gave them a shot. And several people succeeded. I've since met a few people who went through your program. It kept them on the outside. It made all the difference in their lives." He looked directly into Frank's eyes. "I'm doing the same now. I have worked with parolees, and I have recently expanded into a work-release program back in Phoenix."

"Work release?" It came together for him. "Are you here to talk about a work release?" The possibilities began moving quickly through his thoughts.

"Not here to talk...here to offer. I've spoken with the warden.

My program is in Phoenix…it was really the one you started all those years ago. I have never taken someone from outside Arizona, but I have a friend who knows your warden, and it's an offer he will accept based on the success of my program. You haven't done good time, Frank," he said, and Frank was surprised by his directness, "and you still have more than five years left on your sentence. But I pulled a few strings, and you can be in Phoenix in a few weeks…if you're willing, and if you follow the strict guidelines. Drug tests, regular check-ins, et cetera. You'd be required to fly back to Pennsylvania once a year to be examined and interviewed."

There was an echo in his mind. Far off. A voice across the ravine. Not from a former Frank, but from another promontory, this time a young boy he left behind over a decade ago. *Work release?* Those words bounced around the walls of his canyon. It hit edges and careened into others. It slowly moved closer. Building momentum. *Work release. Release!* He heard the word, and at first it meant nothing to him. A fantasy word. Like unicorn or Minotaur. Didn't exist. A fable. A serpent in the Garden, or gods assembled on a mountaintop.

And then it came to him in a furious rush. This young man, once a skinny little boy with scruffy curls, was here to help him leave this cage. This pit. Leave the fear and the danger and the torturous *aloneness*. Leave behind the stabbings. Leave behind the rapes. Leave behind the constant hyper-vigilance. The clank of metal bars. The rattle of cuffs. The beatings from brutal guards. The every day, every way, fear and hate and violence and pain and agony and suffering that was prison…was the *point* of prison…could be behind him. He could see this prison from the outside, more than five years early.

And then those thoughts were pushed away by just one: the boy had become the man Frank was not, though perhaps once was. The young man had built a full, complete life and was able to help others unselfishly. Offer gratitude with real actions. Exemplify goodness, not just talk of it. He was tall now, taller than Frank. His hair was trimmed short and neat. His clothes were well-pressed and obviously tailored. The watch. The shoes. The crease in his trousers. This man in front of him was facing a less-than-man. Subhuman. An angry, bitter, aggressive man. A man so bad, so dangerous, he had to be locked in a cage with other animals. Society had to be protected from him. Two men from other worlds. Two men as distant as continents.

And then tears came. Frank's face fell into his hands, and scalding teardrops streamed out of his eyes. His shoulders humped. The years of tears held inside all came out furiously. He bawled openly. He didn't care about the others in this room. He knew it would get back. He knew he might catch hell for it. He didn't care. It all came out of him. And…then…he felt a warm hand touch his shoulder.

That human contact. That *love*. That compassion. It took his strength, and he bawled harder. He gave way to the insecure child inside of him and let it all out.

"It's okay, Frank…" but the voice was far away. He was lost in his gut wrenching.

Perry didn't know it, but those tears were shed for more than just the thought of release from prison. They were tears for Shelly. The boys and little Ruth. They were for his lost friends. Tony. Trenton. They were for his lost love, Mariah. They were for the teenager he left behind when he was taken to prison. And they were for the man who was now offering to take him out.

Perry wouldn't know all this, of course. He didn't know how many tears had been held inside. All the self-pity. All the self-loathing. All the anguish. All the fear. It all came out of him, sitting in the cheap plastic chair, the half-finished Diet Coke in front of him. He couldn't have known.

Having never been in prison, Perry didn't know that prisoners sit alone in their cells, watching the television of their mind showing the wreckage they left behind. All they had lost. All they would never have again. Video of lost loves. Their victims. Their crime. Their children. The damage done by their own hands. That was the worst aspect of prison…what you were forced to live with every day. Prison was the realization of every mistake you had made in your life.

Frank cried until he was empty. A hollow vessel. He wanted to be filled again. He wanted to fill himself with love again. He wanted friendship. He wanted to be a man again. He dried his eyes and wiped his hands on his denims.

"I can help you, Perry. I can help you…" Frank's voice cracked, but he was determined to tell him.

"I know you can, Frank."

"I mean, you know…I had a head for business…always did…"

"Yes, you did."

"And I don't mind using a torch again. I liked working with pipe and…"

"It's okay…I know that…you don't have to sell yourself…"

"But I want you to know, I can make a difference for you…"

"Yes, I know you can. I wouldn't be here if I didn't think you could."

He looked into his eyes again. He saw kindness and compassion. He knew his own eyes were red and swollen.

For the first time in over a decade, Frank took a cleansing breath and felt purified by it. He once again took in what was around him. Perry's kindness. The hell of state prison. His own shattered past. The images of his children, lost and broken without him. He breathed them in and let out the hate within. Let out the indignations and anger. Let out the violence.

For the first time today, he smiled at Perry. A real smile, not a smirk. "Perry, I'm very proud of you for all that you've done." He stuck out his hand to him. Perry took it, and they shook firmly.

Frank saw the small boy inside the man in front of him. *Hi, mister. I'm Perry. What's your name?* He knew that Perry hadn't yet faced many of the challenges he had. Maybe he would face fewer. Maybe more. Life dealt everybody a different hand. Yet Perry had already faced obstacles he couldn't imagine. Frank had succumbed to his challenges. Had failed at critical moments. So perhaps he could learn again from this young man who had overcome his own struggles and conquered them, at least so far. They could teach each other. He could help him prepare for the buffeting winds of future challenges and stumbles, and Perry could help him restore optimism.

He resolved to do those things. To take those steps. To rebuild a relationship and give Perry all he had to give.

We, each of us, hold a lantern, a guiding light, for those around us. A docent in troubled times and weary trails, if we're so inclined. Or we embrace the darkness and snuff out hope and love in the greedy quests of life. At varying times, each of us can be light or dark, and it is in the degrees of each that our lives are measured. Often perception defines and distinguishes the differences. Frank chose in that moment to follow Perry's bright light, which had cast rays into the darkest of midnights. He would let that light warm him and chase the darkness from his soul. He would reflect that light and use it to light a new fire within himself. He hoped the blackness, the fearful, turgid pit inside him, would be banished by this flame.

They were family, after all.

# EPILOGUE

As he pulled open the door he saw Tony sitting at a booth. Tony's eyes came up as he entered. Their eyes met and unmet several times as he walked toward him. Tony didn't stand up.

"Hey Tony," he said, standing next to the table for a moment.

"Hi, Frank." He was there for a moment, and then Frank's hand came forward. Tony eyed the open hand, then put his own hand out. Frank felt it was clammy. His own wasn't. They shook briefly.

He slid into the booth and said sorry as his work boot kicked Tony's loafer.

"No worries."

They sat and eyed each other for a moment. Frank saw that his old friend was completely bald on top, and had gained about twenty pounds since the last time he saw him. Tony eyed the heavy black tattoos on Frank's hands and forearms. Frank knew what he was thinking and answered him. "Yeah, I got these inside."

"I wasn't..."

"It's okay. I don't mind." There was no reassurance on his face. "Everybody knows I was inside. Ten years inside changes you. Tats are just part of the life. If you don't fit in, you're going to stand out." Frank knew this talk was making Tony nervous, so he tried to lighten the conversation. "Thank you for meeting me, Tony."

Tony smiled in response, but Frank wasn't smiling. He could feel Frank's presence, and it was different than the man he knew before. He felt tension. He could feel the danger in his old best friend. Though lean, he seemed larger than he had before. He had an intimidating air. "Yeah, no problem."

"I thought it would be good for us to bury the hatchet, so to speak. We were best friends for decades, after all."

The young blonde waitress walked up to them, and both of their faces turned up to her. "Are you guys ready to order?" Both looked at each other. "Do you need a couple minutes?"

"I haven't eaten here for probably twenty years." Frank's tone was almost apologetic. He picked up the menu. *Alonzo's Ham & Eggs.* "They still offer the same things as before?" he asked Tony.

"Yeah, I think so." He too opened the menu.

"I'll give you guys a second." She rolled her eyes as she walked away.

"Funny, you and I both grew up in this neighborhood," Frank began, still eyeing the menu. He saw Tony putting on reading glasses. "But honestly I can't remember eating here, though I know I did."

"Yeah, I know we did a couple times. Just so long ago..."

Frank folded the menu and put it down. "This Fruitridge area has gone to shit, hasn't it?"

Tony chuckled. "Yeah, it's all gangs and criminals now." He saw Frank look up at him. "Sorry, that's not..." There was silence for a moment.

"When we grew up in this area," Frank continued, letting Tony off the hook, "it was old families. Now it's the ghetto."

The waitress returned. "You guys ready?" She couldn't hide her impatience.

Frank looked up at her and didn't hide that he was looking at her body as he spoke to her. "I'll have two eggs, sunnyside up, bacon, coffee, black." She ignored his leer.

She turned her eyes to Tony. "I'll have the Denver omelet. And OJ."

She took their menus and walked away. Frank watched her ass all the way to the counter.

"So how did you find me, Frank?"

"Well, I actually saw your profile online. Then I asked around, and Robert Prince from high school had your number."

"Ah."

"I was surprised to see you back in Sacramento."

"Well, it's home. Never really liked LA." They both accepted their drinks. "After me and Shelly split…" Their eyes met. "I decided I'd had enough of the traffic and smog. I'm glad I came back…good to be home."

"Yeah, I know what you mean. Familiar."

"Yeah, that's it." Tony smiled at him. "All my life's memories are here."

"All the good ones anyway, right?"

"Ex-actly!" And Tony pointed his finger at him. "You and I went to high school here. We partied here. We became men here."

Frank blew on his coffee and then sipped. "Yeah. I remember how we used to ride our bikes in the summer. All day. Shoot BB guns and throw dirt clods. It was such a different city back then."

Tony smiled broadly, even though Frank didn't. "Those were good times. Great time to grow up here."

"Yeah. Probably not the same anymore."

"Yeah, probably not."

"And, of course, your friend Red is here, and his uncle is still the chief of police."

Tony looked up from his OJ. He again smiled nervously, and this time Frank smiled back at him. He read it as friendly sarcasm.

"So how about you, Frank. What brought you up here?"

"Well, I'm living in Phoenix. Welding again. Parole ended a couple months ago. So I thought I'd celebrate my freedom and take a little road trip."

"Just to Sac?"

"Well, I started by going to Las Vegas. Then San Diego. Finishing up here."

"Seeing family while you're here?"

"Nah, nobody left. Saw a couple friends. Visited my mother's grave. That's about it."

"I'm sorry for your loss…I always liked your mom."

"No worries…" Both men leaned back as the waitress slid their plates in front of them. "She died some time ago." And then Frank remembered seeing her at the home. Telling her he couldn't afford her private care any longer. *She had wilted in that public home. Sharing a room with five other ladies, the stench of urine.* He poured ketchup on his eggs, then broke one of the yolks.

"How about you? Mom and Dad still doing okay?"

Tony finished chewing a bite. "Yeah, both are well, but of course getting up there. Dad is eighty-three now. Mom turns eighty next month. Living on 27th Avenue still."

"You're lucky to have them both."

"Yeah, I am. Oh, before I forget," he said and reached into his shirt pocket to pull out a USB drive. "Ruth gave me this to give to you. It's some of her wedding pictures. She wanted you to have them." Frank opened his hand and accepted it. "She said she isn't quite ready to talk yet, but she wanted you to see them."

"Thank you, Tony," he said, and he felt genuine gratitude. "I appreciate that."

"It's the least I can do, Frank." He again tried to elicit a smile with one of his own, but it wasn't returned. "Her daughter is the flower girl in these pictures. Joy is five now."

"Five?" *How the years do fly by.* "Hope I have a chance to see these pics."

"Yeah..." he agreed and then thought about what Frank said. "Why wouldn't you have a chance to see them?"

"Well, things are always interesting in my life, Tony. They really are."

"Sure. I mean, do you not have access to a computer? I can print some off if you want..."

"No, it's not that." Tony saw the seriousness in his old friend's eyes. "I just probably won't have the chance. You never know, though."

The hair on the back of Tony's neck rose. He felt chills roll through him. He knew in that moment. Beyond all doubt. His eyes began to dart, and he looked for a way out. Frank sat between him and the door.

"Don't try it, Tony. You won't make it." And Frank's steely eyes told him everything he needed to know.

"Don't do it, Frank. It's not worth it." He felt his hands trembling, knees weakening.

"Oh, it's worth it, Tony. I've thought long and hard about this day."

He knew Frank was palming something, but he couldn't see it. "Please, Frank..." he started, and his voice was trembling like his hands.

"Please? You don't know how long I've planned this, Tony. I've waited years for this moment." His hand was in his lap now. "I lacked the courage in the Raley's parking lot all those years ago. I should have done it then, but I wasn't man enough. Wasn't hard enough. Do you know what it was like for me in prison? Do you know the horrors I've seen?" *Stitches in my anus.*

"You'll go back inside, Frank."

"Probably not, but if I do that would be okay. Kinda looking forward to it. Once you adjust to life inside, you can never really quite adjust to life outside. I know that now. I can't pretend anymore. The charade is over. I was surprised by my own delusion, thinking that I'd make it on the outside. I know better now."

Tony's eyes were searching the room for a solution, but Frank continued talking.

"Everything in my life changed that night at the bar. Just a few miles from here. I Street. I-Ball Bar and Grille. There's a symmetry in that name, which I will enjoy immensely. You see, Tony," and now his hand came up, and it was holding a six-inch ice pick. "I'm going to jam this pick into your eye. Right into your eyeball."

"Jesus, Frank!" And now his voice was loud. Heads turned.

"The last thing you'll see in this life is this metal blade jamming into your brain."

"Frank, fuck!"

Now people were moving around him. Chairs were sliding. Plates rattling. Silverware falling. Someone called out, "Call 9-1-1!"

Tony shifted to try to bolt for the door, but Frank was up, standing over him. He grabbed Tony by the collar of his shirt and pulled it up. A woman shrieked. Several people ran out the door, setting off the *deedoo* from the door sensor over and over. Frank aimed the blade's point at Tony's right eye.

He spoke calmly, though his teeth were grinding. "You took everything from me, Tony. You stole my whole life. Do you wonder that this is going to happen to you? You don't think you deserve this? How can you not?"

Tony shrieked. "PLEASE, FRANK! PLEASE, NO!" He tried pulling away, tried to put his legs between them, but the narrow booth didn't allow him to move much. He was too fat now. His hands were flashing, trying to block the impending stab.

"I'm glad your parents are alive. I wish I could be there when they get the news."

And then Frank drove the blade in with all his force. It sunk in about four inches and stopped. Blood and clear fluid squirted all over them. Tony's body jerked and spasmed, throwing him backward onto the bench, and then he rolled onto the floor. The ice pick was still lodged in his face as he lay there kicking and bleeding under the table.

"See you in Hell, Tony," he shouted, then spat blood from his mouth and lips. He looked to his arms and saw the grisly evidence. He shook off some, then wiped his hands on his jeans. From the tabletop he grabbed the USB drive. *Just in case.* He shoved it in his pocket.

He looked around the restaurant and didn't see a single face. He knew some would be hiding in the kitchen, but that didn't concern him. He turned to the door and walked toward it. He grabbed the only jacket that was hanging on the rack. He pushed the door open, and was wiping his hands on the jacket as he walked out.

He turned toward Fruitridge Boulevard and moved with pace. People were running, some into the market next door, some toward their cars. He looked down and saw that his shirt was drenched in blood, and he was leaving a dripping trail. He knew he must look gruesome. *Guess I'm not going to get very far like this,* he thought. He had forgotten how much people bled and how sticky blood is.

As he moved past the Holiday Market, he saw the first of several police cars flying down Stockton Boulevard, headed his way. He looked the other direction and saw another speeding into the parking lot, lights flashing.

*There's no turning back now*, he thought. *This is it.*

He rolled up the jacket around his right hand. As the car came flying toward him, he ran a few steps into the parking lot, in the path of the cruiser. The car screeched to a stop, and the driver's door flew open. He looked into the eyes of the officer in black. He looked so young. Or maybe Frank was just old now. He knew their lives were interlocked forever.

"Freeze!" the officer shouted. "Don't move, man!" He could see the revolver shaking in his hands.

Frank smiled at him. He knew he was about to ruin this officer's life. He would be telling this story for decades.

*Fuck it.*

He raised his hand, still covered in the jacket and pointed it at the officer.

The *pop-pop-pop-pop* was so fast and the first two shots whizzed by him. The third and fourth felt like punches from a heavy-handed boxer, and his legs folded under him. He was on his back, looking up at the clear spring Sacramento sky. Already blood was filling his lungs, and he could feel it moving up his throat and running down his sides from the two wounds. His vision narrowed, then his sight went black.

His life left him, and he smiled as it did.

# THE END

# AFTERWORD:
## A NOTE TO FRIENDS

A new point of learning. In my first two novels, I included my thoughts in Forewords and Introductions. When I would go online and view my books, I would see mostly those, as previews usually included only the first twenty pages or so. It occurred to me that doing so puts the reader, who is reviewing my book for purchase, in the position where they're making a buying decision based on those introductions...more so than my writing. That is, when you go to the *Look Inside* on Amazon, you end up seeing mostly the Foreword and Introduction, and not the book that I'm trying to sell you.

Therefore, I'm moving my comments and updates to the back from now on. That way, those who are interested (and I hope you are) can read about my musings and life updates, but it's not part of your buying decision. As well, I hope to...aspire to...make these comments meaningful notes to my friends...and by friends I mean those of you who have graciously read this book. You don't know how much I value those of you who have taken the time to read the words I've written.

...And here's why: the writing industry has changed so much, and it's such a challenge to build an audience. Therefore, each one of you who reads this gives me the drive to write more. Without readers, a writer has no purpose...*if a tree falls in the woods* and all that. So thank you for reading... you mean more to me than you could ever know. That's why I'm giving this Afterword a title: A Note to Friends. And you are my friends, if you're reading this. If you take the time to read my words, you are the best of friends to me.

So a lot has happened, and I want to catch you up.

After I bought back my book *The One* Way from my previous publisher, I edited it and re-released it. I'm much happier with the finished product, and Monark Design Services did a great job of punching up the cover, while Mayhem did some wonderful formatting. I also love having full control of my work. I have learned so much since then; it feels *weird* (for lack of a better word) to be putting the book back out. Yet I thought it was important for continuity of the series, and, well, I have a real soft spot for Danny. He is, after all, my first protagonist...and so wonderfully flawed!

In the meantime, I started working on this novel. This one was a bit more challenging to write than my previous two. My first novel, I just started writing without an outline and only a vague idea of what I hoped to do. I knew I wanted Danny to go overseas, but I didn't have any clear idea of how he would get there or why. As Danny was partially autobiographical and partially an amalgam of people I knew, that novel wrote itself. My second novel began as a writing exercise, and having set a specific mindset of *I need to do the opposite of what comes naturally* by itself gave me a target, and that kept my focus as I wrote. So, then, both novels were easy(ish) to write and were done reasonably quickly, all things considered.

With this one, I knew very clearly how and why I wanted to write it. I had outlined this novel very carefully, which I now think was a mistake. Doing so took away the freedom to let my characters roam about, as they had in the other two novels. I ended up pitching the outline about halfway, and I know that I will never keep my characters so restricted again. You certainly need a structure, but a loose one you're free to ditch if your characters guide you in another direction. Put another way, when I write my next novel I will eschew the outline, and instead just develop (what I think are) interesting characters and just let them do what they do. I realized this was what I had enjoyed about writing my previous novels, and that is how I will approach future writing. I'll let you know how it goes after my next one.

So while this book was a bit laborious at first, it became much more fun after I dumped the stodgy outline and just let Frank and Mariah do their thing. They, after all, are people, and people are unpredictable. The more unpredictable, the more they show their humanity. And everybody in this book was so flawed...that's the aspect of humanity I enjoy exploring the most.

Now, one friend asked me what my motivation was for this novel, what made me want to write *The Juke*? Well, it's actually a rather convoluted story. It started with an argument with an old friend about, of all things, football. It became heated, and I felt rather dumb about the whole thing later. I also realized we were "fair weather friends" to each other...friends when things were easy, but not so much when things got rocky. So, then, it meant we weren't really true friends at all. My true friends and I excuse each other's madness from time to time. *And aren't we all a little mad?*

I started to think about the arrogance of mankind, and men specifically. I started to think about how we build a pretentious existence, and we use that façade, that mask, to project out to the world. *No, I'm not the insecure teenager everybody knew back in the day...I'm a confident man who has his shit together, and nobody can take that away from me.* But, and here's the sad part, we are so very frail. We are so vulnerable. Any of us can lose all we have in the blink of an eye. And, in our deepest heart of hearts, we are still that nervous, insecure teenager, and that person makes us make mistakes throughout our lives.

I also wanted to tackle the idea of friends and friendship. For the most part, I've had the same friends for thirty years. Yet along the way I've fallen out with a couple. How do friends end up not friends? Well, I know males have an internal competition going at all times, and that can flare up and test the bonds (and bounds) of friendship. I wanted to consider that, and consider how two friends could end up so far apart...just like my old friend and me.

Frank himself began to take shape first as a reflection of *Professional Ted.* During my professional career, I had worn the suits and the expensive ties; I had the office with the plaques on the wall from professional societies and degree programs. Since I was terrible at sports growing up, my trophies came as certificates and degrees. At times, that meant a lot to me, and was part of my identity. What would happen if all that was stripped from me? How would I react? That was the exigency of this novel. And, of course, I had to have some football in there, in homage to the argument that started this whole project.

Once again, the protagonist of my novel is really me, and I'm not sure I can ever escape that.

I recently read an interview with John Lennon, circa 1975. In it, they asked him about the song "How Do You Sleep." He openly wrote it about Paul McCartney at the time of the Beatles' breakup...they were fighting at the time and saying nasty things to each other. Reflecting on it five years later, he said something to the effect that a song like that, while you think you're writing about someone else, turns out to be about you, and when you're poking a finger at someone, you're really pointing at a reflection of yourself. I think that's true about writing. When I began this novel, I thought it would be about my aforementioned ex-friend. Instead, it's really about me. I guess any art (and yes I consider writing a form of art) really has to come from within. It has to be written from and as a reflection of the author. After all, we can only see out of our own eyes, so whatever we view we do so from that vantage point.

And my professional life has required serious reflection all on its own this year, and this novel helped that. I have become increasingly dissatisfied with my career, and over the last year it occurred to me that I was working far too hard and feeling too stressed, and this was keeping me from doing the writing I wanted to do. *Had to do.* When you absolutely *dread* going to work every day, you have a problem, and you need to address it. Your mind and body will tell you things if you listen…and mine were screaming at me.

I know…I know…nobody *loves* their job, do they? Work is, by design, difficult. Still, there's a difference between a job that you don't like and a job that you dread. That dread is like a cancer that will consume you from the inside. Mine was.

Changes had to be made (and this is Book II of *Changes*, so the timing was serendipitous). I have decided to go back to teaching high school, which will give me the opportunity to work with literature again, as well as give me some balance in my life. So another transition is up ahead and still more changes. Life *is* change, isn't it? I'll write to you again when I'm there.

That's all for now, my friends. Thank you for reading another of my works. I'd love to hear from you, so please find me and share your feedback. I want to hear what you have to say.

I appreciate you more than you know.

www.tedpersinger.com
www.facebook.com/tedpersinger1
@tedpersinger

Ted Persinger, 4/24/2015

# ALSO FROM TED PERSINGER

## Literary Fiction:

### Changes Series: *The One Way*, Book I

The black eye of unmerciful ruin turned on Danny Shields one day. Hot May afternoon. Carjacking gone wrong. He stares into the eyes of his dying wife. He fails to protect her...he gives way to panic and fear. On that roadside black asphalt everything he holds dear is crushed under the cruel heel of the gods. Home, career, and investments all become meaningless to him in that crack of a gun. The shame of his reaction overcomes him, and he is unable to adequately cope with the loss he feels responsible for. He has to leave. Every news report condemns him. Every murmur judges him. Every aspect of his life reminds him of his loss. He travels to Mexico to relive their brief honeymoon. After falling ill, he begins a "one way" trip...only moving forward and never going back. He becomes morally ambiguous. Danny travels to Cambodia and Thailand, all in an attempt to find himself...to build a new life after his old life resets to zero. He's on a collision course with karma and fate.

*The One Way* is a character-driven novel that explores Danny's travels and changing life view over a one-year period.

## Erotic Romance:

### Farfalla Series: *Follow You Down*, Book I

*"Rachel Walker, I'd like you to meet David Wright." I still tremble when I remember those words. That day changed me forever.*

Rachel is a biracial woman from Queens in the late 1970s. She aspires to write poetry, and is drawn to Manhattan for the art she finds there. She meets a man who changes her life forever. David has a dark secret. His desires draw Rachel into a world of easy indulgence, a world of lust and sex, a world where anything goes. From a simple schoolteacher, Rachel is transformed into someone she would never have recognized…would never have approved of. As her career grows, so do her challenges. Is she flying or falling? Sometimes it's difficult to understand the difference.

*To this very day, I remember the first time I saw him. It sounds corny, of course, to say "my heart skipped a beat." But it did. Several. I do believe in love at first sight…it has happened to me a few times in my life. But this was the first, and the first is always special. He set my soul on fire instantly. I would've done anything he wanted…and I guess I did.*

*Follow You Down* is an erotic romance, which explores a woman's personal, spiritual, and sexual evolution. Rachel faces a changing world, a changing culture, and a changing sense of self. Where will she find herself? Who will she be on the other side?

www.ingramcontent.com/pod-product-compliance
Lightning Source LLC
Chambersburg PA
CBHW022135240626
47153CB00007B/2370